Left a house and a for
delighted at the unex
glittering society of St F
century.

Yet she cannot help feeling uncomfortable about her
new-found wealth, for her godfather's nephew, Gennadi, an officer in the Imperial Russian Navy, should
have been the rightful heir. But he has been shipwrecked
in the Arctic . . . or has he? Galina is strangely haunted
by the vivid portrait of the handsome sailor hanging in
the library. He is the perfect hero of her imagination—
but surely she cannot be so foolish as to fall in love with a
portrait?

Wheel of Fortune

Dinah Dean

MILLS & BOON LIMITED
London · Sydney · Toronto

First published in Great Britain 1983
by Mills & Boon Limited, 15–16 Brook's Mews,
London W1A 1DR

ISBN 0 263 74421 3

Set in 10 on 11pt Linotron Times
04/1083

Photoset by Rowland Phototypesetting Ltd
Bury St Edmunds, Suffolk
Made and printed in Great Britain by
Cox and Wyman Ltd, Reading

For Rose and Denis

Note

Readers may find it helpful to know that a Russian has three names. The first is his personal name; the second means (son or daughter of) the father's name; and the third is the surname, and the endings change according to whether the person is male or female. This is not as difficult as it sounds! For example, my heroine's name is Galina Stepanovna Razumova. Her personal name is Galina, her father's name is Stepan, and the family name is Razumov. Anyone who knows her well will call her Galina Stepanovna, but strangers will call her Countess Galina Razumova. One of her friends is called Andrei Ivanovich Valyev. His personal name is Andrei, his father's name is Ivan, and the family is Valyev. Even His Imperial Majesty, Alexander I, Emperor and Autocrat of All the Russians, would be referred to, by those who knew him, as Alexander Pavlovich.

CHAPTER
ONE

THE EMPRESS

A warm and helpful person / A possessive tyrant

GALINA stood at the window of the Peacock Salon, watching the passing traffic outside the house. Although it was still only the last week in October, St Petersburg was filling up with fashionable society, and most of the houses and apartments facing her across the little Fontanka river were showing lighted windows this dull, overcast afternoon. The lamplighters were out along the roads on either side of the river, doing their best to get through the throng of servants and poor people on the footways.

It had been snowing heavily earlier in the day, and the walkers were now slithering and plodding through inches of dirty wet slush, and were constantly showered by more from the wheels of the never-ending stream of carriages and carts passing along the roadway. Most of the carriages were heading to Galina's left, towards the Anichkov Bridge and the fashionable shops in the Nevsky Prospect. It seemed incredible that not one of the hundreds of passers-by was known to her, and it was beginning to seem that, after a week in Petersburg without a single caller, she would never manage to make the acquaintance of any of them.

With a sigh, she turned away from the window and

looked about the room, which derived its name from the wall-coverings of silk brocade depicting peacocks and hens amid flowers and rocks, and the moulded peacocks on the great white porcelain-tiled stove in the corner. Even the chair-coverings and window-hangings were of the same peacock-woven silk, and three of the eight large mirrors on the walls had peacocks in the mouldings of their frames. Galina looked at her reflection in one of them, and saw a slim figure of medium height, with dark brown hair drawn a little too severely into a fashionable high chignon, very large dark eyes, a straight nose and a mouth and chin which were shapely enough, but perhaps a little too firm and determined – something which any prospective suitor would do well to observe.

The other five mirrors were odd ones placed at random wherever they would go amid the pictures which crowded the brocaded walls with no regard to symmetry, and the various glass-fronted cabinets which lined the edges of a great Persian carpet on which a variety of hunters and animals careered madly in all directions against a gratingly brilliant vermilion background.

Galina regarded the carpet with acute distaste, and resolved to start turning the room into something more comfortable and pleasing in appearance. It was so cluttered with all those pictures and mirrors and chairs, most of them heavy and ugly, and hardly any matching, and the cabinets were crammed with pots and figures and knick-knacks of all kinds.

The whole house was much the same, a great mansion of the mid-eighteenth century, Baroque in style, with eight salons of various sizes, a library, two ballrooms, a small theatre, and goodness knew how many bedrooms, boudoirs, store-rooms, kitchens, offices—all crowded with furniture and *objets d'art*, precious things cheek by jowl with ugly rubbish, with no order or sense, and so difficult to keep clean, despite the two hundred or so house-serfs employed about the place. It was like living in the warehouse of some merchant who traded in everything man-made and ornamental, with the difference that at least collectors and customers would visit a warehouse, but no one came to the Zhadnov house, no one at all.

Galina was debating whether to stand at the window again, or to go into the library in search of something to read, when the double doors from the gallery were opened ceremoniously, and two footmen in morning livery stalked in, bringing the many-branched candlesticks which over-illuminated the room every evening.

'A dozen candles will be sufficient,' Galina said firmly. 'You may take the others away.'

The footmen looked disconcerted, and the senior of them ventured, 'But, Countess, we always have four dozen.'

'I don't require so many,' Galina replied. 'And neither do I require to be told what you always have. My ways are not necessarily those of your former master. General Zhadnov. No doubt I can contrive to ring if I need more. Thank you,' she added, for the two men were hanging their heads and almost cringing, as if they feared more than a verbal rebuke. She wondered what sort of master the old General had been. 'You may go.'

The footmen withdrew with most of the candles, attempting to efface themselves completely as they did so, for their exit coincided with the entrance of a plump lady of middle age, dressed in a gown of dark grey woollen a year behind the fashion, with her greying hair almost completely hidden by an elaborate lace cap— Galina's mother, Countess Natasha Razumova.

'Do you think, dear, that I might ask someone to remove the bear from my bedroom?' she enquired as she entered. 'It's quite frightfully in the way, and Eda has a fit of the vapours every time she comes face to face with it, which hardly makes for a tranquil atmosphere. I must say that I don't much care for its teeth myself, particularly as one of the larger ones is missing, which makes the beast appear to leer, and it quite breaks through my concentration if I happen to catch sight of it as I'm reading the cards. It must have been a very ancient animal—its fur is quite white.'

'I wasn't aware that you had a bear in your room,' Galina was puzzled. 'I'm sure it wasn't there when we arrived last week . . .'

'No—it appeared yesterday. Eda says that it was in one of the rooms which you told the major-domo fellow to clear—I can't recall his name . . .'

'Osya Ivanich,' Galina replied absently. 'I collect that it's a stuffed bear, not a live one? Oh, Mama! What am I to do with all these things? The whole house is full of stuffed bears and pictures and furniture and pots and peculiar contrivances . . . Wherever did the General get them all, and why did he want them? According to Osya, he was hardly ever here, yet he was forever sending waggon-loads of things to put in the house!'

'Loot, I suppose,' Countess Razumova sat down at the smallest of the five tables in the room, took a pack of Tarot cards from her reticule and began to shuffle them. 'After all, a General must surely have the pick of whatever the army collects as it goes about, and he was in Italy and Turkey and Austria and several of the German states at least in the past twenty years or so, and I'm sure there must have been a great many treasures to be picked up as the French retreated from Moscow last year.' She automatically crossed herself at the memory of the horrors of 1812, but hardly ceased from shuffling her cards to do so.

'But they were all Russian treasures,' Galina protested.

'Maybe so, but I doubt if many of them found their

way back to their proper homes.' The Countess produced a pair of spectacles from her reticule, perched them on her nose, and looked at her daughter over them. 'You should really do something about this house. It would be quite pleasant if only one could move about in it without knocking something over. Perhaps you could send some things back to wherever they came from, and sell some of the monstrosities, and just keep the more attractive objects?'

Galina sighed. 'I'd like to, but I don't know how to go about it. Godfather's man-of-business seemed quite shocked when I suggested it. He said that Godfather would never even have the things catalogued, let alone consider parting with any of them. Oh, I do wish we knew someone in Petersburg who could advise me – in fact, I wish we just knew someone – we could easily stay here all winter and never speak to a soul apart from the house-serfs!'

The Countess, who was laying out a circle of cards with great concentration, replied vaguely, 'I told your father he should obtain some letters of introduction for you . . . Ah, that's interesting! The Empress!'

'Well, I've no doubt she's the only Empress we shall contrive to meet in Petersburg!' Galina said a trifle tartly, for she found her mother's addiction to the Tarot exasperating, and, seeing that she was about to receive a discourse on the possibilities revealed by the art of divination, she hastily excused herself and passed through the double doors into the library next door in pursuit of her earlier intention of finding something to read. She found that the servants had already brought candles, and she extinguished half of them before she did anything else.

Like all the other rooms, the library was crowded with furniture and objects from General Zhadnov's collection. Long pier-glasses in ornate Baroque frames hung

between the bookcases, and half a dozen fair-sized
tables stood about the room, the top of each covered
with a clutter of snuff-boxes, candlesticks, vases, porcelain figures, swords, and books for which there was no
room on the overcrowded shelves. Galina looked about
her with a feeling of helpless bewilderment, wishing she
dare order the whole lot to a bonfire, and wondered why
her godfather had acquired no less than eight cases of
duelling pistols, which were stacked on one of the
window-sills.

There was, however, only one picture on the walls,
and it seemed to have some significance, rather than
being just another item in the collection, for it hung
alone to one side of the door frame from the gallery. It
was very large, and showed a fair-haired, handsome
young man wearing a dark uniform under a black,
scarlet-lined cloak, bare-headed, and seated on the
driving-seat of a racing sledge drawn by two fine horses.
The artist had caught the courage and noble spirit of the
animals, and there was something of the same look
about the man, who was half-turned to look out of the
canvas at the observer. Galina had no idea who he was,
but, with a wry reference to her mother's eternal Tarot
pack, she had privately named him the Charioteer.

The books in the tall cases seemed to have been
collected in the same totally undiscriminating way as
everything else. Poetry, philosophy, history, drama,
travel, art, religion, memoirs, biography, were crammed into the shelves without regard to language or
subject, or even consideration for fine or elderly bind-
ings. When she pulled out a copy of Derzhavin's in-
nocuous verse, it brought with it a French volume illus-
trated with engravings which made Galina blink with
shock, and hastily push the book back into its place,
hoping that her mother would not come across it.

None of the books seemed particularly interesting,

but eventually she returned to the salon with a well-illustrated account of a journey through the German states, and settled down to work out where the Russian army fighting Bonaparte far away to the west had been during the past eight or nine months, and rapidly came to the conclusion that they must have been marching in circles most of the time.

It was very quiet. The double glass in the windows kept out the sounds of the street below as well as the damp cold, and there seemed to be no movement in the house, apart from the barely-heard whirr and click as the clockwork of the strange automaton in the gallery moved on a place. Countess Razumova murmured over her cards from time to time—she seemed to have settled to a game of Patience now—and the fire in the stove occasionally crackled.

Suddenly, there was a change, scarcely more than a distant stirring at first, and then footsteps hastened along the gallery and a footman entered, a look of expectation on his round, snub-nosed face as he announced 'Countess Kalinskaya has called, ma'am, and wishes to know if you will receive her.'

'Oh, yes. Pray show her in,' Galina replied, and turned to her mother in perplexity as the footman hastened away, leaving the door unlatched in his excitement at having something to do at last. 'Who on earth is Countess Kalinskaya?'

'The name seems vaguely familiar . . .' the older Countess sorted through her cards and found the Empress. 'Now, was she upright or reversed? I can't recall . . .'

'Oh, Mama!' Galina exclaimed.

'It's important to know—it affects the character so much,' her mother said reprovingly. 'Upright, she's a helpful, kindly person, but reversed . . . oh, we'd not wish to know her if she's reversed!'

Galina was saved from an unfilial reply by the entry of
Osya Ivanich, the major-domo, with two attendant
underlings carrying the candles which Galina had earlier
rejected. He swiftly directed the men where to put them,
and then sent them out through the library, while he
turned to the door and announced, 'Countess Tatyana
Petrovna Kalinskaya,' in portentous tones as the visitor
entered, then bowed himself out backwards, as if from
the Imperial Presence.

Galina looked at the newcomer a trifle apprehen-
sively. She was tall for a female and very beautiful, with
a clear-skinned, heart-shaped face, large grey eyes
fringed with black lashes below swallows'-wing eyebrows, black, glossy hair caught up in a chignon with
ringlets crowned by a pretty scrap of lace. Her slender,
shapely figure showed to advantage in a high-necked
long-sleeved gown of amethyst velvet, cut in a style
which made Galina's dark green woollen look provin-
cially *démodé*. She moved across the room in a graceful
glide, and Galina, moving forward to meet her, found
her own face breaking into a smile in response to the
serenity and kindliness of the stranger's expression.

'Galina Stepanova Razumova?' she asked. 'I think we
must be second or third cousins, I was an Orlov before I
married,' and she put her hands on Galina's shoulders
and kissed her in a thoroughly friendly fashion.

'Oh, of course! You'd be Pyotr Sergeivich's girl who
married that horrid old General Kalinsky!' exclaimed
Countess Razumova, rising to embrace the visitor and
scattering her precious cards over the floor as she did so.
'You've a brother, too, I recall—in the Chevalier Garde,
isn't he?'

'He was,' Countess Kalinskaya replied, smiling. 'But
he was twice quite badly wounded in the arm last year, so
he's resigned from the Army and married. I'm expecting
him and Irina back from their wedding-journey any day

now. Have you been in Petersburg very long?'

'A week,' Galina replied, inviting her guest to sit with a gesture, then resuming her own seat. 'Have you, Countess?'

'I arrived yesterday, and please call me Tatya, and I shall call you Galina, if I may? I learned only this morning that you were here, so I came to call in the hope that I might find you at home.'

Galina made a little grimace. 'We've hardly been out at all since we arrived. Mama doesn't care much for going about, and—well—we don't know anyone, you see. I can't think who could have told you we were here, for we've no acquaintance at all in Petersburg.'

'You were mentioned in the list of new arrivals in the city in the *Petersburg Gazette*,' Tatya replied. 'You'll soon have a wide acquaintance, for your inheritance has caused such a stir! I'm afraid your godfather was quite notorious for his magpie tendencies – they called him Yuri Sticky-fingers in the Army. And then there was the tragedy of his nephew's loss—he was something of a hero among the younger set—followed by the General's death, and the news that he'd left everything to an unknown beauty from Tver! You've been the subject of much speculation and gossip, and now your presence here has been announced, you'll soon find any number of people calling on you.'

'You'll probably think it very odd . . .' Galina began nervously, but she was interrupted by the entry of a ceremonial procession. At least, that was how it appeared at first sight, but it resolved itself into four footmen bearing the necessary equipment for serving tea to the three ladies. With well-drilled precision, one placed a small table by Galina, and the others deposited samovar, gold teapot, caddy, porcelain cups and dishes, a gold covered dish of lemon slices, and a basket of little sugar-cakes. Galina wished that they had selected her

mother to preside, but realised that, as she was the
owner of the house, the responsibility was her own, and
she set about the business a little nervously, for it was the
first time she had served tea to a visitor in her own house,
although she had often done it at home.

No mishaps occurred. The tea was safely brewed,
poured, and handed by one of the footmen, then the
servants withdrew and conversation was renewed by
Tatya enquiring what she would probably think odd.

'I don't really know very much about my godfather,'
Galina replied. 'I don't remember him at all—I don't
think I ever saw him after my baptism—and all I know is
that he was a General in the Army, and he died early this
year, and left everything to me, quite unexpectedly. The
lawyers didn't tell me anything more, nor his man-of-
business, and I didn't like to ask . . .'

'But you're entitled to know, my dear, and, remember, you employ the lawyers and the man-of-business!
Yes, Yuri Semyonovich Zhadnov was a General of
Infantry, and quite a good one, according to some of my
Army friends. He was wounded in a battle at Krasnyi,
about midway between Smolensk and Orsha, last
November, when the French were retreating, and died
just after Christmas. He was never married, for he
seemed always to be busy with one campaign or another,
and his heir was his nephew, Gennadi Yakovich Zhadnov. Gennadi was a Captain in the Imperial Navy, and
he was sent in the summer of 1812 to survey the coasts of
Novaya Zemlya. His ship didn't return when it was
expected, and last November two sailors arrived at
Archangelsk, over the frozen sea, and said that the ship
had been caught and crushed in the ice. Gennadi had set
out to lead the men over the ice to safety, but there was a
bad storm, and the two sailors were separated from the
others. They searched for them after the storm, but
could find no trace of them, so they must all have

perished. Everyone was very sorry, particularly as the news reached the General as he was himself dying. He was very proud of Gennadi, who was a brave, adventurous man—and very handsome into the bargain!'

'Was he fair in colouring?' Galina asked, recalling the Charioteer's uniform had an anchor on the collar.

'Yes. You'll have seen his portrait, no doubt. It used to hang in the library.'

'It still does. I wondered who he was. He looks quite young in it—was it painted long ago?'

'No. He would be—oh, about twenty-seven or so by now, had he lived,' Tatya replied. 'General Zhadnov must have been very upset by his death, for he had no other family.'

'So I suppose that's why he left me his property,' Galina said. 'A god-daughter being the next best thing to a blood-relation, although there was no connection—my father just happened to be serving under him when I was born.' She felt strangely moved by the discovery that the handsome, spirited man in the portrait was dead, drowned in the cold Arctic. She bit her lip and told herself that it was foolish to feel emotional over someone she had never met. After all, thousands of men had died since Gennadi Zhadnov, and far more horribly, in the bitter fighting of the last year or more, especially in the fearful cold of last winter.

There was a short pause, and then Tatya asked, 'Do you really not know anyone at all in Petersburg?'

'Not a soul, other than my godfather's—no, *my* man-of-business! We've always lived in Tver, you see, and never gone to Petersburg or Moscow for the Season.' Galina hesitated, and then, encouraged by the interest and kindness of Tatya's lovely eyes, went on, 'My grandfather had the misfortune to offend the Emperor Pavel, and all his possessions were confiscated, except one little estate near Tver and a house in the town, so we couldn't afford to come to Petersburg, even if Papa had been willing, which he wouldn't be, for he really dislikes Society.'

'What did your grandfather do?' Tatya asked with great interest.

'He came back to Petersburg from a journey abroad somewhere, not knowing about some of the Emperor's decrees, and, to start with, he was wearing a round hat. A policeman snatched it off his head and started to nail it to a lamp-post, and Grandfather snatched it back and belaboured the man with his stick! He was arrested because, of course, the Emperor had made round hats illegal, but they let Grandfather off with a warning when he explained that he'd been abroad and didn't know. Unfortunately, the next day he was driving in his carriage and met the Emperor, also out driving, and Grandfather just bowed as he passed, instead of stopping and getting down to kneel in the roadway. The Emperor confiscated all his possessions at first, but someone explained that Grandfather didn't know about the new laws, so the Emperor relented and let him keep the smallest estate. I—I suppose he was a little mad . . .'

'If you mean the Emperor, more than a little, 'though it's still not advisable to say so in public!' Tatya said, laughing. 'Of course, he did some very good things, too, but people never remember about those. The General's legacy must have been very welcome—it's made you one of the richest heiresses in Russia, I should think! We must do something about making a few people known to you—pleasant, trustworthy people, I mean, for you'll have more than enough of the other sort after your acquaintance!' She hesitated a moment, and then said tentatively, 'Are you engaged at all this evening?'

'No,' Galina replied sadly.

'Will you both dine with me, then? I've a small party of friends arranged—just a few people, but it will make a start for you, and I'm sure you'll enjoy meeting them.'

Galina looked uncertainly at her mother, who avoided her gaze, and appeared very interested in the pattern of the carpet.

'Mama doesn't care much to go out,' she said, looking beseechingly at Tatya, who smiled and gave her a little nod of reassurance.

'Then you must come by yourself,' she said firmly. 'It's quite in order, if your maid accompanies you, and she can pass the time with my own maid—she may learn a few helpful little things.'

'I should like that very much,' Galina's relief and pleasure were clear in her voice. 'What time should I come—oh, and where do you live?'

'We're dining very late—not until seven, because two of my guests are coming some distance, and I live in Gorokhovaya Street—your coachman will know whereabouts.'

After Tatya had taken her leave, Galina was tempted to rush upstairs at once to survey her wardrobe and decide what to wear, but she checked herself and asked her mother, 'Do you mind my going?'

'Of course not, my dear. We've come to Petersburg so that you may meet people and enjoy yourself. As long as I know you're in suitable company, and don't make me go to balls and parties with you, I'm quite content. Now, off with you and choose your gown—demi-toilette for an informal party, remember.'

Galina walked sedately along the gallery, and stopped to look at the automaton which towered above the line of assorted chairs, small tables and cabinets which lined the wall like flotsam along a tide-mark. It both fascinated and puzzled her, for she was unable to decide whether it was meant to be a clock, or merely an ornament, or an amusing toy.

It was contained in a square glass case mounted on a

stand, and looked much like the works of the sort of clock one might find in the tower of a kremlin or a cathedral, with numerous large black iron cogwheels slowly turning one another, driven by a weight within the lower part of the frame, but it had no hands, no means of telling the time, and the dial was simply a hollow ring of gilded metal, some three feet in diameter. Where the numerals should have been, eight little manikins, each a few inches high, were mounted on the ring, apparently tied to it by a twisted metal rope about the waist of each. As the mechanism ticked on, the ring moved round clockwise and the figures were jerked slowly round the circle. Each one was jointed like a puppet, and as it rose on the left-hand side, its limbs gradually moved until, at the top of the circle, it was upright, head straight and arms hanging at its sides, but once the apogee was passed, it began to fall into a tumbled posture—head sideways, arms and legs swinging loosely, until, at the bottom of the circle, it appeared to have fallen head downward, limp and dead, only to start to rise again as the wheel turned.

The figures were arranged in pairs, opposite to one another, a king and a bishop, a maiden and a knight, a peasant and a soldier, a child and an old man, each modelled in the appropriate clothing and coloured in enamels—the king and bishop robed and crowned, the maiden in a simple white gown, the knight in armour, the peasant in tunic and hood and the soldier in helmet and leather jacket, the old man white-haired and bent, the child fresh-faced and curly-haired. Above the ring a golden-haired angel spread curving golden wings round the circle and gazed benevolently down on the bound figures, but below, a leering devil in black with outspread arms and talons waited eagerly for each to fall towards him.

It was obviously meant to be the Wheel of Fortune,

the figures, Galina supposed, representing Church and State, male and female, peace and war, youth and age. She thought it must be very old, and not Russian, to judge by the style of the crowns and the armour—perhaps it was German. It was a fascinating thing to watch as the little puppets were drawn in turn up to triumph and then fell to death and disorder, but something in the inexorability of the rise and fall made her uneasy, and her spirit rebelled against the implication that she, like the puppets, was bound to a wheel and had no control over her own fate. The same feeling was aroused by her mother's constant reference to her Tarot pack whenever any decision had to be made or any new factor considered.

A small cough from behind her made her aware of the presence of Osya Ivanich, discreetly arrayed in his day-time livery, but nevertheless a tall and stately figure, his impassive, rather Kalmuck-type face set in a mask of polite attention, his greying head a little inclined to one side and his dark eyes shrewd and watchful.

'Will you be requiring a carriage, Countess?' he enquired when he saw that he had her notice.

'Yes, please.' Galina hesitated, then went on half-enquiringly, 'To dine at seven, at Countess Kalinskaya's . . .' She noted that he still called her 'Countess', and not by her personal names, so she was not yet fully accepted as mistress of the house.

'To depart at twenty after six, in order to arrive half an hour before dining,' Osya supplied smoothly. 'One assumes that the Countess is still in residence at her brother's house? In the Gorokhovaya?' he added, seeing Galina's slight confusion.

'Yes. Thank you. Would you please send someone to ask Dasha to come to my room?'

Osya bowed slightly, and stood watching his new mistress as she went along the gallery and disappeared up the stairs. He allowed himself a small smile of approval at her pleases and thank you, and her use of 'ask' instead of 'tell'. Very different from some people he could name, but one shouldn't think ill of the dead . . .

Upstairs, Galina faced the problem of every female who receives an unexpected invitation—what to wear. She was quite well aware that the gowns which had been fashionable in Tver were *démodés* in St Petersburg, and had made a modest outlay on new ones in the modistes' establishments in the Nevsky Prospect, but had not yet found a modiste whose garments satisfied her. Tatya's amethyst velvet had a certain simple perfection of fit and draping which she thought must be due to expert cutting and stitching, and she wished she might emulate her. However, there was nothing she could do in the next hour or so to improve on what she had, so, by the time Dasha's pert little face preceded her short plump body through the bedroom door, she had selected a crimson silk gown with an almost transparent over-tunic in pale rose. The ankle-length gown had a modest *décolleté* and long, tight sleeves, and the tunic fastened from the neck to the high waist with tiny silver buttons, then hung open to a little below the knee. Its sleeves were wide and unseamed along the outer arm, the edges caught together at intervals with more of the little buttons. Originally, it had been much trimmed with lace, but Galina had patiently unpicked all but a tiny ruffle at the neck.

The gown had matching slippers and reticule, and gloves of the same shade as the tunic, and, when Dasha had helped her mistress to dress and had brushed her hair to a suitable glossiness, she piled it into a chignon, coaxing a few little curls to break the brow-line, and pinned a small aigrette of pale rose-tinted feathers to stand up at the back. Galina looked through the contents of her small jewel-case, found her long eardrops set with garnets, and decided that they were sufficient jewellery.

She set out punctually at twenty after six in the small town carriage which had been her godfather's, attended by the coachman, two grooms perched behind, and Dasha in her second-best Russian costume. The footmen seemed very anxious that their mistress and her maid should both be comfortable for their short journey, and Galina, already swathed in a long sable *vitschura*, found herself additionally burdened with three fur rugs and a can of hot water.

The Orlov house was not in the most fashionable part of the city, but it was a remarkably fine-looking house with a great portico, set back a little from the street behind a wrought-iron screen. As Galina's carriage turned in at the gate, she caught a glimpse of some earlier arrivals—a man and a woman—entering at the door as their carriage moved out of sight round the side of the house, presumably to the stableyard.

Galina felt slight qualms of apprehension as she waited for one of the grooms to let down the carriage step and remove the rugs. Sleet was still falling in the open, but under the overhang of the portico it was dry underfoot and sheltered from the wind. Nervousness made her hurry up the steps and into the great entrance hall, which was brilliantly lit by four huge crystal chandeliers.

She had little more than an impression of a great deal of white marble and gilding and a quantity of hothouse flowers, a magnificent staircase rising to the *piano nobile*, and a small army of footmen, who were dressed in plain livery with unpowdered hair, which conveyed the comforting realisation that this was indeed an informal gathering. One footman skilfully removed her *vitschura*, a second, who had stepped forward with a chair, looked at her feet and retired again as she was not wearing overshoes, and a third spoke quietly to Dasha, and then ushered her away through a side-door.

The guests who had entered the house just before Galina were still removing their outdoor clothing, and they both looked towards the newcomer and smiled in a friendly fashion. The man was under thirty, Galina thought, tall, broad-shouldered, lean and long-legged, with thick dark hair, a beaky nose and an air of alertness. He was soberly dressed in a dark coat and small-clothes, apart from a blue brocade waistcoat. His companion was quite a pretty young lady, rather pale and mousy-haired, but dressed to advantage in a rich blue silk which strengthened the colour of her eyes. She made a little gesture to Galina, an invitation to walk with her, while the man followed behind as they went, not up the stairs, but to one side of them and into a pleasant room with walls painted in the style of the Raphael loggia which Quarenghi had copied for the Empress Ekaterina's Hermitage, and furnished in satinwood and green silk.

Tatya, gracefully elegant in silver-grey, was standing a little way within the doors, talking to a stoutish young man with ginger hair and bright little blue eyes set in a pudgy face, dressed in the blue dolman and scarlet pelisse of the Lifeguard Hussars. She broke off with a murmured excuse to welcome the new arrivals, kissing Galina, then both of her companions.

'Now, let me make you known to one another,' she said, indicating the couple with whom Galina had entered. 'This is Nadya Igorovna Valyeva, and her husband, Andrei Ivanovich Valyev . . .'

Galina smiled and gave a little half-bow of acknowledgement to Nadya, and held out her hand to Andrei, who gave her a oddly questioning look before lifting it on the back of his own to brush it lightly with his lips, and it was only then that she realised that his hands were badly maimed, with several fingers missing from each.

Whether this was congenital or the result of injury she could not tell, as he was wearing gloves which must have been specially made for him.

'Nadya is an old school-friend from the Smolny Institute,' Tatya continued. 'And Andrei is a neighbour from near one of our estates. He was in the Lifeguard Hussars until the end of last year, as Sasha here still is—Sasha Alexandrovich Tuchin.'

The ginger-haired man took a lurching step forward to kiss Galina's hand, steadying himself with a walking-stick, and said pleasantly, 'We're a pair of old invalids now—Andrei's lost most of his hands, and I'm minus half a leg. That's why we're not galloping about Germany in pursuit of Bonaparte.'

'But you're still in the Army?' Galina asked shyly.

'I'm just a sort of uniformed clerk at the War Ministry,' Sasha replied. 'I can still ride a horse, so they let me continue to swagger about in uniform.'

Suddenly, the double doors of the room opened again with rather more abruptness than usual, and Tatya's major-domo appeared, his sense of propriety trying unsuccessfully to stop his face breaking into a grin of pleasure.

'Oh, Tatya Petrovna,' he exclaimed, his voice trembling with excitement. 'The Master's home!'

CHAPTER
TWO

THE MAGICIAN

The adept, the knowledgeable guide/A trickster, a power-seeker

GALINA drew back, away from the door, and watched as the others went forward in a body to welcome the two people who now entered—a slender young lady with glossy brown hair arranged in a small coronet of plaits, an oval, merry face, and brown eyes which reflected the rich softness of an amber velvet travelling-gown, and a big man with a shock of unruly black curls and heavy black brows which gave him a misleading look of severity, wearing a remarkably bright red waistcoat amid his otherwise sober clothes.

'Lev!' Tatya cried, embracing her brother. 'Trust you to arrive just in time for dinner. Irina, dear! How well you look!'

There was a general exchange of embraces and exclamations, for Tatya's friends obviously knew her brother and his wife very well. Galina was left feeling a little envious and out of things, but, within seconds, Tatya had drawn her back into the group, saying, 'Lev, this is our cousin. My brother, Lev Petrovich Orlov, and Irina Arkadyevna, his wife. This is Galina Stepanovna Razumova, who's just come to Petersburg and doesn't know anyone yet . . .'

'Yes, she does,' interrupted Andrei. 'She knows us, and who else matters?'

Lev gave his friend a gentle buffet on the shoulder which nearly knocked him over and caught Galina into a bearhug which left her a little anxious about the state of her ribs, and then Irina gave her a more gentle embrace and said quietly, 'I can guess how you feel—I came here for the first time myself just a year ago.'

'How was your wedding-journey?' asked Sasha Tuchin. 'Where did you go?'

It was clear that everyone was about to ply the new arrivals with similar questions, but Tatya swiftly cut in with a firm, 'I think, if you could hurry just a little, and Pavel Kuzmich can delay dinner for a quarter-hour, you'll just have time to change.'

Lev stood himself to attention, clicked his heels Prussian-style, and marched himself off at once, catching his wife by the arm as he passed and taking her with him.

'You have him well-trained,' Andrei commented. Tatya gave him a knowing little smile and went to murmur a few words to the major-domo, who had meanwhile been standing by the door. He gave a small bow of acknowledgement as she finished speaking and turned to go out, adroitly stepping aside as the door opened to admit Tatya's last guest.

'Igor! I'm so pleased you could come, despite the short notice,' she said, going to greet him.

Galina, who had somehow been left standing alone again, watched as the newcomer bowed over Tatya's hand, saying, 'Dinner anywhere, at a second's notice, is bound to be preferable to eating the food at the Winter Palace!' His height was not much greater than Tatya's, but he was straight-backed and well-proportioned, so he seemed taller. His thick black hair was brushed smooth, but looked as if it might curl if he would let it, and he was dressed in plain black, with only his white shirt for contrast. As Tatya took his arm and led him towards her, she saw that his face was lean and grooved from the curved nose to the chin, framing a long, thin-lipped mouth. She began to smile as he drew near, but the smile faded as she met his eyes and found them watchful and unreadable under heavy lids.

'This is Igor Grigorovich Charodyev,' Tatya made the introductions while the man kissed Galina's hand. The touch of his gloved fingers was minimal, and he looked at her without any apparent interest, yet in a wary fashion which made her uneasy, which he seemed to sense, for his mouth twitched in a secretive little smile and his heavy lids drooped over his eyes. Galina stammered something which sounded foolish in her own ears and felt herself colour.

'Igor, Galina has a problem, and I hope you may be able to advise her,' Tatya said.

'Razumova,' he said consideringly, looking at Tatya, but continuing to keep Galina's hand resting on his own. She attempted to withdraw it, but his fingers immediately tightened on hers, and he shot her a quick hooded glance of what looked like malicious amusement, then turned back to Tatya and let Galina's hand drop. 'Yes, she must have a very considerable problem if she's attempting to live in General Zhadnov's house. We'll discuss it after dinner.'

'Do tell us, what's wrong with the food at the Winter Palace?' Sasha enquired, coming to join them. Looking past him, Galina saw Andrei turn towards Nadya and put one maimed hand up to touch her cheek, exchanging a long, smiling look with her. She wondered what it must be like to love someone like that, and was quite desolate for a moment because she had never experienced such a feeling.

'It suffers from too great a distance between the kitchens and the dining-room,' Igor replied tartly.

'Allied to over-elaboration, too many rich sauces, and unrecognisability. I like to know what I'm eating, to eat it while it's hot, and not suffer indigestion afterwards.'

Sasha made a little grimace of agreement, and said, 'Well, I won't quarrel with that, but why live in the Palace, in that case? Wouldn't you be more comfortable in an apartment somewhere?'

'It's convenient. I can do my work without actually getting out of bed on cold mornings.'

Galina was so surprised by Igor's reply that she blurted out, 'Why, what do you do, then?' and coloured again to hear herself ask such a gauche question.

Igor gave her a sidelong glance with that same glint of amusement and replied, 'I catalogue the never-ending Imperial collections, with the help of a few other people.'

It sounded an odd occupation to Galina, not at all what one would expect a nobleman to do, and she must have looked doubtful, for Andrei said kindly, 'We're both employed in the Emperor's Cabinet—I buy things and Igor writes them down in a book and finds somewhere to put them—it's all part of the machinery of the Imperial Court.'

'Which reminds me,' Igor interrupted suddenly. 'Was it today you were going to Oranienbaum?'

'Yes—that's why Tatya kindly made dinner so late, to give us time to return. I took Nadya with me—she hadn't seen the Imperial Porcelain Manufactory before.'

'Tell me the worst!' Igor shut his eyes as if expecting bad news.

'Nothing to concern you—only orders for Christmas and New Year gifts,' Andrei reassured him. 'Are you being inundated with things from the German States?'

'No. Oddly enough, Alexander Pavlovich doesn't seem to have bought anything for months.' Igor sounded puzzled. 'I suppose he's too busy being Commander-in-Chief!'

'Yes, and it's a pity he doesn't make a better job of it,' Andrei replied astringently. 'The French were broken and in full retreat at the end of last year, and now look at them! They beat us at Lützen and retook Dresden in April, beat us again at Bautzen in May, and at Dresden in August, and we've done nothing but twiddle our thumbs and make truces ever since! I expect everyone's gone into winter quarters by now.'

'Th-there's . . .' Sasha stammered, then broke off as Irina and Lev re-entered the room. Galina wondered what he had been about to say, for he looked quite excited, but whatever it was, he had no chance to get it out, for Pavel Kuzmich, the major-domo had re-appeared.

'Dinner is served, Irina Arkadyevna,' he announced.

Irina looked disconcerted and turned towards Tatya, who smiled and made a little gesture, as if to indicate that she abdicated the position of mistress of the house to her sister-in-law.

'Well, yes, I suppose you're right,' Lev said to Pavel. 'But it's Tatya's party. Oh, dear!' He looked helplessly from his sister to his wife. Pavel stared impassively straight in front of him, implying quite clearly that *he* had been correct and it was now up to the family to sort it out for themselves. Tatya, laughing, said that she had intended the guests to go in informally, so that is what they did.

The dining-room was also on the ground floor, and Galina realised that the house must have a set of informal family rooms down here as alternatives to the more grandiose ones upstairs, not that those she had seen were at all lacking in elegance or convenience, but they were fairly small and intimate. The dining-room was neo-classical in style, with pale terracotta walls decorated with white plaster swags of leaves and ribbons. The chairs had similar swags carved in their mahogany backs, and their seats were, like the curtains, of a striped terracotta and olive green damask. The long table was covered by a white linen cloth, caught up between the place-settings with nosegays of fresh flowers, and more flowers were arranged down the centre in low gold bowls, alternately with dishes of hothouse fruits. The golden flatware glowed in the candlelight, the glass sparkled, and the gleaming porcelain dinner-service was painted with terracotta leaves and ribbons, echoing those on the walls in reversed colouring.

The original seating arrangement had obviously been changed, for Lev was at the head of the table, with Nadya on his right and Galina on his left, and Irina sat at the foot, with Sasha on her right and Igor on her left, while Andrei was next to Galina, with Tatya opposite him.

During the first two courses, Irina and Lev were plied with questions by their friends about their wedding journey. It appeared that they visited several of Lev's estates during the summer, and then, Austria having changed to the Russian side in the war, had gone there, staying for a few weeks in Vienna, then venturing into the Alpine regions and northern Italy in the early autumn.

Lev made some amusing comments about the differences he had noticed between travelling abroad as an Army officer and as a civilian, and the other men had a number of questions to ask about the effect of the long war on their own particular interests—Andrei asked about the Imperial Porcelain Manufactory in Vienna, Igor about the art galleries, and Sasha about the attitude of Austrian officers to Russians, and Tatya and Nadya enquired of Irina about the latest fashions in Vienna, when they could get a word in.

Galina sat quietly through all this, listening with interest and enjoying the excellent food, thinking herself unnoticed, and she was startled when Igor suddenly said, 'Galina Stepanovna, Old Sticky-fingers is said to have "collected" a handsome chalice from a church in Vienna during the Austerlitz campaign. Have you seen anything of it?'

Conscious that all eyes were on her, Galina looked across at him, expecting to see that malicious smile again, but he was looking at her quite kindly, awaiting her reply with real interest.

'There are enough assorted chalices and crucifixes to equip a dozen churches, I'm sorry to say,' she replied. 'Has the one you mention any distinguishing features?'

'The Austrian ambassador has given me a drawing of it,' Igor said, looking as if her answer amused him. 'He's making rather pressing enquiries about the possibility of its return . . .'

'He's welcome to it,' Galina replied with feeling. She was about to say what she thought of people who 'collected' things in general, let alone from churches, but stopped herself, thinking it might be inappropriate, for she was unaware that the Emperor Alexander acquired the objects in his collections legitimately, and substituted, 'I'd be very glad if you would come and identify it and take it away!'

Igor gave her a long, considering look, and nodded two or three times as if in approval, then suddenly smiled, not in his former downward-looking private fashion, but in a straightforward, pleasant manner, so that she could not help smiling back.

'It would certainly be a good thing for friendly relations with our allies,' Andrei said thoughtfully. 'I have a feeling that the Wet Hens don't love us as much as they should.'

'Wet Hens?' queried his wife.

'That's what the Army calls the Austrians, from the way they react to anything unexpected,' Andrei told her with a grin. 'They must be regretting that they changed sides after the past few months.'

'I-I started to say earlier . . .' Sasha tried again. He had seemed to be only half-involved in the earlier conversation, and had several times opened his mouth to say something and then shut it again as someone else forestalled him. 'There's b-been another b-battle!'

'What sort of a b-battle?' Andrei asked, half-teasingly.

'Hush, Andrei!' Tatya said seriously. 'Where, Sasha, and when?'

'At the beginning of this month, at Leipzig,' Sasha replied, his stammer disappearing now that he had succeeded in capturing their attention. 'I don't know much about the details, because the news only arrived late this afternoon. It seems that practically everyone was there—all Bonaparte's levies from the conquered states, as well as the French, of course, and on our side there were Austrians, Prussians, Swedes, Saxons, even a few British. They're already calling it the Battle of the Nations! One report said there were over five hundred thousand men involved over the three days . . .'

'Three days!' exclaimed Andrei. 'One was more than enough for Borodino! I suppose they needed more time to allow everyone a chance to join in.' The bitter expression on his face belied his light tone.

'Were the casualties very heavy?' Irina asked anxiously.

Sasha shrugged. 'I don't know. We've no proper figures yet, only estimates. I'm afraid it sounds as if they may have been.'

'Shall we pray for them?' Tatya asked quietly. It seemed odd to Galina, and yet perfectly natural, that they all stood and turned towards the icon in the corner of the room, heads bowed and eyes closed, all in the middle of dinner, for they had not yet started the third course. The footmen stood still, dishes in their hands, and joined in as fervently in the Amen as everyone else at the end of Lev's recitation of the prayer for the souls of the dead, and then they all crossed themselves and were silent for a few seconds as they sat down and the servants resumed serving.

'I-I did hear one name,' Sasha said presently. 'Prince Poniatowski.'

'Killed?' Igor asked harshly.

'Drowned, apparently. I know he was on Bonaparte's side, but, well, one couldn't help but admire him.'

'One can hardly blame a Pole for siding with Bonaparte, although even he cheated them!' Igor commented. 'As one of a nation annexed by Russia myself, I can understand why they mistrust Russia, Austria, Prussia and practically everyone else, even if it would make my ancestors shudder to hear me sympathise with them! I hope Bonaparte has the decency to regret his loss, but I expect he's too busy enjoying yet another victory. By the way, Saxony's on his side, not ours, you know.'

'No. They changed sides in the middle,' Sasha shook his head and spoke very positively. 'I'm afraid I om-m-mitted to mention one quite important fact. Bonaparte didn't win!'

There was a stunned silence for a moment, and then Galina heard herself ask in a slightly squeaky voice, 'You mean, *we* won?'

Sasha nodded. 'Apparently Bonaparte's in full retreat through Thuringia. They don't think he'll stop until he gets to the Rhine—well, there isn't anywhere he could halt long enough to re-form, is there?'

There was an excited discussion among the men about

this, except for Lev, who occupied himself inscribing lines on the white tablecloth with the point of his dessert knife, and Galina gathered from his muttering that he was drawing a map of Europe.

'He might manage it at Frankfürt,' he pronounced at last. 'Am Main, not am Oder, of course. If I were him, I'd re-form on the Rhine, though.'

'Ah, but you're not,' Irina said firmly. 'And if this is my dining-table, I'd prefer not to have it turned into a battlefield. Thank you, Sasha, for telling us the news, and now, would someone please inform us what's been going on in Petersburg?'

'Scandal, back-biting, politicking, over-eating, gambling, extravagant spending, and a constant round of entertainment, as usual,' Igor informed her with a sardonic twist to his mouth. 'Sergei Dmitriev and his friends tied a policeman to a bear last week—not that there's anything new about that, for Dolokhov and Bezukhov did it years ago. The Society hostesses are gravely displeased with the Emperor for keeping the Guards officers away from Petersburg for the second Season in succession, and any man who can walk a polonaise is sure of an invitation to every ball, there's such a shortage of handsome young men. Any bachelor who isn't actually repellent in appearance has gone into hiding for fear of losing his freedom, and the regiment of mamas with marriagable daughters is taking on the aspect of a wolf-pack in the worst of winters. I'm afraid that even married men may find themselves forcibly divorced and remarried before Lent begins!'

'I hear that Countess Scherer and some of her friends are planning to petition the War Ministry to allow some of the Cadet Corps to attend evening parties and balls,' added Andrei in the same vein. 'And if there's no ball at the Winter Palace this Season, the Court Chamberlain thinks there may even be a *revolution*!' He mouthed the last word instead of saying it aloud, looking about him with exaggerated caution.

Lev snorted, although everyone else was amused, and said, 'Any interesting scandal, or just the usual nonsense?'

'Well, apart from Anna Volkhova . . .' Sasha began, then broke off suddenly and blushed a bright red that clashed with his hair, muttered something unintelligible and dropped his knife, for most of the others had stiffened and gone strangely still.

Galina, alone unaffected by Sasha's apparent *faux pas*, looked from one to another in some bewilderment, until she met Igor's dark, hooded eyes diagonally across the table.

'A pity to spoil a good dinner by mentioning that woman,' he said conversationally. 'She's expecting a child, and even the most innocent among us can hardly believe it to be her husband's. You didn't come across Nikolai Volkhov on your travels, did you?' This was directed at Lev.

'No. We hoped we might find him at his Novgorod estate when we passed through there in the summer, but they said he'd gone to join the Emperor in Germany,' Lev replied, taking up the tactful change of subject. 'In fact, we met hardly anyone we knew while we were abroad—not Russians, that is—except Vassily Karachev—his brother Vladimir is Nikolai's First Battalion Major, or was, I should say, for I doubt if Nikolai will ever be fit enough to go back to his Regiment. We came across him in Vienna—Vassily, that is— 'though I never did find out what he was doing there. One never does with him.'

'He does things for the Foreign Ministry,' Igor said in a final-sounding tone, as if that was all one could say, which it apparently was, for the conversation moved on to general topics and the exchange of news of various friends, with asides of explanation to Galina about who they were from Andrei and Lev, so that she should not feel left out, until Irina and Tatya exchanged glances, and the former invited the ladies to withdraw and leave the men to their wine.

They did not return to the salon where Tatya had received her guests, but to a pleasant apartment which Tatya referred to as the Garden Room. It was a golden room in the candlelight, with Karelian birch furniture upholstered in gold brocade to match the wall-hangings and the long curtains which hid the windows, a white porcelain stove, and a flowered carpet, in the middle of which reposed a very prosperous-looking black cat.

'Why, there's Vron!' exclaimed Irina when she caught sight of him. 'How he's grown!'

The cat condescended to wake up and stalk across to her to be picked up and made much of, although Tatya placed a finger on his nose and said severely, 'You, sir, are supposed to live in the stables and discipline the mice!' At which the cat closed his eyes in a smug smile and settled down on Irina's lap, dabbing at her silk gown with stubby paws, and purring loudly.

The tea equipage arrived, and the delicate porcelain cups were handed by a pair of footmen, and when they had withdrawn, Tatya said, 'I think, Galina, I'd best explain the peculiar turn in the conversation earlier on—about Anna Volkhova, that is. You must have thought everyone behaved strangely, but you see, we've all been affected to some extent by that woman's influence.'

Galina murmured something polite, and wondered at her new friend's use of the word 'woman' to describe a female member of the nobility.

'Anna Volkhova married Prince Nikolai Volkhov at the wishes of both their fathers,' Tatya began in a calm, unemotional tone. 'Nikolai is an old friend of Lev's and mine—an old and dear friend. The marriage was a disaster.' She paused a moment, and then continued, 'I don't know if you've ever come across the term "nymphomaniac"?' Galina shook her head. 'It means a woman who has a—a mania for—for men. It amounts almost to a sickness . . . She's very beautiful, and very skilled at attracting men. In short, she's taken innumerable lovers. Nikolai is not the man to accept such a situation. I think perhaps he blamed himself for—for failing her in some way at first, but now he simply has nothing to do with her. She's now rather obviously with child, and no one knows who the father is—it could be any one of a dozen men—except that he can't possibly be her husband.

'The reason why we were all so put about by Sasha's mention . . . well, Lev and I cannot forgive her for her treatment of Nikolai, and, in spite of himself, Lev was once her lover for the briefest of times, and someone tried to make trouble by telling Irina an exaggerated version of it while Lev was away in the Army. Andrei and Nadya—they each had a brother, and the two of them fought a duel over Anna, I believe, and it made for bitter feeling between them when they first met. I don't know about Igor, for he's a very reticent person, but I believe he has some good reason to mislike her. Sasha, I think, is the only one of us she hasn't hurt, one way or another, and I suppose that's why he made such a blunder, poor boy!

'Now—what else should you know about us? Irina here was left an orphan with no fortune as a small child, and was brought up by an old aunt in the country near Smolensk. She and her aunt fled from the French last year, and the aunt died from the shock in a little inn by the road. Lev came along with a convoy of wounded, found Irina all alone, and rescued her, and then, naturally, fell in love with her—my brother always does the expected thing!' She and Irina exchanged a smile. 'Nadya was living in Moscow, and ran away when the French arrived there, and Andrei rescued her when a man tried to rob her on her way to me at Ryazan—he was on his way to buy horses for his regiment. Igor doesn't say much about himself, but he's three-quarters Ukrainian, and seems to find it a disadvantage at times, which makes him a little defensive and sardonic, and, to put it bluntly, he's not as wealthy as most of our circle— not that it matters all that much. He and Andrei were in the Corps of Pages together as boys. Sasha, bless him, is a simple, uncomplicated person, full of good nature. There you have us!'

'And I'm very glad to know you all, and most indebted to you for calling on me and making me so welcome,' Galina assured her, thinking how sensible it was to give her such a clear idea about them all. 'I was beginning to think that I'd never get to know anyone in Petersburg, apart from my man-of-business.'

'Oh, now your arrival has been reported in the *Gazette*, you'll find that people will start to call,' Tatya told her. 'Who is your man-of-business, by the way? Is he satisfactory?'

'He seems very efficient,' Galina replied. 'He explains everything clearly, and I find that the figures he gives me about produce and income from the estates are all added up correctly, and tally with what the bailiffs in charge of each estate say, so I conclude that he's honest.'

'Yes, he has a good reputation, and I'm glad to hear that you check his accounts, and those of your bailiffs!' Tatya said approvingly. 'So many wealthy females seem to think that being female means that they are exempted from responsibility for managing their own affairs, and that no one will ever take advantage of their ignorance.'

Anything further she might have said was forestalled by the entry of the gentlemen, who had tarried no longer than it took to drink a glass of wine and demolish a couple of military reputations. Lev prodded the cat's stomach with a tentative finger and was bitten for his interference, then engaged in conversation with Nadya and his sister, Sasha sat down on the sofa by Irina, while Andrei drew up a chair near to them and enquired how Irina liked foreign travel, and Igor joined Galina on the other sofa and said abruptly, 'Your problem, I collect, is a surfeit of possessions.'

'It is indeed,' Galina replied with feeling. 'The whole house is *cluttered* with everything imaginable. I'd like to be rid of three-quarters of it, but I don't know where to start. No doubt some of the things are great works of art, so I can't very well send them all to the bonfire, but I know so little about such things, for there's not a great deal of opportunity to learn in Tver.'

'Is there a catalogue?'

'No. Apparently General Zhadnov wouldn't have one made—he had some superstition about it being unlucky to count one's possessions! A few of the things are labelled, but most of them have no indication of where they came from or what they are. I don't know what to do—the house is barely habitable as it is.'

'The first thing you must do is have someone knowledgeable go through the whole collection and make a catalogue,' Igor said in a business-like fashion. 'While he does so, he can throw out the rubbish, and you may send it to be burned as you please. Then you can decide what of the rest you wish to keep, and which to sell.'

'Where may I find such a person?' Galina asked.

Igor hesitated for a moment regarding her searchingly, and then said, 'The Emperor, as I mentioned earlier, is engrossed in playing soldiers, so only a trickle of objects is coming into the Hermitage collections, and there are enough other fellows about to see to those. I can't imagine that the situation will change for several months, so, if you agree, I'll come and stay in the house and catalogue your inheritance for you.'

'Would you really?' Galina felt a wave of relief sweep over her. 'How kind! I'd be so grateful . . .' She hesitated, bit her lip, then went on in a voice made gruff by embarrassment, 'Of course, you must let me . . .' She balked at the word 'pay', but Igor rescued her by saying, 'I'm in the service of the Emperor as a Court official. I can't accept payment for extra-mural activities. I'll make the provisos that if there is anything in the collection which properly belongs to the State (or any other state, for that matter), I must see that it's returned, and if there's anything among the objects you decide to sell which would find a place in the Imperial collections, it shall be sold to the Emperor. I'd prefer to stay in the house, if that's convenient, partly to save time, and partly,' and here Galina caught a distinct flash of humour, 'because the Winter Palace is not the most comfortable of residences.'

'Yes, of course,' Galina replied. 'Although I'm afraid you're quite likely to find a bear in your room . . . The beds are quite comfortable,' she added, anxious not to discourage him.

'Which is more than one can say for those in the Winter Palace,' Igor observed. 'Alexander Pavlovich sleeps on a little canvas folding bed, like an army officer, and expects everyone else to regard anything slightly better as the height of luxury!'

'Little?' queried Galina, who knew that the Emperor was over six feet tall. 'But why?'

Igor shrugged. 'Something left over from the military discipline his father imposed, I suppose. He must be the richest man in the world and owns what is possibly the largest and most expensively-furnished palace in the world, yet he chooses to live in a pair of small, bleak rooms, without an atom of comfort. They all do—Grand

Duke Konstantin Pavlovich and the two younger brothers, that is. Autocrats can afford to be odd.'

Galina quailed inside at such a rash statement and hastily changed the subject by enquiring when Igor would like to take up residence in her house. 'My mother is staying with me, of course, so it's . . .' She paused, not sure what words to employ.

'*De règle,*' he supplied. 'I know. I'd not have suggested it otherwise. I'll come sometime tomorrow—oh, there'll be my valet as well, of course.'

'Of course,' Galina replied, hoping that she sounded quite used to receiving visits of indeterminate length from comparative strangers and their servants. 'I shall be most obliged to you for your help.'

Igor gave her a sidelong look and sardonic little smile, and she realised that what made his amusement disconcerting was its private nature—he smiled to himself, not to or with someone else. It made him seem sly, and she wondered if perhaps she had been rash to accept his offer, and particularly to comply with his wish to stay in the house. After all, Tatya had said that he was a comparatively poor man, and it was not clear how well she knew him—was he altogether honest? There had been no mention of a wife, so presumably he was unmarried, and she was a rich heiress . . . It was too late to withdraw from the arrangement now.

Igor said nothing more, and Galina was busy with these unwelcome thoughts, so there was silence for a few seconds, and then he excused himself and crossed the room to talk to Lev, pausing on the way for a few quiet words with the cat, much to Galina's surprise, and, for some reason, comfort. Sasha limped over to sit with Galina, followed by Andrei, as part of a general post, and she spent the rest of the evening being entertained by the two of them.

Before the party broke up, Nadya invited them all to

dine with her and Andrei at their apartment in the Anichkov Palace, which was, apparently, where Andrei's duties were centred, and Tatya proposed to include Galina in a variety of planned entertainments, so that she went home feeling that at last she was assured of an *entrée* into Petersburg Society, thanks to Tatya's kindness.

Her first action on reaching home was to tell Osya Ivanich of Igor's impending arrival—a piece of news which seemed to please him, and he immediately suggested a suitable room for the guest.

'Er—is he to have a bed-warmer, Countess?' he asked, looking particularly expressionless.

'A what?' demanded Galina, not because she did not understand, but because she was disgusted by the implication that former guests in this house had expected and received such a service.

'A bed-warmer, ma'am—a female serf to—er—'

'Yes. I know what you mean,' she replied testily. 'Certainly not!'

Osya's face became, if possible, even more expressionless as he said, 'He may ask for one,' in a detached tone, his eyes on a point somewhere beyond the top of Galina's head.

'If he does,' Galina said ominously, 'you had best inform me! I'll not have any of my serfs abused in that way.'

Osya's mask slipped for a moment and he looked almost human. All he said was, 'Very good, Galina Stepanovna,' but the significance of that was not lost on Galina.

She was disappointed to find that her mother had already retired for the night, and so could not immediately be told about the excitement bubbling up inside her. There was no one else to confide in, so she calmed herself by taking a stroll through the reception rooms on the first floor, making a mental note of some of the things which must certainly go as soon as Igor Charodyev had passed an opinion on them.

Eventually, she came to the library, and found herself standing before the portrait of Gennadi Zhadnov. A branch of candles stood on a girandole nearby, casting a good light on the face, and she studied it with a strange feeling of interest and regret. He was—had been—a remarkably handsome man. There was a proud set to the head, a look of confidence and directness, proclaiming that here was a man who knew his own mind and could deal with any situation, who was open in his dealings. He would not indulge in private jokes at the expense of others, and he was obviously thoroughly westernised— not a man who would expect to be provided with a 'bed-warmer'! How very sad that such a man should have been swallowed up in the cold Arctic—such a waste! He seemed so obviously to have been made for glory and success, not a wretched death and an unmarked grave. She sighed and went soberly to bed.

CHAPTER
THREE

THE PAPESS

Light and inspiration/*A* femme fatale

To GALINA's irritation, her mother showed very little
interest in her account of the previous evening's events
when they met at breakfast, being more concerned to
identify her daughter's new acquaintances with her
Tarot cards. Even the news that a member of the
Emperor's own Cabinet was to stay in the house and
catalogue its contents brought no more than a distracted
murmur of, 'Yes, of course—the Magician! You know,
Galya I can find no trace of Death in connection with the
Chariot. I really can't understand it!' To which Galya
made no reply but a little *moué* of impatience.

Igor Charodyev arrived during the morning in his own
carriage, accompanied by two large trunks and his valet,
a silent, solemn-looking individual. Although Galina
had only thought to mention to him that Igor and his
valet were expected, Osya Ivanich seemed quite un-
perturbed at fitting in an extra carriage, two pair of
horses, groom and coachmen, and neither did he seem
particularly put out when first Tatya and then Sasha
Tuchin arrived, and were impulsively invited to stay for
luncheon by his mistress. If anything, he seemed pleased
at the sudden increase in activity.

Tatya had come to suggest that Galina spend the
afternoon with her in visiting her modiste to inspect the

latest fashions, and to deliver a considerable number of invitation-cards from her own acquaintance, who, she informed Galina, were all most anxious to meet her new-found cousin. Sasha gave no particular reason for his visit, and stammered a great deal when Igor, returning from an inspection of his room and finding him in the Peacock Salon with the ladies, enquired abruptly, 'What are you doing here? Has the War Minister found you out?'

'Found him out in what?' asked Tatya.

'Embezzling medal-ribbons, probably,' Igor answered seriously. 'He collects them, you know. There are reels and reels of them hidden in the cellar under his apartment.'

'H-haven't got a cellar,' Sasha objected.

'Attic, then.'

'What does he do with them?' Galina asked, apparently in earnest.

'He dyes them different colours and sells them to bonnet-makers. You can see the dye on his fingers.'

Sasha had indeed a black stain on his right forefinger, which he insisted was ink, and pulled on a glove to cover it.

'I-it's all n-nonsense, you kn-know!' he assured Galina. 'He m-makes up these w-wild tales ab-bout people. I don't have anything to do with medal-ribbons.'

'In that case,' Igor improvised smoothly, 'you've sneaked out without leave to waste your time in the frivolous pursuit of pleasure, leaving the conduct of the war to incompetent idiots like the War Minister.'

'Oh, well, yes, but I did have leave,' Sasha replied, leaving the slander against General Barclay de Tolly unanswered and not bothering to point out that he was, in any case, with the Army in Germany. 'I don't have to be there all the time, you know. I just thought I'd call on Galina Stepanovna, you know—er—to—er—well, to call on her.'

'Ah!' Igor murmured darkly. 'Too much eagerness, too much presumption on so short an acquaintance. Probably a fortune-hunter. Mistrust him, m'dear!' he advised Galina in a theatrical aside. 'Any fellow who invites himself to luncheon the morning after he first meets you is Up To No Good, you know!'

Galina was incapable of replying in the same vein, for he had echoed her own suspicions of him too closely for comfort, and she wondered if he had guessed her reservations, but Tatya turned the tables by enquiring mischievously, 'And what if he invited himself to stay the very evening that he first meets her?'

Igor gave one of his private little smiles, and, instead of replying, said to Galina, 'I've no wish to start my stay by appearing over-fussy and troublesome, but do you think that the bear in my bedroom might be moved elsewhere? I've no objection to using it as a hat-stand, but my valet finds it unnerving. I didn't realise that your warning last night was intended seriously.'

'Oh, heavens! I'm sorry!' Galina exclaimed. '*That* bear.' She rang the bell, and the footman who constantly lurked outside in the gallery, awaiting such a summons, came in and stood looking expectant.

'Mischa, would you please ask someone to remove the stuffed bear from Count Charodyev's room,' Galina requested. The man looked startled at being addressed by name, for the General, during his brief periods of residence in the house, had been in the habit of addressing all his domestic serfs as 'Hey you!'

'Certainly, Galina Stepanovna,' he replied smartly, then, less certainly, 'Er—where . . .?'

Galina, realising from his mode of address that she was now fully accepted as mistress of the house, smiled encouragingly at him and said, 'Wherever you can find room for it, where it hasn't been before,' and the man went out looking thoughtful.

'It has the moth,' Igor observed with his private smile. Galina looked at him and decided that it wasn't exactly malicious, or even mocking, but there was something about the way he looked down and let those heavy lids hood his eyes that seemed to exclude the rest of the world from whatever had amused him.

The impromptu luncheon-party was a success, Galina's kitchen staff proving their skills to be more than adequate, and her footmen admirably well-trained. The smaller of the two dining-rooms would have seemed over-large for so small a party, but for the mass of pieces of furniture which crammed the margins of the room and reduced its apparent size by more than half. Tatya and Sasha tactfully showed no awareness that they were sitting in that middle of what might have been a furniture warehouse, but Igor looked about him with an expression of open amusement, then deliberately caught Galina's eye, pulled a face, and winked, so that she was forced to smile back.

During the afternoon, Sasha reluctantly returned to his duties, and Tatya carried Galina off shopping, leaving Igor to decide where to start his mammoth task. The ladies spent a pleasant and very expensive afternoon seeing the new fashions and inspecting a large shipment of fine fabrics which Tatya's modiste had just received from England. By the end of the visit, she was also Galina's modiste, with an order for ball-gowns and more informal frocks which would keep her workshops busy for some time.

Galina returned home to find Igor installed in the library, where he had cleared one large table of all the various items stacked on its surface, and set out his equipment—a battered inkstand with a bundle of pens, several notebooks bound in dark leather, and a quantity of sheets of paper, on which he had already begun to list the contents of the room.

He looked up as Galina entered, frowned a little, and would have stood up, but she said hastily, 'Oh, pray don't rise—I don't wish to interrupt you. Have you everything you require?'

'Yes, thank you. This desk, if it will not inconvenience you, a bell, and a virtually unlimited number of footmen at the other end of it, are all I require. And Gennadi Yakovich for company, of course.' He nodded towards the portrait, and Galina turned to look at it.

'I thought it must be he,' she said, looking up at the vital painted face and thinking once more how wrong it was that someone who looked so alive should be dead. 'Do—did you know him?'

'Fairly well. He served under my father at one time.'

'Served? In the Navy?' Galina glanced round and found that he had silently risen from his chair and come to stand a little behind and to one side of her.

'Yes. My father's a Commodore. Gennadi was his second or third lieutenant when he was a Captain.'

'Is he—your father—in the Baltic Fleet? At Kronstadt?'

'No. The Black Sea Fleet. He's based at Kherson, so my mother lives there, to be near him.' The information was given a trifle curtly, and the subject changed abruptly back to the portrait. 'It's by Borovikovsky—must be one of his finest. He's caught that intense vitality extremely well. A handsome bastard, wasn't he?'

Galina, shocked by the epithet, wondered if Igor meant it literally, and looked round at him questioningly, then registered a certain note of bitterness in his voice and realised that there was some undercurrent here—jealousy, perhaps?

'I didn't care much for him,' Igor said flatly, apparently reading the changing expressions on her face. 'I apologise.'

'One can't help one's likes and dislikes,' she replied

practically. 'I never met him. I came to ask if you would mind dining with my mother tomorrow night. You see, Tatya has contrived an invitation for me . . .'

'To dine at Countess Scherer's and stay on for her ball,' Igor finished for her. 'I'm doing the same, in fact, so I'm afraid that your mama will be left to dine alone then, as well as this evening.'

'She won't mind,' Galina assured him truthfully, for Countess Razumova would be much happier if she were not obliged to make conversation all evening with a young gentleman.

They each went to the Valyev's dinner in their own carriage, but it seemed a more sensible arrangement that, if they would bound for the same destination, they should go in the same vehicle. Galina asked Tatya if that would be in order, and was assured that it was, particularly as her maid would be with her in any case, so the next evening, they both went in Galina's carriage, with Dasha making herself as small as possible in one corner (unnecessarily, for there was plenty of room).

'I suppose you are acquainted with Countess Scherer?' Galina asked as the carriage glided over the wooden pavé of the fashionable Vosnesensky Prospect towards their hostess' residence.

'Tolerably well,' Igor replied. 'She's a great collector of lions, with a trace of the feline herself.'

'Lions?' Galina was puzzled.

'People of interest. Heroes, actors, generals, ambassadors, royalty, heiresses—anyone whose name is on everyone's lips. She's lady-in-waiting to the Empress Dowager and has a salon where most of the conversation is political. Anyone who is anyone is invited to her house, and anyone who isn't anyone but wishes he were tries to get an invitation. She's a mischief-making female of some considerable intelligence—a maiden lady of fifty or so. Don't let her drag you into political discussions, for she passes on anything indiscreet that she hears.'

'Passes on?'

'To where it will do the most harm. There are several people languishing far from Petersburg because of a careless statement made in Anna Scherer's salon.'

Galina assumed that he meant they were in Siberia, or worse, and regarded their hostess with some trepidation, but found her friendly and flatteringly admiring of Galina's choice of a sea-green paduasoy ball-gown a few shades darker than her aquamarine and gold necklace and hair ornament. Her own gown was dark blue, with a diamond cypher of her office on the shoulder. She made known to Galina a number of important-looking gentlemen, mostly in glittering court dress, and a few younger men in military uniform, but ignored the hopeful expressions on the faces of some half-dozen other young men who were not in uniform. The reason for this was clear enough, for she had greeted Igor with an off-hand, 'Ah, Igor Grigorovich—so glad you could come. I can't imagine why you didn't follow your father into the Navy.'

'My father considered one web-footed son sufficient, and even crossing the Anichkov bridge makes me seasick,' Igor replied solemnly, and remained close to Galina, in spite of their hostess' attempts to make him go away, a crow among the peacocks in his black coat and breeches.

Eventually, Countess Scherer had to leave Galina and welcome some other guests, and Igor said quietly, 'I forgot to mention that she's intensely patriotic. Any man who isn't fighting for Holy Russia is virtually French in her opinion.'

'Is that why she gave you such a froggy welcome?' Galina enquired, the warmth of her own reception going a little to her head. Igor gave her one quick, sparkling glance, then his eyelids drooped and his lips twisted in his odd little smile. But all he said was, 'Tatya Petrovna's just arrived.'

Galina turned her head to look towards the door and encountered a considering stare from a lady standing nearby—a very beautiful lady with large dark eyes, lustrous black hair and a complexion like magnolia petals. She was wearing a gown of ivory satin which left her shoulders and most of her shapely bosom uncovered, and, instead of the elaborate jewellery worn by most of the ladies present, her hair and neck were ornamented by many fine gold chains, set every inch or so with single diamonds. The effect was very striking. She did not look away when she saw that Galina was aware of her, but gave a little cat-like smile, her lips moving only slightly and her dark-fringed lids drooping, and then she turned to her companion, a much beribboned and braided officer, made some half-smiling remark, and drifted away on his arm.

'Who is that?' Galina asked.

'Princess Anna Mikhailovna Volkhova,' Igor replied with a marked lack of expression in his voice.

Galina took another look at the retreating figure before she vanished among the other guests, and noted a thickening about the waist and a certain hollowness to the back, which were the visible indications that the Princess was, indeed, *enceinte*.

'You don't like her either, then?' Galina asked, looking directly at Igor. He met her gaze quite openly, but his dark eyes were unreadable and he simply replied, 'No,' his lips shutting firmly after the monosyllable, then, before Galina could feel rebuffed, he smiled and added, 'You probably won't either if you have the misfortune to know her any better.'

'Galina dear—Igor, good evening.' Tatya had come upon them unnoticed. 'What a crowd! I should think Anna Pavlovna has invited all her ball-guests to dinner.

Oh, this . . .' inviting her escort forward with a graceful gesture, '. . . is Konstantin Fedorovich Durakov. He's on sick-leave from the Chevalier Garde.'

The large young man in the white uniform bowed over Galina's hand, keeping his soulful blue eyes on her face, and then stood looking down at her in an admiring fashion, his fair curly hair quite a foot higher than her own chignon. He was broad-shouldered and built in proportion to his height, so that she felt herself almost hemmed in by the expanse of white cloth, red facings and silver lace.

'You're very tall!' she exclaimed, then wished she had not, in case he was offended.

'I'm the same height as the Emperor,' he informed her in a reverent tone. 'I must say that, for the first time since I was wounded, I'm very glad that it happened as it's enabled me to make your acquaintance.'

'I trust you're on your way to recovery.' Galina's concern was genuine and seemed to please the young man, but caused Igor to suffer a sudden fit of coughing, at which Konstantin Durakov gave him a suspicious stare.

Dinner was served in a room of oppressive magnificence, where gilding had been applied to virtually every surface which could be persuaded to accept it. The tables were set in a hollow square, with guests seated on both sides of them, all a little too close together for comfort, and with not quite sufficient room for the servants to move easily between the outer row and the walls. Galina was taken in by Konstantin Durakov, who invited her to call him Kostya Fedorovich. She found the place on her other side occupied by an officer in the dark green uniform with blue collar and cuffs of the Semyonovsky Guard, with smooth dark hair and a sulkily handsome face, whom Kostya introduced as Sergei Mikhailovich Dmitriev.

To her surprise, Galina found that both men seemed to find her conversation most interesting, and she managed to get through the time pretty well until eventually the ladies withdrew to tidy themselves for the ball in a series of little anterooms where warm scented water and linen towels had been laid out for them.

Here, Galina was accosted by Princess Volkhova, who smiled lazily upon her and drawled, 'How pleasant to see a fresh face in Petersburg. You must be the old General's heiress, Countess Razumova.'

'Yes,' Galina admitted cautiously.

'And no doubt Tatya Kalinskaya has warned you about me?' The Princess made an amused little *moué*. 'Such a silly muddle, my dear! Our interfering fathers spoiled everything for us, you see—they married me to the man poor Tatya wanted, and gave her to some dreadful old man, and made us all thoroughly unhappy! My poor husband and I parted, of course—we'd nothing at all in common, so it was inevitable. It's all very sad, but one must make the best of it! You seem to have made a great impression on my little brother.'

'Your brother?' Galina questioned, a little bewildered by the friendliness of this undeniably beautiful creature.

'Sergei. He sat next to you at dinner, and could hardly bear to turn away from you.'

Before Galina could think of a reply, Tatya appeared, bowed icily to Anna Volkhova, and enquired pleasantly if Galina was ready to go to the ballroom. Anna gave her little feline smile and drifted away, and neither Tatya nor Galina made any mention of her as they found places along one side of a large ballroom with pale green walls divided by white pilasters with gilded capitals. Six vast chandeliers cast blazing light and candle-grease on a colourful throng of people waiting for the orchestra in the flower-massed balcony to finish tuning itself and begin the dancing, and whiling away the time in gossiping groups on the inlaid patterns of the polished floor.

In no time at all, Galina found herself somewhere near the centre of a group of young men, all vying good-naturedly for Tatya's attention, but also sparing a little of their own for Galina, and her programme-card soon began to look quite respectably filled.

'I can walk a polonaise, I think, if you've one to spare,' Sasha Tuchin said hopefully, and seemed unnecessarily grateful when Galina offered him two. As he handed her card back, it was intercepted by Igor, who surveyed the various pencilled initials and remarked, 'I see you've a goodly sprinkling of Tatya's Beaux already, so I might as well add one more,' and put himself down for the supper dance and a waltz without asking permission.

'Tatya's Beaux?' enquired Galina, recovering her programme and too flattered that anyone should wish to dance with her twice to remonstrate against his high-handedness.

'Tatya goes about trailing clouds of glory in the form of a group of gilded youth known collectively as Tatya's Beaux,' Igor explained, his lean face wrily amused. 'She won't marry any one of them, but they can't help following, like moths around a candle.' He suddenly frowned and moved very slightly closer to Galina's elbow as Sergei Dmitriev came to beg and be granted the bespeaking of a mazurka. The Guard officer ignored the dark figure until he had returned Galina's card, and then said, slightly patronisingly, 'Ah, Charodyev—how's your brother these days?'

'Enjoying the Mediterranean sun,' Igor replied austerely.

'And his wife?'

Igor's face became quite blank as he replied, 'I've no idea.'

Sergei bowed to Galina, and she was distracted from the curious exchange by the orchestra suddenly striking up the opening polonaise, which Sasha came to claim. He could indeed do little more than walk it, and very lamely at that, but Galina gave him full credit for trying and assured him that he did it very well.

The evening seemed to pass very quickly, for her card was almost full, and she passed from one partner to another as rhythm and tune changed, and, surprisingly soon, Igor was taking her back to the oppressive dining-room, now set with little tables and gilt chairs for the buffet supper.

'I gather that you don't like Sergei Dmitriev either,' she said as Igor handed her to a seat and took the chair facing her across one of the little tables.

'I've no particular feeling either way. The man's a dissolute fool, and seems to spend all his time in Petersburg, which is odd when his regiment's fighting in Germany,' he replied. 'And before you burst with curiosity—Sergei's sister and my brother were somewhat closely involved for a few weeks a couple of years ago, with the result that my brother's wife left him and entered a convent. Denis—my brother—is with the remains of Admiral Senyavin's squadron in the Adriatic. I did Sasha Alexandrovich a wrong this morning.' The abrupt change of subject was not accompanied by any change of tone. 'He has a more than adequate fortune of his own—he doesn't need to hunt another.'

Galina looked at him thoughtfully, but, although he met her gaze, she could read nothing in his eyes. 'It's a danger I shall have to beware of, I suppose,' she said, and could not help but remember what Tatya had said about his own lack of fortune. 'I could wish that the General had left me a moderate amount of property, and not a house full of—of—'

'Moth-eaten bears?' suggested Igor.

'Oh, heavens! There's not more than one of them, is there?' she asked anxiously.

'I was speaking figuratively.'

'Then pray take something less ursine for your figure!'

Igor laughed quite openly at that, his face softening amazingly. 'Wheels of Fortune, then?'

'Oh, that. Yes. What is it, do you think? It doesn't appear to be a clock, for I can detect no means of telling the time by it.'

'It may once have been part of a clock, but it's been adapted. I think it's three or four centuries old, and probably made in Nuremburg. It has no particular use, except to remind us all that whatever rises will probably fall—and vice-versa.'

'I don't believe in Fate,' Galina said firmly. 'Mama is always consulting her cards and trying to make out that we're all tied in some way—like the figures on the Wheel. It's not true. We make our own lives, with God's help. We're not toys.'

Igor's gaze moved over her face, noting her eyes, made even larger by earnestness, the decisiveness of her expression and the firmness of that shapely mouth and chin, and said equally, 'I don't think your mother believes in the cards either—or not yet, at any rate. It's just an amusement, a pastime, to match real people against the cards and see if what the Tarot says matches what really happens. I agree that it's dangerous when a person comes to believe in it, but I'm sure your mother had more sense.'

'It's such a waste of time.'

'Perhaps she hasn't anything else to do.'

Galina was silent, recognising the truth of his observation. Two footmen brought food and wine, served them, and withdrew, and then she said, 'I'm sorry about your brother.'

'Foolishness generally has to be paid for,' he replied obliquely. 'Some of us make our lives into pig's nests.'

Galina had a mental vision of a fat pink pig building a

nest in a tree, and laughed aloud, a merry, tinkling sound which caused several people nearby to look round to see who had such a pretty laugh.

After supper, Igor returned her to the ballroom, where she was claimed by Sergei Dmitriev for his promised mazurka. He danced with considerable panache and paid her some pretty compliments, but she found herself wondering about the state of his finances, and then felt guilty and anxious at realising that he was the second man whom she had begun to suspect of having designs on her fortune in one evening. Then it occurred to her to wonder why he was so far away from his regiment.

'I thought that all the Guards were with the Emperor,' she remarked as he led her back to her place at the end of his dance.

'Indeed, but a few of us have duties here,' he replied smoothly. 'The rest of the Imperial Family has to be guarded too, you know,' which seemed a reasonable explanation.

All in all, Galina enjoyed her first Petersburg ball very much, and told Tatya so when she called on her next day.

'The Season's barely started yet,' Tatya said, smiling. 'I suppose there'll be no regimental galas again this year, but I think there'll be a Christmas ball at the Winter Palace. We must have you presented before then. Perhaps Countess Protasova will be at the Tutaevs' party this evening. She's the Empress' principal *Dame d'Honneur*,' she added in explanation. 'We must arrange for Irina too, for that matter, for, what with one thing and another, there was no opportunity last winter.'

Countess Protasova was indeed at the Tutaevs' that evening. She was very elderly now, and decidedly fat, but still dressed in the height of fashion, with the diamond cyphers of both living Empresses, and also that of the Empress Ekaterina, pinned to her bodice, and an amazingly golden wig on her head. She surveyed the two candidates for presentation through a gold-handled lorgnette set with diamonds, declared herself satisfied with their suitability, and bade them, in a brisk, business-like fashion, to come severally, each alone and in a coach and six, to the Tavrichesky Palace sharp at noon the following Tuesday, in full white court dress, then dismissed them with a regal wave of the hand, beckoning with the other to a stout gentleman in Admiral's uniform. As Galina made her curtsey and withdrew, she heard the old lady say sharply, 'And why the devil haven't you had those gun-carriages replaced at Kronstadt?'

'Oh dear!' whispered Irina. 'I hope the Empress isn't as fierce as that!'

She was not, but the intervening balls, suppers, conversaziones, skating-parties, dinners, morning-calls and theatre visits all lost a little of their savour in the anticipation of the ordeal. Tatya took them both to her modiste again to be equipped with the proper white crêpe, instructed them to wear pearls—no brilliants of any kind—and sent her own maid to show Dasha the proper way to arrange Galina's hair on the great day.

On the Sunday, Galina found her prayers in church tended to centre around what was, after all, only a matter of social significance, and conscientiously turned her thoughts to more important matters, like the comfort and safety of the Imperial Army in the worsening weather and increasing cold, and the well-being of the officers and men of the Imperial Navy.

She was up early on the Tuesday morning, after a restless night, and wandered about the house, seeking refuge from the female domestics with their brushes and dusters and the morning-liveried footmen scurrying about their duties. The library seemed to be the only room not being cleaned, so she went in there, and was surprised to find Igor already at work, surrounded by snuffboxes.

'Do you suppose the General was much addicted to snuff?' he asked after replying to her greeting and apology for disturbing him.

'I don't know. In fact, I know hardly anything about him,' she replied, her eyes going unconsciously to the portrait of the General's nephew, wishing she knew more about *him*, let alone his uncle. 'I expect he just collected all these because they were there to be collected, not because he had any use for them.'

'You're not nervous about the presentation, are you?' Igor enquired, noting that she was fiddling with the trimming of her morning-gown in uncharacteristic fashion. 'There's no need to be. The Empress is a lady like yourself, from a fairly undistinguished German princely house, who happens to be married to someone more important. You'll find she's rather nervous and shy, and not very happy.'

'Not happy?' Galina was surprised, for she had assumed unthinkingly that being Empress and married to such an Emperor must make any female happy.

'It doesn't make for happiness to love someone who has only the affection of custom or friendship to return, or to bear children and see them die. She and Alexander Pavlovich were children when they married. She's changed very little, but he . . . there are other interests, other loves, and they've little in common now.'

'I see. I hadn't thought . . .' Galina thought now, and felt less nervous.

'Also, you won't trip over the hem of your skirt and fall flat on your face!' he added, with something more like his usual manner.

He was, of course, quite right. Galina's coach was ready on time, and carried her to the portico of the Tavrichesky Palace precisely five minutes before noon,

her hair correctly dressed, her white crêpe gown pris-
tinely fresh and perfect, and her throat roped with
lustrous pearls, under the warmth of her hooded cloak.
She hastened up the steps through falling snowflakes and
entered the vestibule, where she found Irina, pale but
composed, smoothing her skirts after removing her
wraps, and attended by a small army of liveried servants.
The two ladies exchanged nervous smiles, and as soon as
they were ready they were conducted by no fewer than
twelve footmen through a very large octagonal hall
under the flattened dome which gave the building its
nickname of the Russian Pantheon. Galina had time
only to notice a forest of immense Ionic columns and
some statuary before they were marshalled onwards to a
large room full of people, who all broke off their con-
versations to turn and stare, then to another even larger
room, where two languid gentlemen in court dress were
playing chess. They rose to their feet and greeted Irina
and Galina with ceremony, dismissed the liveried escort,
and engaged the ladies in desultory conversation for ten
minutes or so. They seemed quite friendly, so Galina
ventured to ask why the ceremony was taking place here
instead of in the Winter Palace, and was told kindly that
the Empress preferred this smaller residence in the
Emperor's absence.

Suddenly, the door opposite the one by which they
had entered opened, and the Empress came in, closely
followed by Countess Protasova. The gentlemen bowed
very low, and Irina and Galina made their best curtseys,
to which the Empress responded by clasping her hands
together at her waist and bowing slightly in the old
Russian fashion.

Irina was presented first, being a married lady, and
Galina stood looking at Elizaveta Alexeyevna meanwhile, wondering what exactly she had expected her to
be like. Someone magnificent and superhuman, pre-

sumably, but what she saw was a slight, fairly tall figure, dressed simply in a white embroidered silk gown, with a magnificent rope of pearls looped several times about a slender white neck. Her hair was light brown and prettily dressed in a high chignon, with curls about her face, which looked a little older than her thirty-four years. She had a small, pretty mouth, large, widely-set eyes and a delicate little nose, giving a general effect of dainty prettiness rather than beauty. Galina was struck by the sadness of her expression in repose, and remembered what Igor had said about the dead babies and the Emperor's other interests. She added to that her own knowledge of the poor health that often prevented the Empress from carrying out social engagements, and thought how difficult it must make her position, when she was open to criticisms to which she could not reply. Her manner was quiet and pleasant, with a touch of shyness, and her smile very sweet and gentle.

When Galina made her curtsey, the Empress leaned forward to kiss her on both cheeks, as she had already done to Irina, and then she engaged both of them in a conversation, speaking very quickly in French, the usual language in Society, in a low, pleasant voice, for about ten minutes. Galina had no recollection afterwards of what the Empress had said, or what she had replied, and she had hardly grasped the fact that she had actually been presented before it was all over. The Empress smilingly made her adieux and withdrew, and Irina and Galina returned to their carriages to go home, both in a slightly dazed state.

That evening, Igor tore himself away from his work with obvious reluctance to escort Galina to the Ruschevs' ball. He asked a trifle absently if she had enjoyed her presentation in the carriage on the way, gave a grunt of laughter when she pointed out that he had just crossed the Anichkov bridge without bring seasick, and then said, 'I meant to get you some flowers for this evening—that gown really needs some, being so plain, but I didn't have time. I'm sorry.'

Galina, who thought he had not noticed that she was wearing her presentation gown, was silent with surprise for a moment, then said, 'It was kind of you to think of it, but I did have some flowers. Three bouquets, in fact.'

'Don't tell me—let me guess.' In the darkness of the carriage, his voice was sardonic. 'Sasha the unexceptional, Kostya the over-sized, and—er—' He hesitated a trifle too long, so Galina supplied, 'Sergei Dmitriev,' with some trepidation.

There was a moment of palpable silence, and then Igor enquired lightly, 'And which are you wearing?'

'None of them. Dasha picked me some white flowers in the winter garden—little scented ones, like wax.'

'Stephanotis. I can smell them,' Igor said, but he made no other comment on that subject, and talked of other things until they arrived at the Ruschevs' magnificent Baroque palace in Millionaires' Row. Galina gazed around her wide-eyed as she removed her cloak and overshoes, admiring the exuberant decoration of the entrance-hall, and then mounted the great staircase on Igor's arm, between the footmen standing impassively at the sides of every other step.

'It's a pity these liveried fellows are in the way,' Igor said quietly. 'The balustrades are most interesting. They're made of wrought iron—barley and poppies, tied with ribbons, and so delicate that the barley-ears rustle as you pass. There are mice and birds among the ears, too.'

Garlina looked sidelong, hoping to see these interesting-sounding treasures between the stout white-stockinged calves of the footmen, but without success. However, after they had been greeted by their host and hostess at the top of the stairs and had passed along the balconied gallery, Igor said, 'Turn round and look back at the staircase now—you'll see something of it.' She did so, and saw that it was indeed very beautiful, delicate work, with the poppies and barley-stalks apparently growing from the edges of the steps, but bent over, as if in a high wind, to cascade downwards, interwoven and strengthened by the wreathing ribbons. She would have liked an opportunity to look at it more closely.

As she turned to make a comment to Igor, she caught sight of Anna Volkhova, who had just arrived at the top of the stairs with her escort, and was talking to Prince and Princess Ruschev. Galina had a clear view of her, and could not help stopping to look, taking in the elegance of the blond silk gown, which had a short train. Galina had thought trains to be quite out of fashion, but assumed that they must be coming in again. She studied the effect, which she thought not very pleasing, but supposed that she would accept it if the fashion became established again. She admired Anna's graceful, lazy movements as she turned to move along the gallery. Prince Ruschev made some smiling remark, and Anna stepped back again to reply, and then, with horrible clarity, Galina realised what was going to happen.

She gasped and started forward, but already it was too late. Anna forgot her train and stepped back on it, catching her foot, stumbled, put out a hand to clutch at the balustrade, but missed, and before anyone could move to save her, she fell backwards, headlong down the stairs.

CHAPTER
FOUR

THE DEVIL

Hidden forces at work/The misuse of power

GALINA found herself at the head of the stairs, but Igor was before her. He must have moved like the wind, for he was already halfway down, dropping to his knees beside the still figure lying there, her fall arrested by one of the footmen snatching at her skirts. The hall below seemed full of the upturned white faces of newly-arrived guests and servants, all staring, silent in shock. Prince Ruschev ran down after Igor, and Lev Orlov emerged from the crowded figures in the hall and mounted the stairs, giving quiet-voiced instructions to the footmen to stop anyone else from coming up.

They obeyed the accustomed note of authority in his voice, and moved to block the head and foot of the staircase, but as Galina was already half a dozen steps down, they made no attempt to send her back, so she slowly descended to the little group below and asked softly, 'Is there anything I can do?'

Igor looked up and said, 'Yes. Come here and take my place while we get something to put her on. Don't let her move if you can help it, and talk to her quietly and soothingly. She might hear you.'

Galina sat down on the step alongside Anna's head and looked at her. The beautiful face was still and peaceful, and, oddly, not as beautiful as Galina had thought. There were dark shadows like bruises under the eyes, and that almost waxen complexion, she now saw, owed much to the skilful application of cosmetics. Even the glossy black hair was a slightly different colour at the roots.

'What happened? Why did she fall?' Prince Ruschev was asking in agitated tones, wringing his hands and sounding near to hysteria.

'Don't know. Didn't see,' Lev replied tersely. 'Must have happened as I came in the door.'

'She forgot her train and stepped back on it,' Galina said. 'And it tripped her.' She bent over the silent figure and whispered gently, 'Anna. Anna Mikhailovna, can you hear me?'

Anna's head moved a little and she groaned.

'I shouldn't rouse her any more for the moment,' Lev said quietly. 'She's in a precarious position—if she moves now, she may slip.'

There was a stir at the bottom of the stairs, and Igor reappeared, carrying a couple of blankets and accompanied by two footmen with what looked like the rough top of a trestle table. Galina moved to the side of the stairs, out of the way, and crouched against the delicate ironwork, her fingers unconsciously caressing a little harvest-mouse hiding amid the barley. Igor used the blankets to cover the board, and then he and Lev, aided by the footmen, carefully lifted Anna on to it.

'Very carefully,' Igor said sharply. 'If her back's injured, we don't want to make it worse.' As the delicate operation was completed, he looked up at their hostess, still rooted at the top of the stairs with Anna's escort, and said, 'I'd suggest that you continue with the ball as soon as we're out of the way,' and to Prince Ruschev, still hovering uselessly, 'Have you sent for a surgeon yet?' which sent the Prince hurrying down the stairs to see to it.

The two footmen lifted the improvised stretcher and carried it down the stairs, steadied by Lev and Igor on either side. There was a short hiatus at the bottom, for the hall was crowded with guests and servants and a way had to be cleared, and while this was being done, Igor looked up at Galina and made a peremptory gesture which brought her to her feet and sent her hurrying to join him as he helped to carry Anna to one of the many small rooms on the ground floor.

They set the board down on a convenient table, and the two footmen bowed themselves out. As they did so, Anna stirred and opened her eyes.

'What . . .?' she murmured, looking at the three silent figures standing round her. 'What happened?' She tried to sit up, Igor put out a hand to stop her, and she suddenly screamed, a shrill, terrible sound, and began to sob.

'I can't move! I can't move! Oh, my back!'

Galina took hold of Anna's hands and said soothingly, 'Lie still, dear. You fell down the stairs and hurt yourself. The doctor's coming, and he'll make you comfortable.'

'Fell?' Anna stopped sobbing and looked at her. 'That silly train, was it? I can't feel my legs, you know, but I hurt as well. Why do I hurt?' The great dark eyes were puzzled and frightened.

'Well, of course, you must be badly bruised,' Galina replied as confidently as she could. 'You had a bad fall.' She looked at Igor, seeking support.

He had been leaning with one hand on the board about level with Anna's knees, ready to help Galina restrain her if she tried again to sit up, but now he was staring at the palm of his hand. Galina caught a glimpse of a scarlet stain, and then he closed the hand into a tight fist and crossed the room to the door, where he spoke quietly to someone outside. Galina caught the word 'midwife', and realised with a feeling of nausea what was happening.

The next half-hour was dreadful. Anna kept crying out and trying to move, clinging to Galina's hands so tightly that they were bruised, sobbing, moaning, praying, and, once or twice, screaming, while Igor and Lev stood by helplessly. Lev scowled and prowled about the room, like the lion from which his name was derived, while Igor, after one or two attempts to help Galina calm Anna, crossed himself and closed his eyes in prayer as the only useful contribution he could make.

Eventually, the surgeon and a stout midwife arrived, and hustled Galina and the two men out of the room. Igor disappeared, and Lev said anxiously to Galina, 'Shall you be all right until Igor comes back? He's gone to wash his hands. I must go and find my wife.'

'Of course,' Galina replied, stifling an impulse to cling to his safe solidity. 'I-I'll wait in there.' She gestured to another small room, across the hall from the one where Anna lay, the door of which stood open, revealing a sofa and a couple of chairs. She hastened across to its sanctuary, avoiding the curious eyes of the servants waiting in the hall, shut the door, sat down, and tried to compose herself.

There was no sound now from the room across the hall. A lilting strain of music, half-drowned by the hubbub of voices and laughter, drifted down from the ballroom, and there was a murmur of talk from the hall. She pulled a lace handkerchief from her reticule; wiped her eyes with it, although she was not crying, and then sat twisting it between her fingers until Igor suddenly strode into the room, shut the door behind him, and stood looking at her, a frown of concern on his taut-skinned face. Without any conscious movement, she found herself on her feet clinging to him, tears beginning to run down her face as she buried it in the black cloth of his coat.

'Here, hold up,' he said, putting his arms round her and patting her gently on the back. 'No need to take on, you know. You did all you could, and very well too.'

'I'm sorry,' she sobbed. 'I c-can't help it.'

'No, of course not.' He sounded vaguely resigned and held her a little more closely, one hand gently stroking the nape of her neck under the clustered ringlets. 'Do try to stop crying, though. You're taking all the starch out of my cravat, and someone may come in here at any moment.'

Galina, despite a strong inclination to enjoy the relief of a good cry on a comfortable shoulder a little longer, stopped her tears and drew away from him, although whether this was out of consideration for his cravat or for fear of scandal was not clear. She sniffed and dabbed at her eyes with her tiny handkerchief, but Igor put her hand aside and dried her eyes and cheeks more efficiently with his own large cambric square.

'Do you wish to go to the ball, or home?' he asked.

'Home, please,' Galina replied, revolted by the thought of dancing while poor Anna might be dying in the room across the hall. 'If you'll please call my carriage, I can go with Dasha—there's no need for you . . .'

'I'd rather be cataloguing those snuffboxes,' Igor replied briskly. 'Stay here a moment, while I go and arrange things.' He went out, and a minute or so later, Dasha came in with Galina's cloak and felt *valinki*, which slipped on over her dancing slippers. Then Igor returned, cloaked and booted, and they left with the minimum of fuss.

At home, they found Galina's mother about to retire for the night. She listened gravely to a brief account of the accident which had caused her daughter to return home so early, and said, 'I thought there was something evil about. The Devil's been coming up every time this evening—always a bad sign, whichever way up!' and took herself off to bed.

Galina asked for tea to be served in the Peacock Salon. When it arrived, she brewed some in the pretty porcelain pot, then, having dismissed the footmen, herself carried it on the tray with the cups and dishes and sliced lemon into the library, where Igor was back in the midst of the small ocean of snuffboxes. He stood up as Galina entered, took the tray from her, and put it down on top of his papers for lack of any other clear space. She gave him a wan smile, poured the tea, and sat down on one of the few chairs not already filled with odds and ends.

'Feeling better?' he asked abruptly.

'Yes, thank you. Are the snuffboxes interesting?'

'Very—a remarkably good representative collection. There's one that was presented to the General by the Empress Ekaterina, so he did acquire at least one thing legitimately! I'm afraid that the coats-of-arms and so forth on some of the others make their presence here a little dubious, though. Oh—by the way—I found the Austrian chalice. It's here.' He crossed over to a cabinet, opened it, and brought the chalice to show Galina.

It was an exquisite piece of craftsmanship, with a plain bowl rising gracefully from a stem moulded with the figure of Christ in Majesty on the front and the Virgin and Child on the back, framed in delicate vine tendrils, leaves and grapes, beautifully enamelled on gold, with carved amethysts forming the grape clusters.

'I don't wonder that they want it back,' Galina exclaimed, handling it reverently and with great care.

'You're willing to part with it?' Igor asked, watching her face with a curious expression on his own.

'Of course, it was stolen. Should I give you a written request to return it?'

'If you would, please.' Igor found her a sheet of paper and a pen, and she wrote and signed a brief authorisation at his dictation. Then he showed her some of the more interesting snuffboxes, until a footman came to remove the tea-tray, and she rose, intending to leave him to his work and go to bed. She paused in front of the portrait by the door, and looked up at the handsome, confident face, thinking that none of the men she had met so far in Petersburg had anything like the attraction or the panache of the Charioteer, and gave an unconscious little sigh. Igor looked up, stared at the back of her head, then transferred his gaze to the fair-skinned painted face and muttered 'trouble-maker' in Ukrainian.

'I'm sorry . . .?' Galina turned round, encountered an opaque stare, and faltered, 'Oh, I thought you said something . . .'

'Goodnight,' Igor said, smiling suddenly. 'You did very well this evening.'

'I hope she's all right,' Galina replied sadly.

In the morning, there was a note from Princess Rus-chev thanking Galina for her help the previous evening, and telling her that Anna Mikhailovna had miscarried of a dead boy during the night, but the doctors could not yet judge the seriousness of her injuries, beyond saying that her life was not in any danger.

Igor came in a little late for breakfast, and said that he had received a similar note, and then, while they were still at the table, Tatya was shown in. She apologised for such an early call, but had come to enquire after Galina.

'I didn't even arrive at the Ruschevs' until it was virtually all over,' she said. 'My gown wasn't ready, which made me late. Poor Anna! I can't like her, but in these circumstances, I can find it in me to pity her. Igor—do you think—Nikolai Ilyich is with the Emperor, and he should be told, I feel. Anna is still his wife, after all. I wondered if there was any possibility of sending a note by the Imperial Courier . . .?'

'It's already gone,' Igor replied. 'I wrote a short letter and took it to the Palace this morning. That's why I was late for breakfast,' parenthetically to Galina. 'The Court Chamberlain put it in the Emperor's private bag for me, and Alexander Pavlovich will see it safely delivered.'

Galina thought it odd that Igor should employ the Emperor as a messenger, but Tatya apparently found it unsurprising, for all she said was, 'That was a kind thought,' giving him a warm smile, to which he responded, his whole face lighting up in a way which Galina found quite remarkable, for she considered him a very sombre man, and she wondered if he was one of the moths he had spoken of, unable to stop hovering around Tatya's flame. Her thoughts on the subject were interrupted by the entry of a footman with a salver piled with letters, which he put down at her elbow. She murmured an excuse to the others and set about opening them, only vaguely aware that a three-sided conversation had begun between her mother, Tatya and Igor.

Most of the letters were invitation-cards, but one folded and sealed sheet bore an illegible postmark and proved to be a letter from Kiev. It said:

'Honoured lady,

I beg your forgiveness for my presumption in writing to you when I have not the honour of your acquaintance, and, if my situation were not desperate, I should not have the effrontery to trouble you.

'To be brief, your uncle, General Zhadnov, lent me money last year, with my family's sole estate as security. I have hopes of being able to repay the loan next summer, but the term of it expires at the end of this year, and your agent in Kiev informs me that he intends to foreclose and seize the estate, although it is worth far more than the amount of the loan.

'I am sure that, if you knew all the circumstances, you would be merciful, and I beg you to instruct your agent to allow me but nine months extension, when you shall be paid in full, or take the estate. For the love of God, Countess, do not take everything we have for the sum of three thousand roubles, which must be a paltry amount to you!'

The letter ended with the customary compliments, and was signed Semyon Semyonovich Bednyak.

'Oh dear,' Galina exclaimed when she had read it for the second time. 'Now, what on earth should I do about this?'

The others broke off their conversation and looked at her enquiringly, and she read the letter aloud to them.

'The poor man sounds quite distraught,' Tatya said thoughtfully. 'Do you know him at all, Igor?'

'Bednyak,' Igor considered the name for a moment. 'Yes, I think I know him slightly, but you must remember that I've spent very little of my life in Kiev, despite my home being there. It's true enough that they've only one estate, and it's certainly worth a great deal more than three thousand roubles. As I recall, he would be—trusting—enough to pledge the whole estate for a loan of four kopeks!' (He restrained himself from saying 'fool' and substituted 'trusting', but the hesitation was obvious). 'He's an honest man himself and not given to suspecting others of—less pure intentions.' (Again, the hesitation showed what he really meant.) 'Presumably, you've never met your agent in Kiev?'

'No,' Galina replied. 'I've read his reports, of course. They seem meticulous, but rather uninspired. I think I should go and see this man.'

'To Kiev?' Countess Razumova's voice fairly squeaked with shock at the suggestion.

'Yes. I can't judge whether it's fair to give the man more time or not without knowing much more of the matter, and I certainly can't allow my agent to take a whole estate for a comparatively small debt, if that's what he intends to do.' She gave a wry little smile, for only a few months ago, three thousand roubles would have seemed to her an enormous sum. 'There's only one way to find out the truth, and that's to go to Kiev.'

'I'll go with you,' Tatya said firmly, seeing that Countess Razumova looked quite horrified at the thought of travelling nearly twelve hundred *versty* in the middle of winter. (*1 verst = 1.06km.*).

'That's very kind of you,' Galina was hesitant about accepting the offer, for it seemed an immense presumption when Tatya had already been so kind. 'But—in the middle of the Season—I suppose it will take at least three weeks to go there and return . . .'

'The Season doesn't properly start until December,' Tatya replied. 'I don't mind at all. I enjoy travelling, and it's years since I was in Kiev.'

Igor made a sound midway between a snort and a sigh and said a little ungraciously, 'I suppose I'd better escort you. I shudder to think what a couple of helpless females will manage to encounter along the road! Has either of you any idea which way to go?'

'By way of Pskov, Orsha and Gomel,' Galina replied a trifle pertly, for she had studied her lessons with application, having little else to do during her childhood, and was better acquainted than most females with the geography of the Empire. 'I should value your company very much, both of you, if you're quite sure, and on condition that I bear the expenses.' She looked very hard at Tatya, who gave the slightest of nods, and said at once, 'I'll raise no objection to that!' thereby making it impossible for Igor to refuse, as Galina had feared his pride might lead him to do.

'I can visit my grandfather,' he said without much enthusiasm. 'In fact, we can all stay with him while we're in Kiev.'

'I wouldn't dream . . .' Galina began.

'He'll be mortally offended if we don't,' Igor cut in flatly, thereby, as Galina realised in time, salving his pride over the matter of expense. 'D'you think, Tatya, that Lev would lend his travelling-coach? It's the best I've ever seen—far better than anything in Alexander Pavlovich's mews.'

'I'm sure he will,' Tatya committed her brother's property without hesitation. 'He's not using it, and I know it's been overhauled after his wedding-journey. We'll need a *jäger*, won't we?'

'I'll borrow one from the Emperor,' Igor seemed to cheer up at the idea. 'Another advantage of taking me with you—I've an Imperial courier's pass! I'll have prior claim on posting-horses, and a few other useful privileges.'

'But we won't be on Imperial business,' Galina pointed out scrupulously, her godfather's reputation tending to make her even more honest than she was naturally.

'I have the right to use the pass for my own travels, and there's always the possibility that Bednyak might have something interesting to sell to the Emperor,' Igor replied. 'Oh. What's today? Wednesday? I can't leave until Friday. I've something important to do tomorrow.'

'Well, I don't imagine that Galina or I could be ready to leave before then, either,' Tatya pointed out. 'We have to pack, and cry off a couple of dozen engagements, and leave instructions for our households—at least, Galina does,' recollecting that Irina was now mistress of the Orlov household.

In the scurry of dealing with all these things during that day and the next, Galina hardly had time to wonder about Igor's important appointment, although it did cross her mind next day, when he hurried away from the luncheon table, that he was being oddly reticent about it. However, about an hour later, she happened to be standing at the window of the Peacock Salon, watching the passing traffic and waiting for Osya Ivanich to come up from the domestic regions, when she was surprised to see Igor riding in an open carriage with a little girl.

At first she thought she must be mistaken, but she had already seen him many times in that grey fur cossack-style hat, worn at just that jaunty angle, and, besides, she knew his carriage by now, although she had not seen it before with the hoods down. That was odd enough, for, although the sun was shining for the first time in more than a week, it was bitterly cold . . . But a child? Whoever could she be?

Galina vaguely recollected seeing a telescope somewhere in the house, but could not recall where, and, in any case, that was a ridiculous idea. She screwed up her eyes to improve their focus a trifle, and saw a lively little face framed in a feather-trimmed bonnet, all the more easily because the carriage had stopped and Igor was pointing out something to the child. For a moment, Galina thought it was herself, and half-raised her hand to wave, not wishing to be thought to be spying on them, and then realised that he was indicating the windows of the library next door, obviously showing the child where he was working. At that point, Osya Ivanich entered the room, and by the time he had gone, there was no sign of the carriage.

Galina had cancelled all her engagements, and dined at home with her mother and Igor, who came in just before dinner was announced and said that he had made all the necessary arrangements for the journey, and

Lev's coach and all the other vehicles were already in Galina's coach-house.

'I've borrowed some of Alexander Pavlovich's horses as well,' he added. 'We'll be using his after the first post-stage in any case, and I didn't think yours were in good enough condition—no criticism of your grooms— you're not in the habit of travelling long distances at speed, so there's no point in your buying that sort of animal. The *jäger*'s setting off tonight, so everything should go smoothly.'

'I'm grateful to you for all your trouble,' Galina said earnestly. 'I'd not the faintest idea how to set about organising a journey like this.'

Igor's thin-lipped mouth gave a wry twist and he replied, 'Save your thanks until you're safely back in Petersburg—they may be premature now!'

'Nevertheless,' Galina insisted, 'I am most grateful to you. You must have had a very busy time—I hope you managed to keep your appointment?' she had not really intended to fish for information, but he apparently assumed that she had, and replied briefly, 'Yes, thank you,' his expression shutting her out of his thoughts, and there was an awkward silence while Galina wondered if he had seen her at the window, until Countess Razumova started on a long, gentle monologue about the Tarot's indications for her daughter's journey, with several mournful references to the Devil, and one sharp warning to watch out for the Magician, which caused Galina to colour with embarrassment, particularly as Igor's private little smile led her to believe that he understood the reference very well.

They started very early the next morning, long before any sign of daylight, and the small procession of vehicles was the first that day to pass through the police barrier on the Gatchina road. Galina had completely forgotten the need for passports, but Igor had not, and sometime during the previous two days, he had found time to obtain them from the Ministry of the Interior, so they passed through the barrier with the minimum of delay, and were soon beyond the city limits and rushing along the snow-covered highway at good speed.

The luggage went first in two *kibitkas*, two stout footmen in each, followed by Lev's large travelling-coach, a berline of stout construction and considerable comfort, in which travelled Galina, Tatya and Igor. After that came a smaller coach with the two ladies' maids and Igor's valet, and finally, a *trainage*, a low, flat vehicle on sledge runners on which were loaded all the bedding, the various bundles belonging to the servants (for, what with the coachmen and grooms and the luggage-guards, there were more than two dozen of these), and the wheels of all the vehicles, in case there should be insufficient snow further south for the sledge runners at present fitted to them all. This portable mountain was covered with stout tarpaulins and well roped-down against weather or theft. Galina recognised the justice of Igor's criticism of the inhabitants of her stables, for the animals he had borrowed were exceptionally strong and well-conditioned, although typically small, wiry and swift-moving.

The *jäger* was obviously efficient, for fresh relays awaited them at every posting-house, and at each short halt, hot soup or mulled wine was offered (and usually gratefully accepted), and a good meal was provided in a clean inn at midday. By late evening, they had covered (to Galina's amazement) nearly two hundred *versty*, and stopped for a late dinner and a few hours' sleep in an Imperial posting-house.

Galina felt very stiff and thick-headed after sitting so long in the stuffy coach and watching the stark black and white countryside passing by, broken by the occasional village and the constant passage of country waggons on their way to and from the towns. A few deep breaths of sharp air cleared her head, and a little tramping up and down in the stableyard soon loosened her limbs. Tatya, realising that she was unused to long journeys, advised her to spend some time while they were in the coach moving her legs and feet as if she were walking on the spot to combat the stiffness, which Galina did the next day, finding it quite effective.

During the second day, they paused briefly in Pskov for luncheon, and reached Opochka for another very late dinner and short night's rest. The time dragged, of course, but both ladies had brought embroidery, which they could manage fairly well when the snow and the road beneath it were firm and smooth enough for a good passage, and when there was a little daylight, which was not very long at this time of year and in these latitudes, and there were books to read. When it was dark, there was conversation, which Galina enjoyed very much, although she spent more time listening than talking, delighting in the well-informed exchanges of her companions. If all else failed, she dozed or thought.

The third day's run was a little shorter, and they stopped in Nevele quite early in the evening and took a brisk walk about the small town after dinner. Galina managed a brief moment of conversation with their *jäger*, a large, solemn man in a smart uniform under a coat apparently made of and lined with bearskins, who bent his head to listen as she thanked him for the smooth arrangements he had made so far—a speech which appeared to surprise and certainly pleased him.

There was a very long run on the fourth day, for they made only a short stop in Vitebsk, and then ran on far into the night to a small village not far short of Mogilev. Galina felt that she would have preferred a little more time to stretch her legs and look about her at the posting-houses, but, on the other hand, it was better to get on with the journey when they had so far to go. She had feared that it would be very boring, and that Igor might prove irritating or irritable while she was shut up in a coach with him for such long periods, but, on the contrary, he seemed to enjoy travelling and had many interesting facts and anecdotes to offer about the places through which they passed, and, even more important, knew when to be quiet and let the others read or think or doze.

During this part of the journey, she spent the brief hours of daylight looking for signs of the passage of Bonaparte's *Grande Armée* during the advance and retreat of the previous year, but saw nothing except the charred shell of a peasant cabin, which might have been burned at any time. She was not sure what she had expected to see, but felt vaguely cheated that there was nothing, and concluded that it—whatever 'it' was—must be hidden under the snow.

The fifth day took them to Gomel, the sixth well past Chernigov, and they arrived in Kiev, not unduly fatigued, in time for luncheon on the seventh day, which Galina thought quite remarkable, and she consulted Igor about some extra payment to the *jäger* for his efficiency, which appeared to cause Igor some amusement.

'He'd have had a severe reprimand from the Emperor for taking over six days to bring him here from Petersburg!' he said. 'But still, if you're pleased, by all means reward him. I'll see to it for you, if you wish.' And, indeed, Galina was glad to let him see to this payment on her behalf, as he had all the others, giving her a neatly-written account each morning for the previous day's expenses.

This conversation took place as they were approaching Kiev, with Tatya conveniently dozing in her corner of the coach. She woke as they stopped at the city barrier, merely opening her eyes, blinking a little, and smiling, contriving to look as serene and unruffled as if she had just stepped out of a bandbox, whereas Galina felt thoroughly crumpled and untidy, her bonnet awry, her pelisse buttoned wrongly and her fine sable cloak somehow full of straw from the coach floor. Even Igor had a limp cravat, and his hair was unusually ruffled, showing that it would indeed curl if it had the chance.

Galina found Kiev an interesting city, for, unlike flat Tver and flatter St Petersburg, it seemed to be built on steep hills, with granite setts instead of wooden pavé to give a grip to horses' feet on the sharp inclines. Also, the city was full of trees—not the little birches and rowans or the tall pines of the north, but great thick-trunked deciduous trees, oak and chestnut, bare-branched now and wrapped in straw against the bitter cold, which was much drier and brisker than in Petersburg.

Craning her neck to see as much as possible from the coach windows, she observed that most of the houses— even the largest and finest—like those in Tver, were made of wood, in the upper floors at least. She caught the glint of the gilded onion-shaped domes of churches every now and again, and realised how much she had missed them in Petersburg, where most of the churches had spires or western-style domes.

Eventually, after lurching up a very steep hill crowded with vehicles and people, the coach and its consorts turned into a quiet side street, and then drew into the forecourt of a rambling old house, rough stone-walled on the ground floor and wooden above, with white-painted pilasters and window-frames of ornate plaster against sky-blue walls.

'Welcome to Petersburg's poor relation,' Igor said bitterly, and Galina, in a sudden flash of insight, realised that he was afraid that she and Tatya might despise his native city and his grandfather's house.

'Oh, but much richer in trees—and what a lovely house!' she exclaimed sincerely.

The doors were opened by a porter wearing the soft boots, full-cut trousers and girdled tunic of the native Ukrainian costume, shaggy-haired and bearded, and, as the new arrivals entered the square, wood-panelled hall, they were met by three young women in embroidered skirts and blouses, and gabled *kokoshnik* head-dresses, each carrying a loaf of bread and a dish of salt on a tray resting on a long towel of pattern-woven linen, who bade them welcome in a language that was almost Russian, but differed slightly in pronounciation and in a few words. Galina realised that it must be Ukrainian.

With the formal greeting over, another shaggy-haired man, dressed like the porter, ushered them into a pleasant room furnished in the style of a quarter-century before, and Galina guessed that it must have been new-decorated for the Empress Ekaterina's visit to the city in 1787. The gentleman who was standing in the middle of the room waiting to receive them obviously belonged to the same era, for he was dressed in buckled knee-breeches, white silk stockings, a red and yellow striped waistcoat and green coat, and wore a powdered tie-wig. The face framed by the side-curls of the wig was yellowed and wrinkled, but had the same hooded dark eyes, strong curved nose, grown beaky with age, and long, thin-lipped mouth as Igor. His height and build were much the same too, but he was thin rather than slim.

'My grandfather, Leonid Matveyich Charodyev,' Igor said. 'Tatyana Petrovna Kalinskaya and Galina Stepanovna Razumova.'

The old Count bowed, but without the old-fashioned flourishes which Galina half-expected, and bade them welcome in a pleasant tone and in excellent French. Count Leonid might choose to live in the provinces and wear old-fashioned clothes, but he was obviously well-grounded in the social graces. A few minutes later, he instructed a servant in equally fluent Ukrainian to send for luncheon in half an hour giving the travellers just time to go to their rooms to wash and change out of their travelling-clothes.

Galina, as it happened, was the first down, feeling much better after a good wash, a complete change of clothes and a brisk attack with her hairbrush. She found Igor's grandfather in the faded comfort of his salon, enjoying a glass of wine. He greeted her with a pleasant smile, and poured her a glass of the clear white liquid, saying that it was produced in his own vineyards in the Crimea.

'I'm grateful to you for bringing my grandson home for a few days,' he said, raising his glass to her in a smiling toast. 'I don't see much of him since he entered Alexander Pavlovich's service, but there's no outlet for a man of his particular talents here. Art and culture are centred in Petersburg—now Kiev is a mere provincial capital, it might as well be a desert.'

'We shall not be here very long, I'm afraid,' Galina replied apologetically, and was surprised when Leonid Matveyich replied drily, 'Just as well—Igor and I would probably quarrel if he stayed longer!'

'Quarrel?'

'Oh, we rub along very well at a distance, but we're too much alike to live in accord at close quarters. I have the dictatorial nature of the elderly paterfamilias, and Igor—has a mind of his own. It's his Cossack blood, I suppose.'

'C-cossack?' Galina felt that she was doing nothing but echo everything he said, like an idiot.

'His grandmother was the daughter of an *esaul* of the Zaporozhskaya Sich. Not my wife (God rest her soul), but his other grandmother. You wouldn't think it to look at him, would you? Pefectly civilized in his sober black and smooth courtier's face! It's there, though, and he's the very devil when he's roused—strong as fine steel, and the courage to match it! Don't tell him I said so, will you?' The old gentleman scowled fiercely at Galina. 'No need to let him get a swelled head!'

CHAPTER
FIVE

JUSTICE

Agreement by negotiation/Injustice

AFTER luncheon, the ladies returned to their rooms to rest for an hour, but Galina found she was too restless to lie down after so many hours of sitting in the coach. She prowled about, ostensibly helping Dasha to unpack her trunks, and then, realising that the maid was rapidly becoming exasperated, sat down on the window-seat and looked out over the city.

It seemed to fall away from the house, which she realised must stand on the top of a ridge, and the low outbuildings and yards at the back of the main block were below her, running down the slope on two or three terraces. Beyond them, she could see the backs of the houses in the next street showing between clumps of trees, and then, much further away, buildings rising on the far side of a valley, with a church or two showing above the shingled roofs.

Later in the afternoon, a servant came to ask if she would care to join Countess Kalinskaya and Igor Grigorovich for a stroll before dark, and they took a short walk through the darkening streets to a small park, in the midst of which was a large grassy mound, which Igor said was earth piled over the remains of the famous Golden Gate of Kiev, to protect it from the consequences of age and mistreatment, and, once they had passed it, they were within the inner kremlin which was the cradle of Russia, where Oleg had set up the Kievan Rus state in the 9th century, where St Vladimir had summoned the Greek missionaries to establish Christianity among the Rus, where Yaroslav the Wise and the other Grand Princes of Kiev had held court.

'This is the true heart of Russia,' he said. 'Not Moscow or Petersburg, but here, where it began. It was sacked by the Golden Horde and by the Poles, but never totally destroyed.'

'It's strange that a nation can change its capital from one city to another, just because its ruler or someone says so,' mused Tatya, looking about her with interest. 'I wonder if it happens anywhere else?'

Galina thought about the question while the other two went on to talk of something else, and then surprised them by saying, 'Norway and the American States. I can't think of any others.'

'Denmark, England and Prussia,' Igor added, with only the slightest hesitation, while Tatya was still adjusting her mind to the sudden backward step in the conversation.

They dined at six in the evening, and it was impossible to tell whether Igor's grandfather always kept this fashionably late hour, or if he was politely adapting to the habits of his guests. After dinner, he entertained them with reminiscences of the Empress Ekaterina's famous journey to the Crimea, when he had been in attendance on her during her stay in Kiev and on the rest of the journey by water down the Dnieper and across the Crimea to Sevastopol.

Igor, who must have heard it all many times before, appeared to be listening as intently as Tatya or Galina, but he sat in a patch of shadow, his face almost invisible, and Galina had an odd sensation two or three times that he was watching her. She thought he was probably looking for some sign of boredom or of impatience with the old man's tales, but told herself that Master Magician would be unlucky in that, as she was genuinely interested in the story, then wondered why she should care what he thought, for she did not much like him, with his sardonic face, sly smile, and over-sensitivity about being Ukrainian.

On the other hand, he had been very helpful, tackling that dreadful collection of her godfather's, escorting her about to social occasions which he did not really seem to like, inviting her to dance so that she would not be left by the wall too often, and arranging this journey, which would have been a nightmare without his help. Perhaps his smile was not exactly sly, and she did not really dislike him, only he made her feel—what? Uneasy? Something of the sort.

A sudden peal of laughter from Tatya drew her attention back to Leonid Matveyich's anecdotes, and she abandoned her line of thought, and only recalled it, with a tinge of shame, when Igor kindly offered next morning to go with her to visit her agent in Kiev.

'We'll all go!' declared Tatya. 'In a body, and intimidate him!'

The agent, however, was more self-righteous than intimidated. His place of business was in the old merchant quarter of the city, and, to get to it, the town carriage which Igor's grandfather lent them traversed the city centre, passing the great cathedral of St Sophia with its amazing forest of twenty-one elaborate Baroque domes, which, Igor said, concealed under its later accretions the oldest surviving church in Russia.

'I should like to go to service there,' Galina said, pressing close to the carriage window and peering upwards in an effort to see the top of the bell-tower.

'You'd find it very bare and dilapidated after the

splendours of the Kazan or Holy Trinity in Petersburg.'
Igor's voice had that bitter, defensive tone in it again, so
Galina's reply was partly intended to be polite, but was
also quite genuine.

'But of course—if it's so old, one would expect that!
Everything in Petersburg is new! The city's not a hundred years old yet, and St Sophia is—what? Nearly eight
hundred?'

'We'll go in the morning, if you really wish to,' Igor
sounded doubtful, but Galina gave him a beaming smile
and said that she wished to very much.

By then, the carriage had reached an elegant blue and
gold church perched on the edge of a street which
plunged downhill so steeply that the driver stopped and
one of the grooms opened the door nearest Igor and
said, 'Moise Nikitich says he daren't risk Vladimirskaya
St—it's icy and the horses won't be able to hold the
carriage. He's going round the long way.'

'Very well,' Igor replied, accepting that the driver
knew his own business best, and the carriage turned
about, manoeuvring slowly on the slippery cobbles.

'Is that St Vladimir's church?' Galina asked, looking
up at the soaring domes.

'No. St Andrei the First-called. It was built by Ras-
trelli for the Empress Ekaterina's visit. I suppose her
ministers thought that all our other churches were too
old and shabby for the Empress to worship in,' Igor
replied.

'It's very pretty,' Tatya observed. 'But more like a
large jewel-case than a church.'

'The Empress Ekaterina didn't have as many jewels as
that!' Galina exclaimed, and even made Igor laugh.

Meanwhile, the carriage had returned almost as far as
St Sophia's, and then plunged down the opposite side of
the ridge, the brake-shoe squealing gratingly as the back
wheels dragged on the cobbles.

'St Andrei's stands on the highest point of the old city. We're going down to the Kreschatik, then round the foot of the hill. It's longer, but safer.' Igor explained. He did not say what the Kreschatik was until they turned into it—it proved to be a narrow, ill-paved street lined by a few shops, but he said that there were plans to make it the Nevsky Prospect of Kiev, with a broad, tree-lined carriageway and shops to rival those of Petersburg and Moscow. At its end, the street wound downhill to the river, and a short drive along the Dnieper bank soon brought them to the Podol, the merchant's quarter, where they passed an interesting row of shops. Galina was on the wrong side for a good view of the river, but she thought it looked very wide.

The agent—a lantern-jawed, grey-haired man in a black coat and snuff-coloured small-clothes—looked decidedly startled when Galina and her companions were ushered into his office by a threadbare clerk. He got to his feet making incoherent remarks about surprise and honour and not having expected, which Galina brought to a halt by sitting down in a shabby wooden chair before his large desk, smiling at him over the bundles of papers and odd deed-boxes which covered its surface, and saying firmly, 'I thought it necessary to come, and there was no time to inform you. I had a letter from Count Bednyak. He says that you intend to take his entire estate in settlement of a debt of three thousand roubles.'

'Er—yes—well—that is—in a nutshell—the position . . .'

'How much is his estate worth?'

'Oh. Er—well—that is—of course, until an inventory is made . . .'

'In excess of three thousand roubles?'

'Oh, much in excess.' This hardly surprised Galina, for she knew perfectly well that an estate would have to consist entirely of arid desert, and be occupied by the Turks into the bargain, to be worth so little. 'Your er—the General—General Zhadnov, that is—made a very shrewd bargain there! He arranged it himself, and most admirably—entirely sound—no loopholes—perfectly legal.' The man rubbed his hands together gloatingly.

'It sounds downright dishonest,' Galina said bluntly.

'Oh, not at all! *Per*fectly legal!' the agent assured her.

'Morally dishonest,' Galina insisted.

The agent considered the point, and then said a trifle patronisingly,' In the world of business, my dear Countess, what matters is the letter of the law. Bednyak knew what he was signing, and presumably thought he could repay the money in time, and no harm done. Unfortunately, he's not a businessman, and although I can approve his actions up to that point, afterwards he behaved very foolishly—*very* foolishly indeed!'

'How?' asked Galina, who was beginning to feel a strong dislike for him.

'Well, I'll not bore you with the details, but he borrowed the money to buy seed—rye. Had he planted it and grown a good crop—well and good, but he didn't you see. He gave most of it away.'

'Why?'

The agent shrugged. 'Sheer sentiment! He said his serfs had nothing to eat, so he gave them the seed. Did you ever hear the like? Of course they had something to eat—peasants can manage on so very little, and if they've no grain, there are always roots and berries, and grass, for that matter. However, he was fool enough to be taken in with their pretence of starvation, and gave them the seed, so now, of course, he can't pay his debt. I much regret that he troubled you with the matter—quite unnecessary, and, if I may say so, a disgraceful presumption on his part!'

Had he been an observant man, he might have been warned by the firm set of Galina's mouth and chin, but he smiled blandly upon her, revealing a surprisingly good set of teeth (Galina had expected yellow fangs) and probably thought that her next words signalled the end of her intervention.

'I see,' she said. 'You'll not be doing anything about it before the end of December, I assume?'

'Indeed not. He has until midnight of the thirty-first, but on the first of January . . .'

'Quite,' said Galina. 'Thank you. I shall see you again before I leave Kiev. Good morning.' And with that, she stood up and swept out, the clerk, who had remained hovering just inside the door, barely managing to fling it open in time, and Tatya and Igor hastening in her wake, caught unawares by the suddenness of her departure.

Back in the carriage, Galina took a gold rouble from her reticule and sent one of the grooms to give it to the clerk, thinking that he looked very shabby and hungry, and then said, 'I've no doubt the man's a good agent, in his way, but I shall have to instruct him to change his point of view on certain matters. Igor Grigorovich, do you think your grandfather may be acquainted with Count Bednyak?'

'I should hope so! Grandfather is Marshal of the Nobility for this area!' Igor was looking at Galina in a thoughtful manner, and continued to do so from time to time all the way home, hardly saying anything the whole way.

'I don't think that a man should have to lose his home as a result of caring for serfs,' Tatya said positively. 'Roots and berries, indeed!'

'I should like to see him eat grass,' Galina agreed.

'People are more important than property,' Tatya added.

'Serfs *are* property,' Galina pointed out. 'I take your

meaning, though, and I agree. I certainly wouldn't let mine starve, even if it cost me every kopek I possess, and I'm sure you wouldn't either.'

'I don't actually have any serfs,' Tatya replied cautiously, not sure how Galina would react to what she was about to say. 'Lev and I have both freed ours. They rent their land from us, and we pay wages to those who work for us.'

'House-serfs—servants as well?' Galina asked, showing no shock, only interest.

'Yes. Of course, we don't have the excessive numbers that most people seem to find a use for, but ours work more efficiently than serfs, because it's to their advantage. The amount of their wages depends on how efficient they are.'

'Is it very difficult to arrange?' Galina enquired. 'Freeing them, I mean. I didn't even realise that it's possible.'

'Oh, it's been legal to do so since 1803—one may sell land and freedom to serfs—but very few people have done it. Nikolai Volkhov has, and four or five others that I know of. My nephew by marriage would like to, but his father won't let him. Lev worked out a system for arranging the freedom part at a very low price, spread over several years, and prefers to rent the land, rather than sell it, and I followed suit. The difficult part is making the peasants understand the process and agree to it—they're so suspicious of anything new—but we've always said that no one *had* to join the scheme. Some preferred to stay unfree, until they saw how well it worked. We lost about a quarter of our income at first, but that soon rose again when our lands yielded better crops because the paid workers were more efficient.'

Galina looked very thoughtful, drew out a small notebook and a pencil from her reticule, and began to write something down, which Tatya, who was sitting next to her, could see was a column of figures, which she deduced were the numbers of serfs on Galina's various estates, and she marvelled that a young female who until a few months ago had not owned a single estate or any serfs, could apparently carry approximate figures in her head.

The addition was finished before they were halfway along the Kreschatik, and Galina, looking up and seeing where they were, said, 'I should like to visit some of the shops here and in the Podol before we leave. What are the best things to buy, Igor Grigorovich?'

'Linen, pottery, embroideries, carpets and carved wooden articles,' Igor replied promptly. 'They all differ in design from the Great Russian equivalents.'

At luncheon, he asked his grandfather if he would be kind enough to tell Galina about Count Bednyak, explaining the situation.

'Oh, I know him quite well, poor fellow,' replied Leonid Matveyich. 'His father was heard to speak in defence of a friend who had been arrested for complicity in the Pugachev business in '73, and had all his property confiscated—the friend he defended was executed, of course, 'though it turned out later that he was innocent. Anyway, the Bednyaks lost everything except the one estate, which was the present owner's mother's dowry. He's done well with it, on the whole, growing rye for the city market, but the year before last, when his crop was almost ripe, there was a violent hailstorm. It only lasted five minutes, but it destroyed his crop, and all he managed to salvage was enough to feed his family and his souls, and for seed. Last year, he used the seed, but the crop came up diseased with black mould and had to be burned. He borrowed money to buy fresh seed, but during last winter, realising that his souls were starving, he gave most of it to them to eat, and had only enough left to grow for subsistence again this year, but that was diseased again, and—well, some of us sent some of our own surplus to feed his souls, but he's no seed for planting, and can't pay his debt. When does it fall due?'

'He *always* grows rye?' Galina asked instead of answering the question. 'That's foolish—he should grow something else every two or three years, to break the disease cycle.'

'Disease cycle?' queried Leonid Matveyich. 'And what do you mean by that?'

Galina suspected that he knew very well, but she replied, 'If one grows the same crop every year, the diseases which attack that crop stay in the soil and get worse each year, but if one grows something different at intervals, it breaks the chain. I thought all farmers knew that.'

'Apparently not,' Leonid Matveyich's eyes were twinkling. 'I know many people who go on growing the same thing year after year, grumbling because their yield is a little less each harvest, or cursing their bad luck because they get blight, or something of the sort. Your new scientific ideas from the West haven't spread to us ignorant savages in the provinces, you know! I offered, by the way, to lend Bednyak the money to pay his debt and buy more seed, but he's a proud man, and said he had plenty of time. How long has he?'

'Until the end of December,' Galina replied. 'It's ridiculous—to pledge a whole estate for a mere three thousand roubles!'

'It's nearer twice that, with the interest,' Leonid Matveyich pointed out. 'Your uncle was a hard man.'

'He was my godfather,' Galina had no wish to own the General as a blood relation. 'I think I had better visit Count Bednyak. Does he live far away?'

'A two-hour drive, across the river,' Leonid Matveyich replied. 'I suggest you write him a note, proposing yourself for Monday, and one of my grooms can deliver it this evening.' An offer for which Galina thanked him very much.

During the afternoon it snowed a little, but not enough to necessitate staying indoors, so Galina and Tatya went shopping and acquired a quantity of good linen and fine embroidered fabrics, but no pottery, as both ladies found it not quite to their taste, although very good of its kind, for the decoration was more in the old Russian style, unlike the western patterns produced by the manufactories in St Petersburg and Moscow.

Leonid Matveyich had invited a few guests for dinner and there was dancing and cards after, which helped to pass the evening pleasantly.

At Igor's suggestion, Galina, Dasha and he set off directly after breakfast on Monday to make the best of the daylight. Tatya had come down to breakfast looking pale with the onset of one of her migraines, although Galina was intrigued and envious to see that she still contrived to be elegant and beautiful. She offered to accompany Galina and Igor on their visit to Count Bednyak, but was clearly relieved when Galina insisted that she stay indoors and rest.

They took the road down to the riverbank and made a lurching, jolting and thoroughly uncomfortable crossing of the ice, with Dasha weeping and praying, convinced that the carriage would overturn and kill them all, or that the ice would break and they would be swept away under it by the current below.

Once across the river, they found the rest of the journey was no trouble at all. The road was smooth and the snow firm, and they were travelling in a *kibitka*, a hooded sledge normally drawn by one horse, but Leonid Matveyich had a troika team trained to draw it, a fast trotting horse in the middle, and a galloper on either side, so they raced along in fine style, well huddled up in furs, with thick straw about their booted feet and a hot, flannel-wrapped brick each to hold on the lap or put under the feet, and reached the Bednyak estate well inside the estimated two hours.

The village looked neat and clean, but the house, a rambling old wooden construction, was shabby and in need of repair and painting. They were greeted with bread and salt, and a serf in Ukrainian dress showed Galina and Igor into a little salon—more of a parlour in fact—while Dasha waited by the stove in the hall.

The room was comfortably furnished with well-worn estate-made furniture, solid and serviceable, but hardly elegant, and there were a few ornaments and pictures on the whitewashed walls, with a fine silver-covered icon in the corner. Count Bednyak stood in the middle of the room, waiting to greet them, in a clean, well-pressed brown coat and small-clothes, shiny on the seams and threadbare in places, with a patch on one leg of the trousers. Galina thought he looked a typical representative of those thousands of nobles who, either because of the old Russian tradition of sharing the family estate between all the sons instead of the eldest inheriting everything, or because of punitive or capricious confiscations by earlier Tsars, had too little land to support the dignities of the title, and she wondered how many of the tiny proportion of extremely wealthy aristocrats in Petersburg ever thought of their poor relations in the provinces, and resolved never to forget herself, thanking God that she was no longer one of them.

Count Bednyak bade them welcome in a nervous, stammering voice, running an agitated hand through his greying hair, his thin face and body tense with anxiety. He invited them to sit down in the only two upholstered chairs in the room, while he faced them unsteadily on an unupholstered one with one leg a trifle shorter than its companions.

'I—I didn't imagine you'd come all the way from

Petersburg . . .' he began in a rush. 'I never intended to put you to any trouble. I'd not have written at all, but my wife said we must try everything . . . I'm sorry she's not here to greet you, but she was too embarrassed . . .' He stopped suddenly, and looked at Galina with sad brown eyes. She thought to herself that Countess Bednyak probably had no frock to wear that she would think good enough to be seen by visitors from the capital.

'I gather from my agent that the agreement you signed with General Zhadnov is perfectly legal,' she said quietly. 'I think it is morally indefensible, so we must see how we can resolve the matter without you losing all your property. I suppose that if I offer to cancel the debt, you are still left with no means of buying the seed to start producing again?'

'If I were a lawyer,' Igor observed aloud, but apparently addressing the ceiling, 'I should advise you to be much more careful what you say, but, as I'm only a student of artistic objects,' transferring his gaze to Galina's face, 'I applaud your sentiments, while quailing inwardly at the possible implications of your words. I trust that you are not inadvertently raising any false hopes?'

'You should know me well enough by now,' Galina replied severely, 'to know that I don't say things which I don't mean.' Igor's secret smile flitted across his mouth, and he bowed slightly in his chair to acknowledge that he had been put in his place.

'I—I couldn't possibly . . .' Bednyak stammered, obviously too much concerned with what Galina had said to him to take in the exchange between her and Igor. 'I owe the money, and I have to pay it back somehow. T-to answer your qu-question—no. Even without the debt, I couldn't buy enough good seed. I—I should say,' he added scrupulously, 'I knew the imp-implications when I signed the agreement, but I was so sure I could settle in time. I didn't reckon with the disease, you see.'

'Haven't you something you could sell?' Galina looked about the room, seeking inspiration. The pictures were a mediocre lot of amateurish landscapes, and she could hardly suggest that he sell the family icon, but there was a small alcove in the middle of the wall, and in it, on a shelf, stood a large vase, quite three feet high, pleasantly decorated with flowers and birds in pretty, light colours. It was behind Igor, so she looked firmly at him, caught his eye, frowned a little, and tried to will him to understand her meaning.

'Igor Grigorovich, do you not think that vase over there might be worth a considerable amount?' adding parenthetically to Bednyak, 'he knows a great deal about these things.'

Igor obediently rose to his feet, located the vase, and went to look at it. He brought it back to his chair, sat down with it carefully balanced on his lap, and inspected it minutely for some time. Then he gave Galina an odd look, and said 'You don't happen to have its lid and its partner, do you?'

'Why, yes!' Bednyak exclaimed. 'I'll fetch them.' He hurried from the room, and Igor said drily to Galina, 'You're a very clever girl!'

CHAPTER
SIX

THE HERMIT

Discretion and silence / Suspicion

THERE was a wait of a few minutes, during which Galina basked in the satisfaction of knowing that Igor had understood her meaning very well, and Igor continued to examine the vase, apparently a square inch at a time, and then Count Bednyak came hurrying back clutching another vase, the twin of the first, with one of his servants following with the two lids. Igor stood both vases carefully on the floor, put the lids on them, and looked at them from various angles, then knelt down and gave the second one as close an inspection as that to which he had already subjected the first.

'They came to us from a d-distant relation of my wife,' Bednyak said, sitting down on his wobbly chair and unconsciously twisting his hands together nervously. 'Very distant, in fact—he was a m-merchant.' He confessed this terrible fact in a hushed tone.

'In tea or silk?' Igor asked casually.

'Well—both, actually,' Bednyak was surprised. 'How did you know that?' Without waiting for an answer, he plunged on, 'He was always going off to Tashkent and Bokhara . . .'

'And Samarkand,' Galina added, her voice lingering lovingly on those three romantic syllables, at which Igor gave one of his private smiles, perhaps because he knew that the famous entrepôt on the Silk Road was now only a barely-inhabited ruin.

'The vases are old Chinese porcelain,' he said briskly. 'The Emperor will be pleased to pay you six thousand roubles for the pair.'

'Six thousand?' Galina and Count Bednyak said in chorus and in identical tones of stunned surprise, then Galina added, 'The Emperor?' Bednyak's echo coming a fraction after.

'But they're only old . . . You said yourself, only old . . .' Bednyak said in a shocked whisper.

'By old,' Igor said kindly, 'I don't mean old in the sense of an old sickle, or an old cooking-pot. I mean *old*—antique, and very rare. I'll give you a draft on the Imperial Treasury. The Nobles' Bank in Kiev will accept it without charge to you. Now, have you a sensible carpenter who could quickly make a couple of stout boxes for them? Oh—I assume you're willing to sell?'

'Indeed,' Bednyak was already on his feet, although still looking as if he had been stunned. 'I'll call Taras Plotnik—he's a good craftsman . . .' and he practically ran from the room.

Igor took a folded wad of papers from his pocket, from which he peeled one sheet printed with an elaborate steel-engraved heading, and looked about him as if seeking pen and ink.

'You should have made it more,' Galina said. 'That will pay the debt and the interest, but he's still no money to buy the seed.'

'I can't give him more than they're worth,' Igor replied mildly. 'I have to answer to the Treasury for what I spend on Alexander Pavlovich's behalf.'

'You—you mean they're really worth . . .?' Galina said faintly. 'Good Heavens!'

'Yes. I thought . . .' Igor stared at her for a moment,

then said, 'Oh, I see. You were going to give him the money to pay his debt and buy his seed, and pretend it was the price of the vase. He'd never have believed that one vase was worth that much!'

'I thought we might convince him it was worth enough to pay back the principal, and I've another idea for the rest.'

'Why did you choose the vase?'

'It looked as if it might possibly have some value, and certainly nothing else in the room does!'

Igor looked about him, smiled again, this time directly at Galina, his face transformed by warmth, and said, so quietly that she could hardly hear him. 'You're not quite as clever, but a great deal more kind than I thought!' and Galina had to turn her face away and hunt industriously for something in her reticule, to hide the sudden increase of colour in her cheeks.

Count Bednyak's carpenter, an old man as gnarled as an ancient willow, quickly understood what Igor wanted, in spite of constant helpful interruptions from his master. He measured the vases by a system of fore-arm lengths, palm-widths and thumb-joints, and went off to make the boxes, muttering about various pieces of wood of his acquaintance. Igor then requested some ink and a pen, which Count Bednyak failed to discover until he thought to ask a servant to find them, and then Igor wrote out the draft.

'Now,' said Galina in a business-like fashion, when the Count was sitting down again, staring unbelievingly at the sheet of paper in his trembling hands, 'I shall instruct my agent in Kiev to accept only the principal of the loan from you. The interest is waived as compensation for the anxiety you've been caused. You'll now have enough to buy good seed for the spring sowing, but I think you shouldn't grow rye again for a few years.'

'Not rye?' Bednyak transferred his gaze to her face.

His brown eyes had a child-like guilelessness, and he obviously regarded Galina as some sort of *deus ex machina*, and was quite prepared to plant a barnacle-tree and grow geese if she advised it.

'Well, I gather that you've had trouble with disease,' she said, and gave him a very clear little lecture on disease cycles and the rotation of crops. After that, she told him to grow wheat, which was a far more profitable crop, in any case, as there was a good market for it overseas (at a high price) as well as in the towns. 'One of my estates near Kharkov produces a very good wheat-crop,' she finished. 'I shall instruct the steward to send you what you need at a fair price, and that should set you right.'

Bednyak was so hypnotised by then that he agreed without the slighest demur. Igor, who had succumbed to a sudden fit of coughing at Galina's didactic tone, was saved from disgracing himself by the return of the carpenter with two stout boxes, a sackful of sawdust and shavings, and an old but clean sheet.

It took only a short time to tear the sheet in half, and wrap the vases in the pieces, then pack each in its box with plenty of sawdust and shavings, and nail on the lids. Count Bednyak offered refreshment, obviously discomfited that he had not thought of it before, but Galina politely declined, saying that she particularly wished to be home before dark, for she was afraid that, if they did not leave very quickly, Bednyak would start thanking them, and it would all become very emotional and embarrassing.

Once they were safely on their way, the two wooden boxes set rather uncomfortably between their feet in the straw, Igor rummaged in one of the small compartments built into the sides of the *kibitka* and found some fresh white bread and cheese, a bottle of wine, a flask of brandy and three horn cups, which he said were always put into any one of his grandfather's vehicles when the horses were harnessed to it, for Leonid Matveyich had once been delayed somewhere with a broken wheel and nowhere to obtain refreshment, and had gone several hours without food—an unpleasant experience against which he now took every precaution. They made a good luncheon as they sped along, even Dasha being persuaded to eat and drink, despite being sandwiched between her betters.

'Tell me,' Igor suddenly asked as they raced along the smooth, straight road through an unending tunnel formed by the stark black trunks of pine-trees and the clear blue sky above them, 'where did you learn so much about agriculture?'

'From my father's steward,' Galina replied. 'We may have only one estate, but it's well-managed and productive, and it will be mine one day. The steward's a literate man—father sent him to school in Moscow for three years—and he reads books about farming. He has some from England which Father had translated for him—the English are very good farmers, you know. I think that, if I'm going to own land, I should know how to look after it, so I read them too.'

'Won't you leave all that to your husband?'

'If I have a husband, yes, 'though I should still take an interest, of course, but there's no guarantee that I'll marry.'

'You should look in your mirror,' Igor said quite kindly. 'You'll find your guarantee there! On the other hand,' his voice suddenly harder and a shade bitter, 'you could look at the list of the property you've inherited—that's an even better one!'

There was an awkward pause, and then he said in a normal, conversational manner, 'You seem to know a great deal about your estates, but you've only had them a few months.'

'I receive reports from my stewards.' Galina was surprised. 'I asked for a detailed description of each estate to start with, and I shall try to visit as many as I can during the summer, and see that they're using proper scientific methods.'

'So you can make more from them and charge higher rents,' Igor said, half-questioningly.

'They should certainly yield more—some of them, at least, although one or two are already doing very well in that respect. I see no need to raise the rents, though, in labour or money. There's no sense in discouraging the peasants from growing better crops by penalising them if they do by charging them more rent or making them work longer hours! In any case, I shall probably look into this business of freeing my serfs, and that will change the whole rent structure, and, I hope, make it fairer.'

Igor murmured, 'Whoever said that Westernisation will never spread to the provinces? It seems to have penetrated to Tver!'

'I do hope that Tatya Petrovna is feeling better,' Galina changed the subject. 'I'd like to start back for Petersburg in a couple of days. If it's convenient, of course.'

'Perfectly convenient. I expect she'll be quite well by now,' Igor replied to the implied questions in reverse order. 'She has the migraine only occasionally. It's very bad while the attack lasts, but she's perfectly well again by the end of the next day. Don't fuss her about it—she dislikes drawing attention to it.'

'Have you know her a long time?'

'Several years. I'm not a founder-member of Tatya's Beaux, nor even a particularly closely attached one— more of a caterpillar among the moths! I was in the Corps of Pages with Andrei Ivanovich, whose home is near the Orlovs' Ryazan estate, and I got to know

them—Lev and Tatya—through him. I like and admire
her a great deal, for she's even more beautiful in her
nature than she is in face and form.'

'Yes,' Galina agreed whole-heartedly. 'Has she been
a widow very long?'

Igor counted on his fingers. 'Eight years, almost. Her
husband died of wounds soon after Austerlitz.'

'I'd have thought she'd be married again by now, but
perhaps she loved her husband very much . . .'

'Feared him, more like,' Igor replied, his face becoming remote and stern, like some heroic statue. 'He was
an infamous bully, and no one doubts but that he treated
her abominably.' He looked at Dasha, but she was
sitting between them fast asleep. 'It's quite likely that he
got his death-wound from his own men—they all had
reason enough to hate him. That's gossip, you realise,
and shouldn't be repeated!'

'I wouldn't repeat any of it,' Galina assured him. 'I'm
grateful to you for telling me, for I might have said the
wrong thing to Tatya at some time, and I'd not at all wish
to upset her.'

Igor glanced at Dasha again, but Galina said, 'She
hardly knows more than a dozen words in French. I
suppose we all become so accustomed to speaking
French nearly all the time that we tend to forget that few
of the servants know the language.'

'My valet speaks fluent French,' Igor said a trifle
smugly. 'But then, he is French—a refugee from Bonaparte! I think he probably deserted from the army, but I
don't enquire.'

'But his name is Russian?'

'He's properly Eugène, but he prefers Yevgeny.'

Dasha woke up, unfortunately, when they reached
the river, and Galina had to speak quite sharply to her to
prevent her throwing a strong fit of hysterics. Instead,
she disappeared under the fur rugs and moaned gently

until they were safely across, and was quite calm and cheerful by the time they reached home. Igor enquired more seriously of her why it was that she feared crossing the Dnieper so much, when she must be quite used to going over the ice in Tver and Petersburg, which each had a river not so very much less broad than the Dnieper, and it emerged that she had heard some garbled version of the story of how Marshal Ney had lost two thousand men in trying to crawl across the ice of the half-frozen Dnieper the previous winter, and nothing would convince her that the river was safe to cross anywhere or at any time after that.

Tatya was quite recovered when they reached home, and ready to leave Kiev on Wednesday morning for the long journey back to Petersburg. Leonid Matveyich did not invite any guests for Tuesday evening, for he said that the travellers should all retire early to gather strength for the ordeal ahead—he obviously did not care for travelling. He even said his goodbyes after dinner because he might otherwise delay their start in the morning.

The journey home was much the same as it had been going to Kiev, except that on the second day it snowed heavily, and the *jäger* recommended that they remain in Chernigov until the weather improved. They made the best of the enforced delay, and visited the very old and famous Cathedral of the Transfiguration, with its curious pointed-topped, semi-detached towers, which reminded Galina of pepper-mills. It was very dark inside, but an obliging sacristan lit the candles to enable them to see the fine marble of the pillars, which were much older than the church, and probably came from some antique Greek or Roman building. He drew their attention to what was left of the frescoes after so many centuries of warfare and invasion, which he said were the work of Greek artists.

At Tatya's request, they also visited the church of Sts Boris and Gleb, so that she could pray there for her nephew Boris, who was serving in Nikolai Volkhov's old regiment, somewhere far away to the west.

During the night, the snow-storm blew itself out and they were able to proceed in the morning. The temperature had dropped and the snow was now hard-frozen, so they managed to make up some of the lost time, and arrived back in St Petersburg very late at night on the seventh day out of Kiev.

Despite the late hour, Osya Ivanich had most of the servants lined up in the hall to greet Galina when she eventually managed to extricate herself from the rugs in which she had been wrapped in the coach and enter the house. She thanked them and dismissed all but those on duty, noticing that the others had obviously pulled on their clothes in great haste, and could hardly stifle their yawns, so she said privately to Osya Ivanich that in future, when she returned from a journey, only those servants who were already up and about need assemble to greet her. He asked if she wished to dine, but, having ascertained that all was well, she declined, said goodnight, and went straight up to bed, leaving Igor in earnest conversation with Osya about the respective merits of a dish of cutlets or some cold chicken. As she reached the top of the first flight of stairs, she heard them reach a compromise on an *omelette aux fines herbes*.

She slept fairly late in the morning, and on her way down to breakfast, was surprised to encounter the bear in the gallery of the *piano nobile*, for she had not noticed it the night before. It was certainly an unprepossessing creature, and not the sort of thing one would wish one's friends to come upon unexpectedly in the shadows, so she summoned one of the footmen who hovered about the place, and firmly instructed him to see the animal safely stowed away in a remote attic, then left him contemplating the problem while she passed on, pausing to look at the Wheel of Fortune.

The soldier was standing in martial glory at the top of the circle, and the poor peasant lay sprawled grotesquely at the bottom. Galina was reminded of Leonid's words on Pugachev's rebellion, and stood for a few moments thinking about the wretches who existed in the poor districts of St Petersburg, shivering in tumble-down hovels, or crowded into makeshift barracks in old houses, supporting with their work the fine houses, beautiful palaces and churches of the city. Even as she watched, the mechanism whirred and clicked and the soldier began to tumble sideways, while the peasant seemed to make the first effort to gather himself together. She shivered and moved on.

One of the five footmen who waited on her told her that Igor had already breakfasted and gone out, and that her mother was upstairs writing letters. Judging from the pile of invitations and notes waiting by her place, Galina thought that she would have to do the same, and wondered how she should decide which invitations to accept, but that problem was solved when she found on top of the pile a note from Tatya inviting her to spend the afternoon at the Orlovs' house to sort out their arrangements for the next few weeks.

After breakfast, Galina went upstairs to bid her mother good morning, and then summoned Osya Ivanich to the little office which she had established on the ground floor, and received his report. He told her a number of humdrum things, and then said nervously, 'I'm afraid we had a small fire in one of the little rooms off the second courtyard. Nothing much, as it was put out quickly, but some bedding was burned.

'How did it happen?' Galina asked, for she was under the impression that the house-serfs slept in rooms and dormitories over the stables and coach-houses round the third courtyard, so there should have been no bedding in the room Osya had mentioned.

He hesitated for so long that she became suspicious and said, 'Was the bedding stored there?'

He opened and shut his mouth twice, and then said wretchedly, 'I can only tell you the truth, because you're bound to find out before long, Galina Stepanovna, and beg mercy for all concerned. One of the kitchen girls was sleeping there, and knocked a candle over. It shouldn't have been alight, but she needed to see to attend to her baby, because it was crying.'

'Yes,' Galina prompted as he stopped again, some part of the back of her mind thinking that she had never seen a child of any age about when she had gone into the domestic areas at the back of the house.

'One of the footmen put it out.'

'Indeed. How?'

'With—with the contents of a—a domestic utensil.'

Galina assumed (correctly) that he meant a chamber-pot and that this was the reason for his embarrassment, so she said reasonably, 'Well, I can hardly be angry with the girl for lighting a candle to attend to her baby, and her husband seems to have acted very sensibly—I take it the footman is her husband?'

Osya looked as if he was about to be sick and said wretchedly, 'No Galina Stepanovna, and that's why I have to speak to you about the matter. You see, the General wouldn't allow any of the house-serfs to marry.'

There was a stunned silence for a full second, and then he went on in a rush, 'It wasn't possible to stop them forming attachments—not even human to try. He was so seldom here that they could manage, and when he or Gennadi Yakovich came, the children were put out among friends in other houses, and everyone went back to sleeping in the dormitories . . .'

'And how many of the serfs live together and have

children?' Galina asked, hardly able to believe her ears.

'About forty couples,' Osya admitted miserably. 'They want to marry, but they can't, of course—not without written permission from their owner.'

'In that case,' Galina said briskly, 'you had better make out the necessary permits for everyone who wishes to be married, and bring them to me to sign. Why on earth did General Zhadnov refuse?'

Osya looked blank, and answered in an expressionless voice, 'He said they wouldn't do their work properly—they'd be forever wasting time with each other and their children. Of course, we know that a lot of owners take the same view and don't allow marriages, but we wondered if perhaps you . . . You really mean it, Galina Stepanovna? You'll let them be married?'

'Certainly,' Galina was tempted to tell him exactly what she thought of General Zhadnov and other owners who refused to let their serfs marry, but thought it better to make no comment at all as, once she started, it would be difficult to stop, and one should not deliver a diatribe against members of one's own class of Society to a house-serf. 'The sooner the better, and I don't wish to hear another word about the matter. Bring me the permits as soon as maybe, and arrange the marriages as quickly as possible. I'm ashamed that such a situation should have existed in my house without my becoming aware of it. In future, if any couples wish to marry, you may send them to see me. Oh, and you may give each couple five gold roubles, and one for each of their children, and I don't wish to be thanked by anyone, either for the money or the permission.'

Nevertheless, Osya tried to make a speech of thanks, but she cut him short out of embarrassment at being the object of gratitude for something which she considered should be every person's right, even if the person was a serf, and asked him to accompany her on a tour of inspection, starting with the domestic area on the ground floor of the main block of the house, and working upwards. This was not, of course, the first time she had done this, and she was pleased to see that the kitchens and other offices were still as clean and tidy as when she had first seen them, and some great improvements were obvious in the reception rooms on the first floor. The ballroom and the large dining-room were almost usable. Her own Peacock Salon looked twice as large with most of the surplus furniture removed, and the unpleasant carpet had been replaced with a beautiful one which had obviously been made for the room, for it too had peacocks and flowers in colours matching the silk on the walls.

'Where did you find it?' she asked.

'It was here all the time, underneath the other,' Osya replied. 'Count Charodyev gave me a long list of instructions during the second week he was here. He said I was to make all the changes and surprise you, and, of course, with you going away, it was much easier. I hope I did right . . .'

'Certainly you did,' Galina assured him. 'I want to be able to use the rooms, so most of their contents will have to go. What did you do with the things you removed?'

'Count Charodyev told me to put most of it in a part of the stable-block we don't use, for the time being, and he said to burn things—not many,' he added hastily. 'Now he's back, I expect we'll get on quickly. The small things are the problem—he has to look at each one, to see just what it is.'

'Thank goodness Countess Kalinshkaya found him for me!' Galina said fervently as she went on to the next room, marvelling at so great an improvement in such a short time.

She passed the bottom of the stairs to the upper floors, where three footmen were struggling with something large, furry, and fairly white, and investigated the other half of the *piano nobile*. Some of the rooms seemed more crowded than ever, but at least she now had enough space to do some entertaining in the others. The small dining room had been cleared of all but the things which belonged in it, and rearranged, and the room which occupied the opposite corner to the Peacock Salon at the front of the house had emerged as a charming apartment decorated in apricot and pale green, with satinwood furniture.

'The Countess your mother has taken to using this room,' Osya said uncertainly. 'She entertains here most evenings and some afternoons. I hope that is in order?'

'My mother!' Galina exclaimed in surprise. 'Oh, I *am* glad to hear that!' for she had hoped that Countess Razumova might make a few friends in St Petersburg and go into Society a little.

The large and small supper-rooms, the Chinese Salon, the picture gallery and the winter-garden also showed signs of improvement, and Galina decided to leave the two upper floors of the house and the warren of rooms around the courtyards at the back for another day as it now lacked little more than a half-hour to luncheon.

She dismissed Osya Ivanich with a little speech of thanks for all that he and his underlings had achieved, and a further assurance that she would give permission to marry to those of the serfs who wished it, and went to the one room on the main floor which she had not yet entered—the library. It was a very dull day, not yet snowing, but obviously about to start, and the candles had not yet been brought in, so she assumed the room to empty, and turned at once to look at the Charioteer.

In the dim light, only his face and hands were visible, the rest merging into the shadows. He was just as handsome and vital as she remembered, and it seemed quite impossible that anyone who could look so alive in paint on canvas should be dead in reality. She thought fleetingly of the living men who had partnered her at Countess Scherer's ball, particularly Sasha Alexandrovich, Kostya Fedorovich and Sergei Mikhailovich. It would be pleasant to see them all again after almost three weeks away, and she felt modestly confident that they would remember her, but how insipid they seemed in her memory compared with the impression of Gennadi Zhadnov conveyed by his portrait!

She had been vaguely aware of a small sound while she stood gazing at the portrait and thinking, but it was so familiar—the striking of flint against steel—and she had been so absorbed that she was startled when a hand bearing a taper suddenly reached past her and lit the candles on the girandole beside the painting.

'There—you can see the Handsome Hero in all his glory now,' Igor said in a distinctly bitter tone.

'Oh! I'm sorry—I didn't realise you were in here!' Galina exclaimed.

'I was ferreting about on the floor,' he replied. 'I dropped my tinder-box. You seem remarkably struck by that portrait.'

Galina turned away, feeling foolish and aware that her colour had risen. Surely she could not have been so foolish as to become infatuated with a portrait? It would be an extremely stupid thing to do if the subject were alive, but Gennadi Yakovich was dead—*dead*—drowned deep in the cold Arctic . . .

'It's—it's a very fine portrait,' she said in something near her normal voice. 'I suppose it interests me because I've inherited the things he should have had. I—I suppose he really *is* dead?'

She was surprised by her own question, and waited for Igor to make a sardonic comment about wishing for the moon, or something of that sort, but he replied quite seriously, 'The survivors from the expedition were sure that all the others must have perished in the storm, but I suppose they might have looked in the wrong direction—or not bothered to look at all! I shouldn't worry—he'd have turned up by now if he was still alive.'

'Yes, of course.'

'Mind you,' Igor went on cheerfully, 'it would be just like him to come back and upset everything!'

'Why did you dislike him so?' Galina asked.

Igor crossed the room to light the only other branch of candles in there, for the snow had started to fall heavily outside and the room was very dark. 'He was everything I'm not,' he replied reflectively. 'Tall, handsome, rich, confident, Great Russian . . . Apart from the last, which I don't mind in the same way, I suppose I was jealous.'

Galina felt certain that this was not the whole of it, but it was none of her business, and it seemed better to change the subject.

During luncheon, Galina said to her mother how pleased she was to hear that she had some friends in Petersburg.

'They left cards, so I had to send some myself, and then they called,' Countess Razumova replied vaguely. 'These things seem to happen of their own volition. I thought it best to use one of the other salons—I don't think my elderly ladies would mix comfortably with your young friends. I didn't think you'd be needing the Apricot Salon very often. I did wonder about the Chinese one, but there are dragons writhing about somewhat profusely, and I thought them too distracting. We drink tea and play cards, or read them, and it passes the time quite pleasantly. Sometimes we stitch our embroidery and gossip . . .'

'And do you visit them?' Galina asked hopefully.

'Oh, dear me, no! Why should I do that? No, they seem quite happy to come here. I've chosen a few good pictures and some comfortable furnishings, and set up my own little hermitage. I knew you wouldn't mind.'

Igor smiled encouragingly at her, taking her reference to the Hermitage which Ekaterina II had built on to the Winter Palace in which to keep her own good pictures and entertain her friends in private. 'Mind that your Hermitage doesn't grow until it engulfs the whole house!' he said.

'No fear of that,' Countess Razumova replied, smiling at him in a friendly fashion which surprised Galina, who had not noticed that her mother had grown to like the Magician.

'If we don't get rid of some of the rubbish in this house, we shall be overwhelmed ourselves,' she observed. 'Osya Ivanich tells me that the clearance which took place in our absence was at the expense of the stables.'

'A temporary measure,' Igor replied. '*Very* temporary, for I don't care to think of all that wood close to hay and straw—too much risk of fire. I suggest that you hire a warehouse and put everything you don't want into it until you can decide what to sell and what to burn.'

'A warehouse!' exclaimed Galina. 'What a good idea! Do you know of one?'

'I've set enquiries in hand, and heard of two near the English Quay. I'll go and inspect them this afternoon, and hire one or both if they prove suitable, and you're agreeable.'

'Agreeable and grateful!' Galina assured him, so after luncheon, Igor set off for the port area of the city, and Galina went to the Orlovs', leaving her mother preparing to receive her cronies in the Apricot Salon. It had, she was pleased to find, stopped snowing, although the sky was an unpleasant yellowish-grey colour.

Tatya was in the garden-room, sorting her invitations into three piles, which she called acceptances, polite refusals, and what-shall-we-do-about-this-ones. She put down the cat Vron, which had been sitting on her lap, presumably assisting, and greeted Galina with a welcoming kiss, admired her new green bombazine frock with black braid frogging *à la chasseur*, and brought her up-to-date on the news of what had been happening in Petersburg while they were away, the most important item being that Irina was *enceinte*, and Lev over the moon with pride at her cleverness.

'No female ever managed it before, of course!' she added, laughing. 'Well, not with Lev as the father, at least.'

'Is she well?' Galina asked, stroking the cat, which had climbed on to her lap, thumped about until it was to his liking, and settled down to rest.

'Yes, very well. She and Lev have gone for a drive, but they'll be home soon.'

'Are there any news of Anna Mikhailovna?' Galina asked nervously, torn between not wishing to mention a subject distasteful to her friend and pity for the poor creature who had suffered such an accident.

'You know she miscarried?' Tatya's expressive face showed only concern and pity. 'Poor soul—she has no life at all in her legs—no movement or feeling, and her back is so painful that she can get no ease, sitting or lying, and she refuses to see any callers. Nikolai—her husband—has not yet responded to the message Igor sent, but, of course, there's not been time, for he's with the Emperor, and I believe that Headquarters is now in Frankfürt, and the Army actually on the Rhine!'

'But that's the border of France!' Galina exclaimed.

'Yes. Everyone's waiting to hear the official news, for it's only rumour as yet, but there's talk of a truce and peace negotiations. Oh, Galina! If it's true, then there may be a chance that Bonaparte will be finished at last.'

'I can remember a time when I'd never heard of Bonaparte,' Galine said reflectively. 'It seems very long ago, when I was a child. I'm twenty-one now, so I must have been about six, I suppose—I recall my father saying something about France having a new sort of government with consuls, like the Romans, and this "Bonaparte" was to be the chief of them, and I asked what a consul was . . . Just think! He's been a shadow in all our lives ever since.'

Tatya sighed. 'He's not finished yet, I fear. I can't quite imagine him surrendering while he still has any sort of army. He may be driven back into France, but I doubt that's the end of it just yet!'

There was a small silence, then Galina asked, 'Do you think Prince Nikolai will come to Petersburg?'

'I don't know,' Tatya replied. 'He's had nothing to do with Anna Mikhailovna for several years, but he's such a good, kind man, he may feel sorry for her and wish to try to help.' Her beautiful eyes looked past Galina into some distant place and time. 'It would be good to see him again,' she said, as if to herself. 'I've not seen him since last winter, when he was still very ill with the wound he got at Borodino, and I could only stay a few minutes . . . I sometimes think that it would have been far better for both of us if our fathers had chosen to marry us to one another instead of to Anna and—and General Kalinsky . . .'

'Did you love him?' Galina asked gently, her eyes huge with sympathy and concern.

Tatya's gaze came back into focus, and she said, 'Love? I don't think I really know what love is—not yet, at least. Perhaps I never shall, for I'm twenty-five now, and too old for thinking of romance. When I was seventeen, I thought Nikolai the finest, handsomest man in the world, but I don't believe he ever noticed me particularly. He was kind enough to ask me to dance when we met at a ball, for he was Lev's friend, and Lev was always good about making his friends take notice of his little sister. I'm fond of Nikolai, and desperately sorry for him, but I couldn't marry him, even if he were free.' She shivered suddenly, as if she had recalled an unpleasant experience, and Galina caught a glimpse of something like fear in her eyes, recalled what Igor had said about Tatya's husband, and said a silent prayer for her, for she thought it a great pity that someone so beautiful and kind should not be happy. She felt very honoured that Tatya had shown so much confidence in her discretion by talking of such personal matters.

'Now, these invitations,' Tatya suddenly recalled the purpose of Galina's visit. 'We should try to sort them out now, I think, before the others arrive—you'll stay to dinner?'

Galina accepted, once she was assured that her bombazine frock would 'do' very well, and they went through their pile of invitations (Galina having brought hers with her) quite quickly, for Galina was happy to agree with anything Tatya suggested. The acceptances amounted to a formidable programme of social activity for the next month or more, but everything paled into comparative insignificance when Tatya remarked that the Christmas Ball at the Winter Palace was to take place during the following week.

'It won't be nearly as brilliant as usual,' she warned, 'not with the Emperor and three-quarters of the Guard officers away, but it's an honour to be invited, and that's the most important thing. What shall we wear?'

There was some discussion of ball-gowns, and then Galina asked Tatya's advice about Christmas gifts for her house-serfs.

'I believe most families give them at New Year, but I prefer Christmas,' she said. 'I generally see to it at home—in Tver, that is—but that's only about three dozen souls, and here—goodness knows how many!'

'Ask your major-domo—Osya, isn't it?—to give you a

list of names, and some indication of what would suit each person, then send an order to this shop.' Tatya wrote an address in the Gostinny Dvor on a piece of paper, which Galina put safely away in her reticule. 'They'll supply all the articles wrapped and labelled. I usually choose most of the gifts for our servants myself, but I know them all, so it's different.'

Galina thanked her, then, on an impulse, told her about General Zhadnov's refusal to allow his house-serfs to marry, and her own reversal of the policy. 'It seemed downright wicked and cruel,' she said.

'Indeed it was!' Tatya agreed. 'And what a miserable excuse. As if it would make the slightest difference. They'd be more distracted from their work by worrying about being found out, and trying to care for their children in secret, and how could he expect good service from people who would naturally be filled with resentment against him? Really! How stupid some people are! I suppose it only shows how thin the veneer of civilisation is in Russia.'

They went on to talk of other domestic matters, and Galina asked advice on holding a dinner, or perhaps even a ball, in her own house now that there was sufficient space. Tatya was delighted with the idea, and they settled down to make preliminary plans for a small dinner for perhaps thirty guests, followed by a ball to which another hundred or so might be asked, to take place sometime in January.

They had finished that, and Tatya was about to ring for tea, when Pavel Kuzmich entered to announce Prince Nikolai Volkhov.

CHAPTER
SEVEN

THE SUN

Success and enjoyment/Happiness is short-lived

GALINA gazed at the new-comer with great interest, and was disappointed, for she had assumed that the paragon of whom Tatya had been speaking must be someone quite extraordinary, in looks at least, but the man who entered seemed to her nothing remarkable at all. He was very tall, with light brown hair and the pale, set face of someone not fully recovered from a very serious illness. There was an air of remoteness about him, as if he were cut off in some way from the rest of the world, which she supposed was also due to the state of his health, and the only really striking thing about him was the intense blue of his eyes, but even they had no more life in them than the sapphires which they resembled. Of course, he had been badly wounded and had hung between life and death for many weeks, but that was over a year ago. She could only suppose that his suffering had left some permanent effect on his spirits.

'When did you arrive?' Tatya asked him when the greetings and introductions were finished and they were sitting down drinking tea.

'Last night. I went to see Anna this morning—she's at her father's house—and then to Prince Ruschev's, to hear what happened. He seemed to have very little idea,

and referred me to Igor Charodyev, but I can't find him.
I thought he might be here.'

'He will be later,' Tatya said. 'I think the Ruschevs
were very upset about the accident, so perhaps they
don't wish to talk about it. How is Anna?'

Prince Nikolai considered the question, then said
hesitantly, 'I'm not sure. She's obviously seriously injured, but her spirit seems to have broken, and I think
that's making her worse than she need be.' He shook his
head. 'Her father seems to have called in every surgeon
he can find to see her, but they are all helpless.'

He sounded unwilling to say much more about his
wife, so Tatya asked him how and where he had left the
Emperor, and he gave them an interesting account of the
Imperial progress as Commander-in-Chief during the
past few months, which lasted until first Irina and Lev,
then Sasha, Kostya, and Nadya and Andrei arrived.
The Prince seemed vaguely pleased to see them all,
but said apologetically that his ability to feel any
emotions had been severely affected by the shock of
his wound.

'The doctors say I shall recover in time, but I'm afraid
that meanwhile, I might as well be made of wood, or ice.
Everything seems remote and meaningless. I'm sorry.'
And he looked at his friends with an air of patient
hopelessness that made Galina feel like crying, and
probably had a similar effect on the others, to judge by
their expressions.

The awkward little silence which followed was broken
by the arrival of Igor, who greeted the Prince with a
matter-of-fact, 'You've got here remarkably quickly—
all credit to the Imperial couriers, I suppose! I thought
you'd wish to know.'

'Yes, and I'm grateful to you for thinking of sending to
me,' Prince Nikolai replied, shaking his hand. 'I gather
you were there when it happened?'

Igor looked at Galina, and seemed somehow to understand that she had no wish to be involved, for she was doing her best to forget that terrible evening at the Ruschevs', which still disturbed her sleep at times. He drew Prince Nikolai away across the room, and presumably told him the whole story, while everyone else talked of other matters.

Presently, they returned to the main group, and Prince Nikolai made his excuses to Tatya, for he was expected to dine at his father-in-law's, and left, saying sombrely that he hoped to see more of his friends during the Season. His going seemed to remove a damper from the party, and soon they were all chattering merrily about the events of the past three weeks, bringing the travellers up to date on the current gossip.

Igor quietly informed Galina that he had rented both warehouses at a reduced rate, as they were both owned by the same merchant, and the furniture stored in the stables was already being removed to them, and then he was drawn away by Lev's friendly enquiry about the well-being of the rest of his family, and Sasha Tuchin limped over to sit with Galina, smiled uncertainly at her, and said confidentially that he was glad she was back in Petersburg as he had very much missed her.

Galina, who thought he was a pleasant, good-natured man and felt sorry for his lameness, replied kindly and enquired if the cold weather made his leg ache.

'It does a bit,' he admitted. 'But it aches worst in the part that isn't there, which is ridiculous, isn't it? I feel sometimes as if my foot and ankle have been trodden on by an elephant, but they aren't—I mean, from the knee down is just wood.'

'Yes, I've heard of that,' Galina said with sympathetic interest. 'It's very strange. You seem to manage well, though—I believe you said that you can still ride a horse, even?'

'Fancy you remembering that!' Sasha exclaimed, going rather pink in the face. 'It's still a—a disfigurement though, isn't it? I mean—it's not a thing anyone would want to—to contemplate . . .'

'It's a great shame,' Galina replied, trying to temper sympathy with something more bracing. 'But I wouldn't call it a disfigurement, for it isn't at all obvious. I mean—some men have ugly noses, or warts, or . . .' Looking round for inspiration, her eyes lighted on Andrei's hands, and she was silent. Sasha's gaze followed hers, and Andrei must have become conscious of them, for he suddenly turned his head and looked at Galina, his eyebrows rising enquiringly.

'Sasha is worried that—that people might think his leg a disfigurement,' Galina said flatly, giving him as meaningful a look as she could manage.

'Well, you'll always find a few idiots who will,' Andrei replied, addressing Sasha. 'But who cares what idiots think? It's no bar to a happy marriage, if that's what's worrying you! I should know—my hands are more obvious and unsightly than your discreet little wooden peg!'

'D'you think so?' Sasha asked hopefully, and Galina found, to her consternation, that he was looking at her with much the same expression as a dog hoping for a kind word.

'I'm sure Andrei's right,' she answered, hoping that her reading of his expression was wrong, but very much fearing that it was right.

After dinner, it emerged that they were all in receipt of invitations to the Imperial Ball, for Galina's had arrived with Igor's that afternoon, and he had brought it with him, thinking she would wish to know as soon as possible. The ladies at once became deeply involved in discussion about what they should wear, while Lev attempted to take the men away to his study to look at some of the things he had brought back from his wedding-journey, but he failed to tempt Sasha or Kostya, who remained in the garden-room with the ladies, obviously at a loss with the feminine conversation, yet obstinately determined to stay, and attempting to discount any discomfiture by carrying on a disjointed discussion of the respective merits of various horses of their acquaintance.

Galina assumed that Kostya wished to be near Tatya, and hoped that Sasha's motive was the same, but noticed with a sinking feeling that both men were inclined to gaze fixedly in her own direction, and she was quite relieved when it was time to go home.

In the evening, Osya Ivanich brought her the marriage-permits to sign, and said that everything had been arranged. He again tried to thank her, but she repeated that she had no wish to hear any more of the matter, and asked instead, 'What is the custom of the house about Christmas gifts?'

He looked at her blankly, and repeated uncertainly, 'Christmas gifts Galina Stepanovna?'

'Yes. What did the General do about them? Did he give them at Christmas or New Year, and what sort of things did he give?'

For the first time since she had met him, Osya looked completely at a loss. He opened and shut his mouth two or three times, as if unable to find the right words, and eventually said, 'Nothing.'

'You mean he didn't give any?' Galina asked, her eyes opening wide in shocked surprise.

'He was seldom here,' Osya appeared to be about to defend his late master, then abandoned the attempt. 'He said that the house-serfs were housed, fed and clothed at his expense and had no right to expect more. Gennadi Yakovich used to give something when he was here at New Year, but he wasn't a rich man, you see,' he added, seeming relieved to find something good to say of the Zhadnov family.

'That is something I'm going to change,' Galina said in positive tones. 'Please have a list made of the names of all the people in the house, stables, yards—everywhere, and put by each name a suggestion for a gift which that person would like to receive, excepting the children—I shall give their parents some money to buy whatever they need. I intend to give the presents at Christmas.'

'Certainly, Galina Stepanovna. Er—is that to be instead of the clothes?'

'Clothes? You mean the new clothes for New Year?'

'Yes. The General used to give a set of new clothes to the senior person in each department.'

'And the others?'

'Oh, they were passed down—I mean, the one who had new ones passed the old ones to the next most senior, and so on down the line.'

'But that's . . .' Galina began, then remembered not to speak ill of the dead and substituted, 'I had assumed that everyone would be given new clothes. The gifts are to be in addition.'

Osya managed with a great effort to retrieve his eyebrows from his hairline and shut his mouth, and, after a preliminary gurgle and a cough, to make a little speech of thanks on behalf of all the house-serfs in Galina's ownership, which she allowed this time, although she felt embarrassed by it, and then he hastened away to start work on the list.

Igor had not appeared at breakfast, but Galina assumed that he had probably eaten earlier and gone out, or perhaps had started on his work, so she was not surprised to find him in the library, but he croaked in reply to her, 'Good Morning,' and she saw that he was very pale and heavy-eyed.

'Are you not well?' she asked.

'Quite well, thank you,' he replied, then, sitting down abruptly, 'No I'm not. I feel as if a regiment had ridden over me. My head aches—in fact, I ache all over, and my throat hurts, and I think you'd best leave me alone before I start snarling!'

'Shouldn't you go back to bed?' Galina enquired. She put a hand on his brow as if he were a child, persisting when he tried to jerk away, and found him to be feverish. 'I think you should, and I'll send you up a tisane to soothe your throat and allay the fever.'

'I can't. I have to go out this afternoon.'

'You can't possibly go out. Send to whoever it was you were to visit and tell them you're ill.'

Igor shook his head. 'She'll be too disappointed. I promised we'd buy her Christmas gift today.'

Galina wondered who 'she' might be, but refrained from speculating.

'There's plenty of time for that. Christmas is still nearly three weeks away.'

'No, there isn't,' Igor sounded irritable. 'She's only allowed one outing a month, and it's today. If I don't go, she'll miss it, and won't be allowed out again until January. A promise is important to a child, and she's only eight! I can't just not go.'

Galina suddenly remembered the afternoon before they set out for Kiev, when he had had an engagement which he could not put off, and the child in the carriage with him.

'Perhaps I could take her instead?' she suggested tentatively.

Igor pulled his handkerchief out of his sleeve, covered most of his face with it, and sneezed explosively.

'I suppose so, but it's an imposition on you. I wouldn't ask . . .'

'You didn't ask,' Galina interrupted. 'I offered. I

collect she's at school? When and where should I meet her?'

'At the Smolny Institute, at three o'clock. She has to be back by half after four,' Igor managed between two more sneezes. 'I'll send a note to the *Directrice* to explain, and Varvara will be waiting in the vestibule.' There followed a positive barrage of sneezes, so Galina ordered him off to bed as soon as he had written and sent the note, and went down to the still-room to see what she could find to help his cold.

The still-room maids looked startled when the mistress suddenly entered their domain. They were sitting by the stove knitting and, no doubt, gossiping, but the room was clean and tidy, the pine tables scrubbed and spotlessly white, the labelled pots of dried herbs in neat rows on the shelves. Galina considered the store, found practically everything she could think of, and set to work.

She sent one maid to the kitchen for a lemon, then told her to squeeze out the juice and beat it with honey to make a soothing syrup, while Galina mixed enough thyme and hyssop for a dozen tisanes in a pretty porcelain jar, which she sent up to Igor's room with the syrup, and samovar, tea-pot, and cup and dish, so that he could make a fresh brew whenever he wished.

On the way to the Smolny Institute that afternoon, she allowed herself to speculate about the child she was about to meet. No one had ever mentioned that Igor was married, nor that he had a child. Presumably she was his, for why else should he have the monopoly of her once-a-month outings? It seemed very odd, for the Smolny Institute, founded by the Empress Ekaterina II for the education of the daughters of the Nobility, was the most respected and select school for girls in Russia. Surely they didn't admit b—illegitimate children? Igor had never seemed to her the sort of man who would have any illicit connections, but one could never tell with men! Then she recalled that Tatya had once said that Igor was reticent about himself, so perhaps he had been married, and his wife had died, and, as that seemed the most likely and comfortable conclusion, she concentrated on looking out of the window, for she had not been through this part of the city before.

The shortest route to the Smolny was eastwards along the Nevsky Prospect to the Zagorodny Canal, then alongside it to the Preobajensky Guards' barracks and past the Horse Artillery arsenal, from whence the golden-yellow classical façade of the Smolny's new building could be seen across the gardens.

Galina's carriage drew up before the eight large columns of the portico promptly at three, for the bells in the cathedral tower were just echoing the carillon of the Peter-Paul Cathedral down the river, and a porter came out to enquire her business. As soon as she mentioned Varvara Charodyeva, he turned and signalled with one finger to a small figure standing in the vestibule, nose pressed to the window beside the door, and the child came out, walking sedately, but in a manner which showed a strong inclination to run, and climbed into the carriage.

'Good afternoon,' she said primly. 'It was kind of you to come for me. *Madame la Directrice* explained about it.'

Galina smiled at her, thinking her a funny, solemn little thing. She was a skinny child with the dark hair and eyes to be expected in Igor's daughter, her face beginning to be quite striking, but without any childish prettiness. She was dressed in a dark grey pelisse trimmed with black fur, but her grey bonnet sported half-a-dozen white egret feathers, trimmed to make a fluffy plume, which relieved the sobriety of her appearance.

'I'm sorry your father couldn't come,' Galina said in a

friendly, sympathetic tone. 'But he's caught a very heavy cold, and it seemed more sensible for him to stay in bed, for he might have given you the infection, and made himself worse by coming out. He was very disappointed, and I expect you are as well, but he sends his love, and these flowers.' She had taken the initiative of bringing a large bouquet from her own hothouses, and felt no compunction about crediting Igor with their origin. He had sent down a parcel at the last minute, just as she was leaving, which she recognised as one Leonid Matveyich had given him before they left Kiev.

Varvara looked puzzled and said, 'My father is away in the Navy, in the Adaratic Sea—no, that's wrong, but it's something like that.'

'Adriatic,' Galina supplied, light suddenly dawning. 'Oh, I see! You're Varvara Denisovna! Igor Grigorovich is your uncle!'

Varvara smiled for the first time, and then laughed. 'Did you think him my father? Poor Uncle Igor! He thinks it quite bad enough to be my uncle! He's very good to me, though,' she added seriously. 'My father's been away for such a long time, because that horrid Sultan of Turkey won't allow any Russian ships to go through the Dardanelles into the Black Sea, so they can't come home except by going all the way round Europe to Petersburg.'

'I suppose you wouldn't have any outings at all, then, if your uncle didn't take you,' Galina said concernedly.

'No,' the child replied sadly. 'My mother is a nun in a convent near Moscow. I never hear anything from her at all, and my grandparents live in the south, so I don't see them very often.'

'Your great-grandfather sent you a gift,' Galina indicated the parcel. 'I expect it's for Christmas.'

'It will be a doll,' Varvara said with happy certainty. 'He promised me a doll this year.' She looked out of the window, realised that they had just passed the Tav-richesky Palace and were now going along Kirochnaya Street, and asked, 'Are we going to the shops?'

'Yes. Your uncle asked me to go with you to choose your Christmas gift from him. Would you like to go to the Gostinny Dvor?'

Varvara gave a wriggle of excitement and pleasure, for the double arcade of little shops was a treasure-house of everything pretty and pleasurable in the way of manufactured articles that one could imagine, and said she would like it very much, so that was where they went, but, to Galina's surprise, the child passed by the toyshops with hardly a glance, and stopped before a shop which sold materials and accessories for needle-work.

'I'd very much like a fitted work-box,' she explained. 'Do you think it would be too expensive? All the other girls in my year have them.'

'Then let's go in and look at some,' Galina replied.

She was surprised to find what a variety of work-boxes one small shop could contain, but Varvara seemed to have a clear idea of what she wanted, pushing aside most of those which the shop-keeper offered with little more than a quick glance, until she came upon one of moder-ate size, made of walnut and inlaid with a bowl of flowers in fruit-wood on the lid. Inside it was lined with green silk, and was deep enough to have two compartmented trays for tools. Galina assured the child that it was by no means too expensive, and added on her own account a silver thimble, a set of netting-tools in a carved ivory container, a dozen spools for thread, a case of needles, a paper of pins, scissors, measuring-tape, and a pretty tatting-shuttle inlaid with mother-of-pearl flowers.

Varvara seemed reluctant to allow Galina's attendant groom to take her parcel, but once he had assured her that he would on no account drop it, she allowed him to carry it, and turned her attention to the other shops, and confided to Galina that she would like to buy a gift for Uncle Igor out of her savings, which amounted to nearly two roubles. She chose a penknife, as her uncle, she told Galina, did a great deal of writing and must be forever trimming old pens and cutting new ones. The knife she particularly wished to buy, which had a pattern of birds and flowers in cloisonée enamels on the silver side-pieces, cost four kopeks more than she had in her purse, but she was persuaded to borrow this sum from Galina, and also asked her shyly if she would be kind enough to deliver the gift to Igor.

After that, there was only time for Galina to make a hurried purchase of sweet-meats for her in a confectioner's, and then they must drive back to the Smolny, with Varvara sitting on the edge of her seat, anxious not to be late for fear of forfeiting next month's outing.

She thanked Galina most earnestly for all her kindness, and sent several messages to Uncle Igor, and Galina watched her disappear sedately into the Institute, clutching her parcels and the great bunch of flowers, with a feeling of warmth tinged with sadness that so likeable a child should be shut away at school, far away from her parents—and, indeed, unlikely ever to see her mother again in this world—and dependant for affection on a brief contact once a month with her sardonic, cynical uncle.

On her way home, she brooded on this a little, and then recollected that Igor had been so concerned that the child should not miss her outing that he had been prepared to go out in spite of his obvious unfitness. Perhaps she was being unfair to him in dismissing him as cynical. After all, he had been very kind to herself, and look how quickly he had sensed her own wish to help Count Bednyak, and lent his assistance.

Of course, his appearance was against him. He had a

lean, sardonic face, and those hooded eyes gave him a predatory look, although his nose was not large or hooked . . . How much easier it was to think of a man with a frank, open face, particularly if he was fair-skinned! The Emperor was like that, and people still spoke of him as an angel and were sure of his innate goodness, despite the open secret that he had connived at his own father's assassination, and was as deviously Asiatic in his dealings with his ministers as any of his predecessors! As Galina guiltily suppressed these treasonable thoughts, one small part of her mind, with the amusement of a detached observer, was aware that even her feeling of guilt was based on fear. She hastily cast around for a better example of a fair and open countenance, and immediately thought of Gennadi Zhadnov.

Now there was a face one could trust, a character one could admire! There was no trace of deviousness or cynicism in those handsome features, and she was sure that no hint of mockery or sardonic amusement ever hardened the smile in those blue eyes. If only . . . She sighed, and Dasha, who had developed the art of self-effacement until she seemed a part of the upholstery of the carriage, startled her by asking if she felt unwell.

It was three days before Igor was sufficiently re-covered to appear downstairs again. Yevgeny, his valet, reported to Galina through Osya Ivanich on his pro-gress, starting off with a gloomy bulletin which said that a physician had been summoned, but had diagnosed only a severe cold, and continued thereafter with cau-tious optimism. Galina, in the brief intervals between morning-visits, fittings at her modiste's, two dinner-parties, a ball, a visit to the Opera, and a rout, sent him more lemon and honey syrup and herbs for tisanes, and a note reporting on Varvara's outing, and otherwise hard-ly thought of him at all.

He came down to breakfast on the fourth morning, and assured her that he was quite recovered, although, contemplating him over the flowers in the middle of the table, she thought he looked pale and tired.

The conversation remained general until Countess Razumova had departed to write letters, and then Igor, resuming the seat from which he had risen as she went out, said, 'Thank you for looking after Varvara. I trust she was well-behaved?'

'A credit to the Smolny,' Galina replied. 'She's a very pleasant child, and so sensible. I was surprised that she chose so practical a gift. I'm sure that when I was eight, I'd have selected something quite frippery, or a toy, never a work-box!'

'A work-box? I suppose all the other girls have them,' Igor seemed to have no difficult in guessing the reason. 'There's a great deal of pressure towards conformity in an institution like the Smolny. I recollect being very conscious of it in the Corps of Pages—one fellow would acquire a particular thing, and in no time we all had to have the same, or feel devilish awkward. I remember being very upset because one simply had to have a certain type of spur, and my father sent me a pair of a different kind, and I hadn't the confidence to set a new fashion!'

Galina's large eyes gazed at him in surprise at this unexpected revelation of a chink in his armour, but the glimpse was fleeting, and he changed the subject by asking how much he owed Galina for the box.

'Is that all?' He seemed surprised, and added as he counted out the money and passed it to her, 'I'll buy her some of those little knick-knacks ladies keep in their work-boxes, 'though I don't believe they know what half of them are for!'

'I've already done that,' Galina replied, and as Igor gave her a startled look, 'Well, I felt sorry for her, to be honest! After all, she's only eight, and her parents are so far away that she never sees them, and she's only allowed to go out once a month. It seems very hard.'

Igor's eyebrows quirked. 'One grows used to it, especially as everyone else one knows is in the same situation! Were you not sent to school?'

'No. I had a tutor at home, and shared some classes with the families of Father's friends. I—er—made rather a foolish mistake,' she thought it might be best to tell him herself, in case Varvara mentioned it. 'I—I thought Varvara was your daughter.'

Igor looked at her with a completely expressionless face, except that the corner of his mouth twitched until he pulled the muscles taut, giving him an even more sardonic look than usual.

'And whom did you imagine was her mother?' he enquired.

'I don't know,' Galina said frankly. 'I didn't have a great deal of time to consider the matter, for it only takes a few minutes to drive to the Smolny from here. I assumed she couldn't be illegitimate, as I don't think the Smolny Institute admits . . .' She tailed off, unable to think of a suitable euphemism.

'Love children,' Igor supplied. 'No, it doesn't, except possibly Imperial ones. Is that the only reason you could think of? I'd have thought that my obviously high moral standards and transparently honourable character would have led you to dismiss any possible doubts on that score! Didn't my habitual melancholia and addiction to black clothing lead you to suspect some deep-felt tragedy in my life, such as the loss of a young wife and mother?'

'I hadn't observed any particular signs of melancholia, and I assumed that you wear black out of sheer perversity,' Galina retorted in the same tongue-in-cheek fashion which she had detected in his speech. 'I can't answer for your character because I haven't known you very long, but I don't imagine that Tatya Petrovna would have recommended you to me if there was anything the least shady about your morals or your honesty!'

Igor actually laughed, looking suddenly younger and neither cynical nor sardonic. 'I suppose you discovered that she's my brother's daughter?'

'Yes,' Galina replied demurely. 'Oh, she sent you a gift. Should you like to have it now, or wait until Christmas?'

Igor elected to wait, and presently went away to continue his cataloguing, for he had now started on the porcelain. Galina busied herself about her own affairs, and did not see him again until the evening, when he accompanied her to a ball at Princess Dengovskaya's, further along the Fontanka, and almost opposite the Engineers' Castle.

Galina was wearing a new gown in pink gauze over silver tissue, and had received no fewer than twelve bouquets from as many gentlemen, only one of which was anything like the right colour, and this was a spray of tiny pink rosebuds a few shades darker than her gown, so she had chosen to wear it as a corsage but, in the usual rush to be ready in time, had omitted to look at the card which accompanied it.

'Oh, heavens!' she exclaimed as the carriage turned out of her own forecourt and rolled along to join the queue waiting to disgorge guests at her hostess' door. 'I don't know who sent my flowers, and I'm sure to commit some dreadful *faux pas* over them!'

'I collect that you received a record number of offerings,' Igor observed. 'Can you not remember who sent any of them?'

'Yes, of course I can. Sasha Alexandrovich sent some purplish things with crimson spots, and there were yellow roses from Sergei Mikhailovich—or was it Tolya

Davidovich? Er—white scented things like little lilies from Kostya Fedorovich . . .' She tailed off, unable to recall which name matched which of the other bouquets.

'And does none of your other suitors impress you as a man who might think to enquire of your maid what colour to send?' Igor asked in a particularly ironic tone which caught Galina's attention, for she had a sensitive ear for the nuances of other peoples' voices.

'Was it you?' she asked bluntly.

'Ah, saved!' Igor replied with even more irony. 'I was about to cast myself into the Fontanka in despair, and you would have been haunted all your life by the tragic tones of my voice calling your name as the dark waters closed over me!'

'The river is frozen solid enough to bear a coach and four,' Galina pointed out unromantically. 'Besides, extravagantly foolish gestures don't accord with your nature!'

'You don't consider me romantic, then?' Igor sounded amused.

'Romantic?' Galina considered the word thoughtfully, and her mind obligingly produced the portrait of Gennadi Zhadnov. Certainly the Charioteer was romantic, but Igor . . .?'

'Not particularly,' she replied, 'but thank you for the flowers.'

Princess Dengovskaya's palace was quite extravagantly luxurious. The entrance hall and staircase were banked with masses of hothouse plants, and each of the footmen on the stairs held a tall flambeau with half-a-dozen candles, as if the two thousand burning in the chandeliers were insufficient. The gallery was lined with orange and lemon trees in flower, and the ballroom made Galina blink as she entered it, for its walls were panelled with lapis-lazuli and divided by malachite pilasters topped with heavily-gilded acanthus leaves, and the ceiling had also been gilded, giving a brilliant effect above the dozen chandeliers set two by two along the length of the room.

'What do you think of this year's scheme?' Andrei asked as he suddenly appeared beside Galina.

'Intolerably oppressive,' Igor replied unenthusiastically. 'It makes me long to go out and walk about the Summer Gardens for an hour or two.'

'It's snowing again,' Andrei pointed out gloomily, as if he thought Igor might actually go.

'What do you mean, "this year"?' asked Galina. 'Is it different every year?'

'Yes,' replied Andrei. 'And each year . . .' he looked around to make sure that their hostess was not within hearing, but she was still in the gallery receiving her guests. Nevertheless, he dropped his voice and went on sepulchrally, 'Each year is worse than the last!'

Galina looked about her, considering the size and proportions of the room, then said, 'I should have it white, with just a very small amount of gold on the capitals—enough to pick out the highlights on the leaves, no more. Then all the colourful gowns and uniforms would show to better advantage.'

Andrei and Igor looked at one another over her chignon, smiled and nodded.

'She hasn't seen it yet, has she?' Andrei asked.

'No, I'm sure not. She's right, of course.'

'Indubitably.'

'It is rude to discuss a third person as if she were not present,' Galina said severely. She was disconcerted when both men went down on one knee and ceremoniously begged her pardon more or less in chorus, but it dawned on her almost immediately that they were in confident expectation that she would be quite capable of carrying her part in the joke, so she graciously accepted their apologies in an extremely regal fashion, realising that this was one of the many signs that her status in this highly competitive and exclusive society had subtly changed from that of a mere protegée of Tatya Petrovna's to that of an individual to be considered in her own right.

She had been made gradually aware of the change since her return from Kiev, but it became very obvious at the Dengovskaya ball, for she found herself so much in demand as a dancing-partner that she was hard-put to save enough dances for her friends. Indeed, she resorted to putting three or four of them down on her card herself, for fear that there would be nothing left by the time they appeared. Not all the claimants were drawn from among Tatya's Beaux now, but included several very important men in the various gradations and elaborations of court dress and military uniform, which apparently conveyed to the initiated whereabouts the wearer ranked in the hierarchy of Palace circles.

Sasha Alexandrovich was particularly grateful to find that she had saved him two polonaises, but, as these were the only dances in which he joined all evening, she wondered if perhaps to encourage him was not really as kind as she intended. On the other hand, Kostya Durakov seemed to take it for granted that she should have saved him a waltz, and was even surprised that it was only one and not two or three, and Sergei Dmitriev attempted to cross out someone else's initials to give himself more than the one mazurka Galina offered. He made the mistake, however, of choosing the supperdance, which Igor had reserved, and that gentleman said something to him in Russian which sent him off looking red in the face and angry. 'What did you say?' Galina asked.

'Something very rude in Army argot,' Igor replied.

'He didn't like it,' Galina observed unconcernedly. 'And what haven't I seen?'

Igor's private smile appeared, and he said 'Wait until next week—you'll know then.'

CHAPTER
EIGHT

THE LOVERS

A time of choice/An inability to choose

As THE day of the long-awaited Court Ball approached,
Galina gave much thought to what she should wear, and,
one morning, sought out Igor in the library, where he sat
amid a considerable fortune in porcelain pots and
figurines, and said to him, 'May I ask your advice?'

'By all means,' he replied vaguely, looking round for
an empty chair, and finally clearing one by tipping a
number of particularly ugly pots off the seat of the one
nearest his desk. There was an expensive-sounding crash
as they arrived on the floor, but he reassured Galina with
a brief, 'Shoddy rubbish. He must have looted a fair-
ground to find that!'

'It appears that full fig is expected at a Court Ball,'
Galina said as she sat enthroned above the wreckage.
'Including a tiara. I haven't yet acquired one, so I think I
should buy a parure while I'm about it, but I wondered if
you would advise me where to go for it, and what to buy,
as I know very little about jewellery.'

Igor considered the matter in silence. He was sitting at
his desk, which was stacked with neat piles of papers,
mostly covered with his small, neat handwriting.

'I take it that you want something of the first quality,'
he said eventually. 'I'll ask Duval to bring a selection of

suitable pieces, and you can try them on in comfort. I'll advise you whether they're worth the asking-price, but you haven't much to fear in dealing with Duval—he's worked for the Empress-Dowager for years.' He hesitated, then said in an oddly taut voice, 'You must realise that he'll insist on paying me commission for introducing him to you, and be mortally offended if I refuse it.'

'Accept gracefully, then,' Galina advised him. 'You can always give the money to charity if it worries you.'

Igor gave her one of his searching looks and said nothing further on the matter, but a footman was despatched to Duval's with a note, and the next morning M. Duval himself, an elderly, affected Frenchman, dressed in the fashion of the years immediately before the Revolution in his homeland, arrived with four attendant myrmidons carrying velvet-lined leather boxes, and spread a quantity of flashing jewellery in gorgeous profusion all over the largest table in the Peacock Salon.

Galina looked at it all with interest, but rejected all the coloured stones at once, saying that diamonds were more useful, a phrase which caused M. Duval to shudder. After trying on several magnificent tiaras, she eventually selected one which was made up of two sprays of diamond-set roses and leaves, rising a little at the front. It felt comfortable and not too heavy on her head, and was ingeniously designed to come apart and reform as a necklace or two bodice ornaments. The rest of the parure consisted of a necklace of single roses which could be used also as a simple tiara, a brooch with flowers and leaves mounted *en tremblant*, and a pair of bracelets to match the necklace.

Igor made no comment on her choice, but inspected the stones through a glass lent to him by M. Duval, and pronounced gravely that the quality of the stones and the workmanship were excellent, and the price quite reasonable, so Galina purchased the parure, giving M. Duval a note to draw the money from her man-of-business. It was a larger amount of money than she had ever spent at one time in her life before, but she hoped that she managed to give the impression that it was not an unusual occurrence.

'A very good choice,' Igor observed after M. Duval had departed, with many flourishes and bows, shepherding his myrmidons before him.

'I'm glad you approve,' Galina said sincerely, thinking that the expression on his face looked a trifle sour. 'It seems a frightful extravagance,'

The sourness vanished, and he said lightly, 'You can well afford it, and a lady in your position is expected to look the part. You're extremely rich, you know.'

'I wish I were not,' Galina said reflectively. 'A little wealth would be comfortable, but a great deal is a burden.'

'And an insufficiency . . .' Igor began, not looking at her, but broke off and substituted, 'is a handicap,' for whatever he might have intended to say.

The great day arrived at last, but did not pass uneventfully. Dasha had toothache and was understandably irritable, which was probably the reason why she managed to scorch Galina's white crêpe presentation gown quite irretrievably, thereby negating some careful planning. Two new gowns had come home from the modiste only the day before, and these were hastily unpacked and considered, but the pomona green silk was too long, and Dasha pricked her finger while taking it up and dripped some blood on the skirt. She wept copiously over it, which did no good at all, and then, more practically, said that a lace flounce would cover the damage, but there was no time left to go out and buy suitable lace, so, by process of elimination, the other gown became the only choice, for Galina did not think it proper to wear something for an Imperial ball which had already been seen elsewhere, other than her presentation gown, of course.

What with one thing and another, she was a few minutes late going downstairs, and found Igor already waiting for her in the hall. She paused in surprise at the head of the grand staircase to stare at his appearance, for he was in full court dress, his coat heavily embroidered with gold thread, his cravat of finest lace, gold buckles at the knees of his breeches and on his shoes, and clocked silk stockings.

He made her an elegant bow and watched her descend the stairs with a marked lack of expression in his face, so that she thought there must be something amiss with her appearance, although her mirror had shown her looking her best in white satin embroidered with silver leaves, with a fall of crisp lace to frame the *décollétage*, her shining hair encircled by the tiara, and the bracelets flashing on her white-gloved arms. She had decided against the necklace or the brooch as well, and had instead pinned a simple spray of stephanotis on the shoulder of her gown, and carried a white lace fan with silver sticks, and a reticule of the same fabric as her gown.

'Is something wrong?' she asked nervously as she reached the bottom of the stairs without any changes appearing in Igor's face, except a possible tightening of the muscles about his mouth.

'I can find no fault whatever with your appearance,' he said. 'If I'm looking at you in an odd fashion, it's because I'm thinking of all the poor fellows who'll lose their hearts to you tonight, and you infatuated with a portrait!'

'I'm not!' Galina exclaimed indignantly, sweeping past him towards the door and the waiting carriage with heightened colour. Dasha emerged from the back regions and scurried after her with her hooded sable cloak, attempting simultaneously to fling her own heavy cloth one about her. Igor caught the maid by the arm as she passed him, took the sables from her, strode after Galina, and carefully draped the furs round her shoulders.

'I'm sorry,' he said quietly. 'I was teasing. You look very beautiful.'

His tone was so unlike his usual one that Galina gave him a questioning look, but he had already turned to see if Dasha had caught up, and by the time they were in the carriage his customary sardonic manner had returned, and Galina decided that she had probably been mistaken in thinking that he had sounded different.

The queue of carriages waiting to deposit guests at the Winter Palace stretched from the *porte-cochère* in the middle of the river front, round the side of the building and along the Palace Square front almost as far as the Winter Canal, but it moved quite quickly, and in little more than three quarters of an hour after leaving home, Galina entered the vast white marble gallery on the ground floor, where a great throng of servants was assembled, each clutching the precious furs of a master or mistress who had already gone up to the ballroom. Dasha had barely time to take Galina's sables and Igor's plain cloth cloak before she too was tidied away by a giant footman in a livery so gorgeous that it outshone the costumes of some of the guests.

'To the left,' Igor murmured, enabling Galina to turn in the correct direction without looking about her and betraying to the supercilious footman that she had not been here before, and in a few moments she came to the foot of the most magnificent staircase she had ever seen, rising in a single first flight, then branching to right and left for three more flights before reaching the *piano nobile*, where the Court Chamberlain was waiting to receive the Empress' guests. The height of the painted ceiling was remarkable, and the gilded statues against the walls and the pink marble columns at the head of the stairs so vast in scale that Galina could not help whispering to Igor how impressive she found it.

'The statues are mostly plaster, and the columns are artificial marble,' he whispered back. 'Galina, don't let the hollow shams of Petersburg mislead you. Much of what you see and hear in this city is corrupt and oppressive. A few hundreds come here to dance in splendid jewels and fine clothes, while millions are outside in the cold, hungry and ill-clad. Don't forget them!'

'I don't forget,' Galina replied. 'I suppose you think me an ignorant, empty-headed fool, but I'm not.'

'I'm well aware that you're not. I shouldn't like to think that what you find here might change you,' he replied. He was speaking very quietly, but not whispering, yet every word reached Galina's ears quite clearly. She realised that he was using a method of conversing which allowed one to talk privately in a public place without much danger of being overheard.

'I shall pray that it may not,' she replied, smiling and bowing to an acquaintance.

'Are you thinking of marrying Sasha Alexandrovich?' Igor asked with an abrupt change of subject. 'If not, don't be too kind to him—it would be an unkindness in the long run.'

Galina had already suspected as much, and gave the matter some thought while she was making her curtsey to Count Koshelev, but when she passed on into the ballroom, the sight before her drove it out of her mind.

The room was extraordinarily large, far larger than any she had ever seen, immensely long, with a colonnade at either end, and a gallery set on columns along the wall to her left where spectators might watch the dancers below. On her right, long windows looked out on the winter night, but within, all was light. Hundreds of candles circled the tops of the columns and filled the vast chandeliers, producing so much light that each individual flame looked dim. The walls and columns were white of a purity that seemed to deny that any speck of dirt could endure in the Palace, and there was not the slightest touch of gold or colour anywhere.

To Galina, this confirmed the feeling that she had expressed at Princess Dengovskaya's ball, for the room in all its magnificence was simply a setting for the display of the people it contained, and, at all the grand balls and dinners she had attended, Galina had nowhere seen gowns so colourful or jewels so magnificent. She might have been content to stand and gaze all evening, but within minutes, the orchestra played a flourish, the doors at the far end were flung open, and the slender white-clad figure of the Empress Elizaveta Alexeyevna entered, followed by a phalanx of *dames d'honneur* and Court officials in a dazzle of diamonds, blue and red ribbons, pale blue silks, and gold-embroidered black velvet, against which the Empress seemed to stand out like a single white pillar before a border of summer flowers. She walked quickly and lightly down the length of the floor, nodding and smiling to right and left in response to the bows and curtseys of her guests, with no sound in all the great room but the susurration of silks and the murmur of blessings and whispered comments. The Court Chamberlain met her a little distance from where Galina had sunk down in her own curtsey, and led her to the throne which had been placed to one side. As soon as she was seated, the orchestra struck up the first polonaise, and the ball began.

Galina was immediately besieged by gentlemen seeking to initial her programme, and she seemed thereafter hardly to have time to draw breath as mazurka followed polonaise, and waltz followed mazurka, with the occasional variation of a contredanse or a cotillion, and she had frequently to change partners two or three times in the course of one dance in order to fit in all who wished to partner her.

'You don't seem to spend much time by the wall!' Lev commented as he whisked her round the floor in a very expert waltz, surprising Galina, who had not expected him to be such a good dancer.

'I think my fortune is the attraction,' she replied. 'In some cases, at least. I'm not grown so cynical that I can't recognise that a few friends would still ask me to dance if I hadn't above three kopeks in the world.'

'You take it all very calmly,' he commented, giving her a kindly smile. 'Tatya was afraid all this might go to your head a little.' He made a sweeping gesture to indicate what he meant by 'all this' and narrowly missed dislodging the toupé of a very important minister.

'I don't quite believe it's all real,' Galina replied. 'There's a dream-like quality about everything in Petersburg. One day I shall wake up and find myself back home in Tver, so I must be sure to retain my ability to lead a humdrum existence.'

'Is there no Society in Tver, then?'

'Yes, but my father can't afford to entertain much, so we go about very little.'

Lev looked as if he was about to say something important, for his black brows drew together in a severe frown, but he was interrupted by Kostya, come to claim his half of the waltz.

He was looking extremely smart in the dress version of his white Chevalier Garde uniform, the high red collar making him hold his head very erect, and Galina was amused to see that Lev, who had been a Major in the same regiment, looked him over critically, as if seeking something to find fault with in his turn-out. He missed the opportunity, however, for Kostya's uniform was perfectly correct. It was his dancing which lacked perfection, and he trod on Galina's toes several times without appearing to notice.

'I was just thinking,' he said, 'that I shall call to see your mother one day before Christmas, if you've no objection.'

Galina was surprised, for Kostya appeared to be an egocentric young man, not at all likely to spend his precious time in visiting elderly ladies, but she replied non-commitally, 'I expect she would be pleased to see you.'

'You mean, you don't mind?' Kostya leaned back a little and gazed soulfully down into Galina's face, and she thought, not for the first time, that it must be difficult for so large a man to carry on a conversation while dancing, as few of his partners would ever come above his shoulder.

'Why should I mind? It's a very kind thought, for she seldom sees anyone but other older ladies.' The hem of Galina's skirt became entangled momentarily with the heel of someone's shoe as she spoke, and in disentangling it and making sure that no spur was involved, she missed the puzzled look in Kostya's sentimental blue eyes, and, as his normal expression was slightly smug, it also escaped her notice that he regarded her with fatuous self-satisfaction all the rest of the evening.

By some unfortunate chance, Sergei Dmitriev had managed to put his name down for the supper-dance, so when the time came for it, Galina made sure to be standing with Tatya, coolly elegant in oyster satin embroidered with roses and leaves in soft pinks and greens, with scattered crystal dewdrops. Irina in gold silk and Nadya in sky-blue taffeta also joined them, with Lev, Andrei, Igor, Sasha, Kostya, and a stout, be-spectacled gentleman called Pyotr Kyrillovich, whose surname Galina failed to catch.

By the time Sergei found her in the middle of this

small crowd, Galina was deep in conversation with Pyotr, who came from Moscow, and had actually been in the city during the French occupation, and had been taken with them on their retreat, until a group of partisans rescued him. She told Sergei this, and, despite his obvious lack of interest, continued to ply Pyotr Kyrillovich with questions as they all strolled through the galleries of the palace together on their way to the supper-room, Sergei looking sulky, and the other men finding some amusement in thwarting him every time he tried to approach more closely to Galina, until she felt quite sorry for him and offered him her one unclaimed dance.

For a moment, he frowned petulantly and looked as if he might decline on some pretext, then, to Galina's surprise, he accepted with good grace and quite a pleasant smile, so, to show some interest and soften her earlier attempt to avoid him, she asked if there was any fresh news of his sister.

'Oh, I don't go near her,' he answered. 'She's always either in a foul temper or crying, so what's the use? She don't like me, in any case. She's no better, I collect.'

'Can the doctors do nothing for her?'

'Apparently not. Nikolai Ilyich talks of calling in somebody from Vienna, but I don't know why he bothers. He'll get no thanks for it.'

The rest of the party were involved in a lively discussion of the activities planned for later in the week, and were not listening to Galina's conversation with Sergei, so she ventured on a slight reproof, 'I don't suppose he does it in expectation of thanks. He seems to me a very kind, good man who would wish to help if he can.'

'Oh, you've met him, have you? Yes, perfectly saintly, ain't he?' Sergei sounded half-jeering, half-bitter. 'Of course, Tatya Petrovna and all her friends blame Anna for the marriage failing—they never stop to wonder how she felt, married without option to an iceberg!'

Galina's large and very fine eyes rested on the sulkily handsome face with an expression of troubled interest, for it had, indeed, never occurred to her to think of Anna's side of the story, and, for that matter, she had adopted the attitude of her friends towards Sergei himself without question. The resulting attack of conscience made her behave more kindly towards Sergei for the rest of the evening than she might otherwise have done.

The table at which they were all sitting had been intended for eight, and it was decidedly crowded with eleven people sitting round it, but this did not deter two young ladies, so much alike that they must be twins, from coming over to speak to Tatya and Nadya, with whom, it emerged, they had attended the Smolny Institute. In the resulting commotion of summoning footmen to draw over another table and more chairs, and to bring more food and wine, several people changed places, and Galina found herself wedged firmly between the white serge bulk of Kostya, and Igor, who asked if she admired the supper-hall.

As she had not really had a chance to look about her, Galina did so now, and found it a very elegant apartment of enormous size, made to appear even larger by an abundance of mirrors giving endless vistas of beautifully-dressed bejewelled guests, banked flowers, blue-lustred chandeliers, and round tables, each with an orange tree growing through its centre, filling the air with the perfume of the blossom.

'It's like a scene from a fairy-tale!' she said.

'And has about as much substance,' Igor replied.

'That's an odd thing to say,' Kostya interjected. 'What on earth do you mean? Of course it has substance.'

'I'm not about to enter into a philosophical discussion with you,' Igor replied with his odd little smile. 'I've something better to do at the moment.'

'Such as?' Kostya stiffened and seemed likely to take offence, but subsided when Igor replied lightly, 'I'm engaged to Galina Stepanovna for the next dance, and I don't intend to miss it.' He stood up and made a slight bow to Galina, who was quite content to return to the ballroom with him, although most of the other guests were still at supper, and there seemed to be no one about in the great galleries of the palace but the sentries and the Emperor's giant Mameluke footmen standing by each door.

'Are you sure it's time for the next dance?' Galina enquired, hearing no sound of music from the ballroom.

'Why is Kostya Fedorovich adopting such a proprietorial attitude towards you?' Igor asked without answering her question. 'I trust you haven't encouraged him to think that you favour him particularly?'

Galina looked at him with some surprise, and without saying anything.

'I apologise,' he said after a few moments. 'Not my business. I'm employed to look after your art treasures, not your marriage prospects.'

'Quite,' Galina said. 'But it's kind of you to concern yourself about me. I think I hear some music now.' She was considerably startled that Igor should think Kostya's attitude proprietorial, but his question put an unpleasant little doubt into her mind, which she hastily dismissed, deciding that Kostya's attitude was always that of a man who is confident that all females must admire him as soon as he condescended to smile upon them. It was simply something he could not help.

The sound of music proved to be the orchestra tuning itself, but, by the time they entered the ballroom, it was about to plunge into a waltz, and Galina found it very pleasant to swoop and spin about such an expanse of perfect floor with only a bare half-dozen other couples to share it. She thoroughly enjoyed performing all the more complicated and space-consuming figures for which there was normally insufficient room, only gradually having to restrain herself as the other guests began to trickle back from supper.

'Um,' said Sasha, attracting her attention to himself as she seemed inclined to stand there smiling after Igor's retreating figure. 'I—er—I wondered if you'd care to take a turn in the gallery instead of dancing, as it's so hot in here.'

'Is your leg troubling you?' Galina asked sympathetically, taking his arm and allowing him to lead her out into the comparative peace of the picture-hung gallery which ran alongside the ballroom. .

'Not particularly, but the floor's rather slippery where the candles have dripped on it, and I'm enough of a fool already, without falling over in the midst of a polonaise. Actually, I wanted to talk to you, and it's very difficult to get a quiet moment now you've taken on so.'

They strolled in silence for a few seconds, then Sasha came to a halt below a large painting of scantily-clad nymphs frolicking in a sylvan glade, turned to face her, and said abruptly, 'You see, I've decided not to ask you to marry me, and I thought I should explain, as you must have noticed how besotted I've been ever since I met you.'

Galina was so startled that she could only look up at his pudgy, good-humoured face and wonder what was coming next.

'My trouble is that I'm always falling in love,' he went on in a matter-of-fact manner. 'And out again. Also, I'm not a suitable husband for you, because you're clever, and you need someone at least as intelligent as yourself, which I'm not. And, supposing by some unlikely chance you accepted me, I'd always feel unequal to you, and you'd eventually grow impatient with me, however hard you tried not to. Mind you, I'm not nearly as stupid as some people think. For example, I've enough sense to realise that my leg wouldn't make the slightest difference to you, one way or the other. What I need is a sensible, kind sort of girl who likes horses, because I intend to settle in the country and breed mounts for the Army when I'm married. I expect I shall marry Andrei Ivanovich's sister, actually.'

'I-I didn't know he had one,' Galina croaked.

'Yes. She's still at school but she'll be Out next Season. She's a bit plump and spotty at present, but she'll improve vastly in the next year so so, and I'm sure we'll suit one another very well. I shall always be fond of you, of course, as I shall be of Tatya—I've been in love with her on and off for years—and if either of you ever needed my help in any way, I'll be happy to be at your service. Being in love don't last, you see. It's a friendship that lasts, and being interested in the same things, and, if you're lucky, a deeper sort of love that's got nothing to do with beauty or attraction. It's more being in harmony about everything, even if you don't always agree.'

'How can people be in harmony if they don't agree?' Galina asked, saying the first thing that came into her head.

'That shows you don't know much about music,' Sasha observed kindly. 'Harmony's made by two or more *different* notes, not all the same one! Of course, there's no need for me to tell you all this, because I know you don't love me at all, and you wouldn't have accepted me if I had asked, but I wouldn't wish you to think you might have hurt my feelings. You're a very kind person, and I expect things like that worry you. Anyway, you haven't. Hurt me, I mean.'

'How do you know I don't love you?' Galina asked, hoping she had not unintentionally snubbed him at some time.

'Because I can see your heart's set on someone else,' he replied simply.

'But . . .' Galina began, wondering what in her behaviour could possibly have betrayed how uninspiring she found most men compared with what she knew of the character of the Charioteer. However, she was unable to finish the sentence, for two men entered the gallery, both dressed like Sasha in the dark blue dolman, scarlet pelisse and white trousers of the Life Guard Hussars, and hailed him with delight. They bowed and murmured polite responses when Sasha presented them to her, and then plunged happily into professional conversation with Sasha.

'Any news of the war?' one of them asked.

'Yes,' Sasha replied. 'Perhaps you know already, though. The peace negotiations at Frankfürt broke down, and we'll have invaded France by now, I should think.'

'Invaded!' the taller of the two men exclaimed. 'What a hope! Does Alexander Pavlovich really think we can beat Bonaparte when he's fighting on his own territory, and capture Paris?'

'We may not have to,' Sasha replied. 'Remember what Marshal Rumantsiev said back in Ekaterina Alexeyevna's time? "What matters isn't the capture of a geographical position, but the destruction of the enemy's forces." We can manage that all right—we've already proved it!'

Galina, both listening and contemplating the cavorting nymphs, marvelled at the strange nature of men until Sasha recollected his responsibilities and took her back to the ballroom, where her next partner was looking for her.

On the way home in the carriage, she recalled Sasha's words, and thought, 'Surely he can't be right? I'm not in love with Gennadi Yakovick, am I? He's just an ideal, that's all, and every female has some picture in her mind of the sort of man she'd like to marry. That doesn't mean that she's in love with an imaginary person. I'd like to meet someone as handsome and brave and clever as Gennadi, and perhaps I will some day, or perhaps I'll meet someone quite different, and my ideal will change to fit him. Oh, I don't know!'

She unconsciously said the last four words in a half-whisper, and was surprised when Igor asked, 'What don't you know?' for she had thought that he, like Dasha, was dozing.

'How one knows if one loves someone.'

'If you don't know, then you don't love him,' Igor replied gravely.

Galina considered this statement and its implications, and said, 'Do you know? That you do, I mean?'

'Yes.'

'You don't sound very happy about it.'

'I'm not.'

'But I thought being in love was supposed to be a happy state?'

'It depends. It's not a subject to which I feel I could do justice at four o'clock of a winter's morning. The cold congeals my brains.'

'I'm sorry,' Galina said. She meant she was sorry that he was not happy, and wondered if he were in love with Tatya, but he chose to take it as a conventional apology and replied, 'Not at all. I'd be delighted to discuss the subject with you on a warm summer's day, preferably in a woodland glade full of wild flowers and butterflies. Did you enjoy the ball?'

'Very much, but I feel quite exhausted. There were so many people, and it was so hot!'

'And you danced every dance.'

'Yes, I suppose I did, or almost every one. Sasha said I'd "taken on"—does that mean it's the fashion to profess to admire me?'

Igor noted the 'profess', and that there was no trace of vanity in the question, and smiled in the darkness. 'Indeed, but that doesn't mean that all the admiration is insincere. Your problem will be to distinguish the real from the counterfeit.'

Galina thought about that remark when she was in bed, and worried a little over Igor's earlier query about whether she had encouraged Kostya's expectations, trying to examine her feelings about Kostya. He was certainly pleasant company, and handsome enough, but obviously had a very good opinion of himself, and, apart from his suggestion that he might call on her mother, never showed the slightest interest or concern for others less fortunate than himself. He would probably be an undemanding and comfortable sort of husband, but . . .

Not surprisingly, Galina slept late in the morning, and did not go downstairs until after she had taken a light luncheon in bed. She had only been in the Peacock Salon a few minutes when a footman announced Lieutenant Count Konstantin Fedorovich Durakov, and Kostya walked in on the heels of the announcement, before she could say whether or not she would receive him.

'I came as soon as possible,' he announced, thrusting a large bouquet of red roses into her hands. She looked at them in a bemused fashion, some part of her mind noticing that the hothouse blooms were spangled with snowflakes.

'I—I beg your pardon?'

'When you said I might call on your mother, I wasted no time! I saw her this morning, and now I come to lay my heart at your feet!'

Galina took an involuntary step backwards and exclaimed 'Oh! I didn't realise that you meant . . . Oh, dear!'

It is doubtful whether Kostya heard what she said, for

he had looked a trifle dubiously at the carpet, then lowered himself on to one immaculate white-trousered knee, clasped his hands over his heart, and made an impassioned speech of which Galina scarcely took in a single word, for she had seen the handle of one leaf of the door to the library turn, and the leaf silently open a few inches.

'What do you say?' Kostya's confident tones suddenly impinged on her consciousness, and she realised that she had actually missed hearing her first proposal of marriage.

'I'm very sorry,' she said firmly, the knowledge that Igor was undoubtedly listening at the door giving her the necessary determination to carry off this awkward situation without making a fool of herself. 'But I'm afraid I misunderstood you. I thought you meant to call on my mother as a kindness to an older and possibly lonely person. I'd no idea you meant . . . anything more personal to me.'

'You mean you don't wish to marry me?' Kostya sounded mildly puzzled. 'Oh. Well, that's a pity.' He stood up and dusted any possible specks of dust off his trousers with a very large clean handkerchief. 'Don't wish to imply that your carpet ain't clean,' he said in parenthetical apology, 'but this stupid uniform shows every mark. Actually, I thought we'd suit one another quite well, but if you don't agree, there's an end of it. No offence taken, or given, I trust?'

'Indeed no! I'm very honoured,' Galina replied in a bemused tone. 'I'm sorry I can't accept your—your most flattering offer, but, you see, I-I don't love you, and . . . I like you very much,' she added hastily, 'but as a friend . . . I hope we may continue to be friends?'

'Oh, by all means! Of course, if it's love you want, I can see it won't do. I must admit I've no patience with all that romantic stuff myself, 'though, of course, one says all that on proposing—it's the custom, I suppose, and people expect it—so I'm told, that is—don't make a habit of proposing! I find you easy to get along with, and beautiful, of course. Also, you've considerable property—not that I need it as I'm pretty well-breeched myself, but it makes the idea all the more attractive. Well, I'll wish you good fortune in finding what you want, and look forward to seeing you at the theatre tomorrow. Er—good afternoon,' and he kissed hands and bowed himself out with good grace and unshaken aplomb before Galina could collect her wits sufficiently to ring for a footman.

She recovered in a second or two, and then, recollecting the open door, marched angrily into the library to confront Igor.

He was sitting at his desk, a large and very ugly teapot in his hands, and he looked up with a slightly quizzical expression as Galina sailed in, put the teapot down very carefully, and stood up, watching her face warily, with just a glint of amusement in his eyes.

'You were eavesdropping!' she accused indignantly.

'I had a good reason,' he replied equably. 'And when I found it was only Kostya Fedorovich, I stopped listening.'

'There is no excuse for spying on people! How dare you!' Galina went on, then, realising what he had said, broke off and asked curiously, 'What reason?'

'I was expecting it to be someone else, and thought you might need a knight-errant if things went badly. I didn't quite hear what the footman said when he announced your visitor—you should tell him to speak up and not mumble! Truly, I didn't listen any more after I realised it was Kostya. Er—did you accept him?'

'You know very well I did not!'

There was a sudden little silence, and Galina wondered why she was so certain that Igor would know she could not marry Kostya, for she accepted his assurance that he had not been listening.

'Well, it wouldn't do,' he said mildly, shuffling his papers and not looking at her. She had a sudden sense of uncertainty, as if she had unexpectedly stepped into a quicksand.

'Whom did you think it might be?' she asked, trying for safer ground.

There was a tap at the door from the Peacock Salon, and the footman appeared again, saying in tones of ill-concealed interest 'Excuse me, Galina Stepanovna. Lieutenant Count Sergei Mikhailovich Dmitriev is here. Will you see him here, or in the salon?'

'The salon, please,' Galina replied, looking at Igor.

'That's whom I was expecting,' he said with a deceptively innocent smile.

CHAPTER
NINE

THE CHARIOT

The successful, triumphant hero/An arrogant bully

GALINA went back into the Peacock Salon, and without thinking what she was doing, left the door ajar as she had found it. She walked sedately across to the window, and turned to face the door as Sergei entered in a hurried, jerky fashion.

'Good afternoon,' he said abruptly, kissing her hand Prussian style, with a stiff bow and a heel-click. 'I waited on your mother this morning, and she gave me permission to speak to you. I should be most honoured if you would accept my hand in marriage.'

'This—this is very sudden,' Galina said, wishing she might disappear into the peacock-strewn carpet.

'Oh, come! It must have been very obvious that things were tending that way!' Sergei sounded downright smug. 'And you've certainly not discouraged me. In fact, last night you were so encouraging that you decided me to offer today instead of waiting a few more weeks! I thought we might announce our betrothal before Christmas and marry towards the end of January. What do you say?'

'I'm afraid I must say no,' Galina was a trifle piqued by his obvious assumption of her acceptance.

'No? You mean, you'd prefer longer to prepare your

trousseau and so on? Well, I suppose I might try to get my tour of duty in Petersburg extended by a few weeks, but it'll be difficult.'

'I meant no, I can't marry you,' Galina said firmly. 'I'm sorry, but I don't love you.'

'Love? What the devil has that to say to the matter? People don't marry for love! As far as I'm concerned, once we're married we'll both do as we please. I shan't trouble you above once a month, and then only for getting an heir.'

'No. I'm sorry, but no!' Galina repeated, shocked by his cold-blooded attitude.

'Well, then—if you must have it the hard way—it wouldn't be difficult to make you only too glad to marry me!'

'What do you mean?' Galina was alarmed by the confidence with which he made the threat.

'A few choice little rumours dropped in the right places—if it's spread around that you're my mistress, for example, you'd have to take me, for no one wants another man's cast-off!'

'Why, you miserable little worm!' Galina exclaimed indignantly, but Sergei laughed—an ugly sound.

'Try to prove it isn't true,' he said mockingly. 'Mud sticks! Be thankful that I'm willing to overlook the fact that you've already taken one lover into your household! Cataloguing your art collection, indeed!' He laughed openly at the mingled shock and fury in Galina's face, and jeered, 'Yes, I know it's not true, but once people start to think it might be, you're finished! If you send him away, they'll assume you've quarrelled. If you deny it, you confirm it in most peoples' minds. Oh, I can wreck your chances in the marriage market in a week, and you'll thank me on your knees for taking you after that.'

Galina cast an appealing look towards the library door, regretting that she had been so sharp to Igor about opening it. As if in reply, Igor appeared and leaned against the door-frame, his thumbs hooked into his waistcoat pockets, looking completely at ease.

'Ah, Sergei Mikhailovich,' he said calmly, sounding a little amused. 'I thought I heard your snivelling little whine. What are you up to this time?'

'Nothing to do with you. Who asked you to interfere?' Sergei asked irritably.

'You did,' Igor's amusement surfaced in a lazy smile. 'When will you learn? If you're threatening a helpless female with something unpleasant, have the sense to lower your voice, and don't address the poor girl as if she's a company on the parade ground! That's the trouble with you rough soldiery—no finesse! So you're thinking of spreading a tale that Galina's your mistress, are you? Or is she to be mine?—it wasn't altogether clear.'

'Don't be ridiculous. Just a joke,' Sergei protested uneasily.

'A joke? I can think of a better. How if I summon the police and say I caught you trying to rape Galina Stepanovna? Let me see—I was working in the library, and heard her scream for help, so I rushed in and found . . . Galina, would it trouble you overmuch to sacrifice that frock by tearing the bodice a little—or perhaps you'd prefer to go and change into another? I'm sure Sergei won't mind waiting if I sit on his head until you return. I can't recall what the punishment is for attempted rape. Imprisonment, is it? Or exile to Siberia? Maybe it's flogging—there are a few exceptions to the Nobility's exemption from corporal punishment, surely? Perhaps you wouldn't care for any of those . . . How about if I smashed your nose flat with my fist? I expect some of the servants would be happy to assist you to stand still. You'd be able to transfer to the Pavlovskys.' In an aside to Galina, he added, 'That's the regiment the Emperor

Pavel founded for flat-nosed fellows like himself. Alternatively,' turning back to Sergei, 'I could have a word with some friends at the War Ministry and arrange for you to be transferred to garrison duty at Archangelsk, or in the Caucasus, or somewhere even more unpleasant, for twenty years or so . . .'

Sergei opened his mouth during this speech, turned pale, and shut it again.

'Yes,' said Igor gravely. 'You know I would. Unlike you, I keep my word. It's that Cossack blood you find so deplorable, you see—it makes me ruthless! May we assume you won't be spreading any nasty little tales about Galina Stepanovna, then, and you've decided that you don't wish to marry her after all?'

'It was only a joke,' Sergei mumbled, scowling. 'No need to get in a wax about it! Didn't really want to marry her anyway.'

'No, just her money,' Igor said understandingly. 'What shall we do with him, Galina?'

'I think,' said Galina thoughtfully, making a determined effort to be very cool and calm, for she was mortified to think how amusing Igor must be finding her predicament, and resolved not to give him any further grounds for laughing at her by showing confusion or distress. 'He can't have a very good opinion of himself if he thinks he has to use threats to persuade a female to marry him! He's quite handsome when he isn't sneering or sulking, and he can be a pleasant enough companion when he tries. I suppose he drinks and gambles and—er—so forth? If he pulled himself together and made more of an effort to be pleasant and good-natured, he'd probably find a pretty girl with a reasonable fortune fairly easily. I suggest we forget about this afternoon, as long as he behaves himself. Of course, if he does anything silly, we can always try one of your suggestions. Good afternoon, Sergei Mikhailovich,' and she held out her hand with the bland smile of the perfect hostess, so that Sergei could only bow over it and take his leave. Meanwhile, Igor rang the bell for the footman to show him out, and made him a mocking little bow as he passed.

'Well, now!' Galina said when he had gone. 'Quite an eventful afternoon! I apologise for being so angry with you earlier. How did you know he was coming?' She waited for some sardonic remark about her foolishness in being too encouraging to Sergei, but his reply was factual, and the mockery in it was not directed at her.

'Yevgeny informed me that he'd called on your mama this morning, and I didn't imagine it was to have his fortune told—not with the cards, at least!'

'Thank you for rescuing me,' again with the expectation of a jibing reply.

'Not at all,' Igor shrugged her thanks aside. 'Porcelain valuations, snuff-box cataloguing, knight-errantry—all part of the service. Do you think some tea might be a good idea?'

Galina shakily agreed that it would, so he rang the bell again, and sent the footman for the tea equipage. It arrived with Countess Razumova in the van, to Galina's surprise, for her mother had lately entertained her own friends in the afternoon, but her arrival was presumably explained when she looked about the room and said, 'Oh. Are your young gentlemen gone already?'

The presence of the footmen and the need to prepare and serve tea kept Galina silent for a few minutes, which was as well, for the shock, and the expectation of mockery from Igor had passed, and she was now more annoyed than upset. As soon as the servants had withdrawn, she said with careful restraint, 'Mama, was it really necessary to give permission for two gentlemen to speak to me, both on the same day, and without a word to me about it beforehand?'

'Well, my dear, you weren't up when they came, and, having given one of them permission, I couldn't very well refuse the other! Besides, you're of age, and must make your own decision! Asking my permission is no more than a courtesy. They seemed quite pleasant young lads—did you not care for either of them, then? The fair one put me in mind of the Knight of Coins—honourable and a lover of virtue, you know.'

'Ah, but in reverse, he's smug and dull-witted,' Igor observed. He exchanged a friendly smile with the Countess, who replied, 'Yes, I see! And the other—the Knight of Cups, perhaps? Bringing offers and opportunities?'

'Cups, certainly, for he drinks too much, and the reverse suits him—full of false promises and lies!'

'Dear me!' commented the Countess. 'I'm glad you didn't accept him, dear!'

'Mama,' Galina said, her determined little chin tilted aggressively. 'I am not planning to marry a Tarot card! When—and if—I meet a man I should like to marry, it will be for what he actually is, not for what your cards say he might be!'

'As you please my dear.' Her mother sounded the merest trifle miffed. 'I wash my hands of the matter as you're so particular! If any other hopeful suitor approaches me, I shall refer him to your father, and let him deal with the matter!'

'Thank goodness!' thought Galina, but aloud she merely changed the subject by making a conciliatory enquiry whether her mother was expecting any guests that evening, and was surprised to hear that she not only expected fifty guests, but had arranged for a string quartet to come and give a concert!

'I think I may have forgotten to mention it,' the Countess added vaguely. 'But I'm sure you don't mind.'

'Not in the least,' Galina replied sincerely, for she was

glad to find her mother coming out of her shell at last and taking some pleasure in social activities.

She was herself going to dine with Nadya and Andrei, and then on to the opera at the Great Stone Theatre. On her way upstairs to change, she was amused to see that the knight on the Wheel of Fortune was lying in a state of abandoned despair at the nadir of his destiny, which seemed a suitable comment on Sergei Dmitriev's discomfiture, although it gave her a twinge of conscience about Kostya Durakov. She was distracted from those thoughts by an encounter with Osya Ivanich, who informed her confidentially that the house-serfs, to whom she had given permission were now safely married, and very grateful to her for her kindness, which gave her a curiously-mingled feeling of pleasure and embarrassment.

Igor squired her to the Valyevs' and the theatre, and on the way home, Dasha having, as usual, dozed off, he said quietly, 'I thought you were splendid this afternoon over Sergei Mikhailovich's little exhibition of spite.'

'Well, I didn't intend him to see that he'd frightened me, but I felt very shaky inside,' Galina admitted. 'He was quite right, of course—if he did spread those rumours, I'd be ruined!'

'I doubt it,' Igor sounded cynical again. 'You're so appallingly wealthy that I doubt if anything in that line would ruin you socially! He won't spread any tales, though—he knows I'm a man of my word.'

'Thank goodness you were there!' Galina replied, and then, to her surprise, gave a distinct sob.

'Steady on, you're not going to throw a fit of hysterics, are you?' Igor said, sounding alarmed.

'Certainly not!' Galina answered with dignity, taking a few deep breaths. 'A person is entitled to cry a little after receiving two unwanted proposals in one afternoon!'

'Oh, by all means,' Igor agreed. 'Galina, you're not falling into the trap of measuring all the men you meet against some impossible ideal, are you?'

'I don't think so,' Galina replied soberly. 'I suppose I have an ideal picture in my mind, but I don't think I'd let it influence my judgment too much.'

'Gennadi Yakovich was a well-built, handsome fellow, with more than average courage and intelligence, and a great many people admired him, but he wasn't perfect,' Igor said bluntly. 'By all means regard him as a hero and regret his untimely death, but don't waste your life by treasuring an idealised picture of someone you never knew, and judging every living man against the standard of an impossibly perfect dead one.'

'I don't!' Galina protested, wondering if she did. 'Do you think I should have accepted Kostya Fedorovich, then?'

'Not if you don't love him. He's a pleasant enough fellow, but not over-gifted with brains or ambition. Sasha Alexandrovich is even more pleasant, but you'd make him unhappy, because his intelligence is inferior to yours.'

'He's already told me as much. He's planning to marry Andrei's sister.'

'Gavrila? He has more foresight than I suspected. She'll suit him very well. So that's one proposal you won't have the trouble of refusing. At least you'll have a little warning in future! If one of your admirers suddenly rushes off to Tver, you can guess what he's going to ask you when he returns, always provided that your father consents!'

The few days left before Christmas passed very quickly, especially for Galina. She went to the Gostinny Dvor with Tatya and bought gifts for all her friends, and relented towards her mother's hobby sufficiently to buy her a silver case for her cards, embossed with the symbols of the four suits of the Minor Arcana—coins, cups, batons and swords—cunningly lodged amid a profusion of flowers and leaves. For Tatya, Irina and Nadya, she bought a pretty fan, a silver-mounted enamelled *necessaire*, and an embroidered silk shawl respectively, and sets of silver waistcoat buttons in three different designs for Lev, Andrei and Sasha. For Igor, she decided on an inkpot, and, after looking at some four or five dozen, found one with an enamelled view of St Sophia's in Kiev on the lid. The owner of the shop also produced a matching box for pens with a panorama of Kiev round the sides and the arms of the Ukraine on the top, so she took that as well.

By the morning of Christmas Eve, the gifts for the house-serfs had all been delivered and checked against Osya's list, and set out on a long table in the Chinese Salon, and four waggon-loads of meat and six of sacks of flour had been delivered and divided into parcels for distribution to the poor—a task which taxed Osya's powers of organisation, for this was another custom to which the General had never subscribed.

During the afternoon, a group of priests from one of the many monasteries in the area came to hear the confessions of all who wished to take the Eucharist during the all-night service, starting with Galina and working their way down to the humblest sweeper in the courtyards.

After making her confession, Galina found time to go on a little tour of inspection by herself through the domestic quarters, and came upon a lively scene in the second courtyard, beyond the stables. Some enterprising person had made an ice-mountain with old floorboards, supported on a ricketty scaffold, from one of the first-floor windows, stretching quite three-quarters of the way across the yard, and covered with packed snow, iced by pouring water over it. Some of the off-duty servants and children were sliding down it on wooden trays, attaining quite an alarming speed, and plunging into a stack of straw at the bottom to brake them and prevent injury.

Galina stood in the archway watching for a few minutes, noticing how quiet they were, even the children not squealing with excitement as one would have expected, and she realised how difficult it must have been for their parents in the past, when they had to keep the very existence of children in the house a secret.

Suddenly, one of the men caught sight of her and called a warning to the others. They all froze and turned horror-stricken faces towards her, the child who happened to be on the slide at that moment hurtling on into the straw, then sitting still, hunched and waiting as if for a blow. Galina walked out into the yard, and then the man who had called out came hesitantly forward and dropped to his knees before her.

'Please, Galina Stepanovna!' he begged, raising his clasped hands beseechingly. 'Please don't punish the others! It was my idea, and I persuaded them! Please don't blame them!'

Looking down at him, Galina recognised him as Mischa, one of the footmen, looking very different out of his livery, for he was dressed in a very old and much-darned kaftan and wide-legged trousers. She was upset to see that he looked really afraid, and she wondered what he expected her to do.

'Please stand up,' she said. 'You say you thought of this? It's very ingenious,' and, with that, she nodded and smiled at the watching group and went back the way she had come.

A little while later, Osya Ivanich came to her and asked anxiously, 'Is young Mischa to be punished, Galina Stepanovna?'

'For devising an amusement for his fellow-servants?

Of course not!' Galina replied. 'As long as they don't
waste time on it when they should be working. I think,
though, that the scaffold needs strengthening, and they
should use proper sledges—those trays aren't safe. Will
you send someone to fetch half a dozen of the little
sledges from the shop near the Kazan Cathedral—at my
expense, of course—and ask the carpenter to see to the
scaffold. He may have the money to buy what wood he
needs if we've none suitable in store.'

Osya stared at her with his mouth open, then said
abruptly, 'If the General saw any of the servants enjoying anything, he had them flogged! He said they
weren't put into the world to enjoy things! Thank you,
Galina Stepanovna. I'll send for the sledges. You're
most generous, and your souls appreciate your kindness
very deeply.'

Galina had arranged to meet her friends at the Kazan
Cathedral for the midnight service, which she found
deeply moving. The dimly-lit interior of the church had
an air of mystery, its pink granite columns shining in the
candle-light and disappearing up into the darkness
above, where the bronze capitals gleamed fitfully as the
candle-flames flickered. In the deep shadows against the
walls, she thought that other things stirred gently in the
draught from the great bronze doors, and eventually she
realised that they were flags—the standards captured
from the French in the previous year, grouped around
the tomb of Marshal Kutuzov.

The service ended well after midnight, and Galina was
thankful to tumble into bed when she reached home,
despite the feeling of reverence and excitement which
the great festival service had aroused in her. She slept for
a few hours, dressed in new clothes, breakfasted, then
went to the Chinese Salon and spent more than two
hours handing out the gifts for the servants, who came in
a seemingly never-ending stream, in at one door, wind-

ing round the room, and then out again by a side door. Osya had marshalled them in the order in which the gifts were laid out, so it was quite simple for Igor, who had offered to help, to pass each package to Galina, who gave it to its recipient with a few suitable words. She was touched by the blessings she received along with the thanks, and some of the female servants were actually in tears with pleasure.

At luncheon, she gave her mother and Igor their presents, which obviously pleased them, and received a reticule from her mother which she had embroidered with tiny beads, and, from Igor, a two-volume history of the Ukraine and a book about estate management, both of which she thought would be very interesting.

Immediately after luncheon, she went to the Chinese Salon, which looked out on one of the courtyards, and watched Osya Ivanich and some of the other servants distributing the meat and flour she had bought for the poor. Igor joined her, and they stood in silence for a while, concealed by the dragon-wreathed curtains, as wretched ragged creatures, some of whom scarcely looked human, queued up for their share.

'Russia's like a small palace built on a vast anthill,' Igor observed. 'A few of us live in luxury in the palace, but the weight of it is supported on the backs of the myriad ants, who go cold, hungry and half-naked, living on the scraps we condescend to throw to them.'

'I wish I'd given more,' Galina murmured, more to herself than to him, for the wretchedness and poverty she saw below horrified her.

'If you gave them everything you had, you'd not even scratch the top of the anthill,' he replied. 'One day, the ants will rise up and eat the palace, but I doubt they'll be much better off, for if they kill everyone with education, there'll be no one left to teach them what they need to know.' And, with that, he turned and left the room.

Galina watched a while longer, and then, subdued and thoughtful, went up to her bedroom.

Another rest during the afternoon refreshed her, and then she went with Igor to dine and dance at the Orlovs', and, to her delight, her mother went too, and spent a pleasurable evening playing cards with some of the other mothers who had come to chaperon their daughters. Galina noticed that all her gifts were in use, and she made a point herself of wearing the embroidered gloves which Sasha had sent her, and carrying the fan from Irina and Lev, the posy-holder full of white rosebuds from Nadya and Andrei, and the silver-mesh reticule from Tatya. She had received a number of other gifts, and wished she had thought to bring a list of the givers so that she might be sure not to miss thanking anyone.

On St Stephen's Day, (which is a day later in the Eastern Church than in the Western), which was, of course, her father's name-day, Galina went to morning service in the Holy Trinity Cathedral to pray and give thanks for him, wishing he would come to St Petersburg, for she missed him very much. She spent the afternoon at a skating-party which Andrei had organised on the Summer Canal, with Chinese lanterns hanging from poles along the banks and over the ice, so that the skaters could continue after the short hours of daylight had passed, and she arrived home with Tatya, the Orlovs, the Valyevs, Sasha and Igor, who were all to dine informally and spend the evening with her, at a little before five o'clock.

Osya Ivanich opened the door to them himself, looking very white-faced and shaken, and said, without any preliminary greeting, 'Galina Stepanovna, you have a visitor. He's in the Peacock Salon.'

Galina paused in the middle of removing her furlined *vitschura* and bonnet to enquire, 'A visitor? Is it someone I know?'

Osya cleared his throat nervously, and said in a very unsteady voice, 'Oh, Madame! It's—it's—I can't believe it, but it's Gennadi Yakovich!'

Galina dropped her bonnet and stood looking down at it as a number of confused thoughts raced through her head. One of the footmen picked up the bonnet, and she pulled herself together and said, fairly calmly, 'It sounds as if reports of his ship-wreck may have been exaggerated! Would you all care to come upstairs with me, and find out what's to do?'

A silent and shaken group mounted the grand staircase, looking uneasily at one another as they wondered how Gennadi Zhadnov was reacting to finding Galina in possession of what he must have thought to be his inheritance.

The footman whose duty it was to open the doors seemed to have become paralysed with shock, so Igor pushed them open, and entered the room a half-pace behind Galina, followed closely by the rest of her guests. A tall, fair-haired man rose from a chair by the stove as they entered, and turned to face them.

It was undoubtedly Gennadi Zhadnov. His resemblance to his portrait was sufficient to prove that, but there were differences. His golden hair had darkened a trifle, and his face was gaunt and slightly scarred by frostbite. He looked leaner and a little older than the portrait, and the blue eyes were harder and more direct than Galina expected, but he was still very handsome, and her heart gave a distinct flutter at the sight of him.

'Good afternoon,' he said, looking at the surprised faces before him and nodding in recognition of those he knew. 'Tatya Petrovna, Andrei Ivan'ich, Lev Petrovich, Sasha Alexandrovich, Igor—um—'

'Grigorovich,' Igor supplied gravely. 'Ladies, may I present Captain Count Gennadi Yakovich Zhadnov.

Galina Stepanovna Razumova, Nadezhda Igorovna Valyeva, Irina Arkadyevna Orlova. Er—I take it you're not actually a ghost?'

Gennadi bowed without undue ceremony to each lady as she was named, and replied, 'Of course not,' rather shortly to Igor's last remark, which apparently brought his old acquaintances out of their respective trances, for they suddenly began to express pleasure at seeing him safe and well, varying from Tatya's fervent, 'Oh, God be praised! How good it is to see you not lost after all!' to Sasha's somewhat tactless, 'Good to see you, but what a sell! This'll tie the lawyers in knots!' Unfortunately, his lameness had made him slower than the others in reaching Gennadi, and his remark rang out heartily after they had spoken.

There was an awkward silence, which Galina made an effort to break by saying, nervously, 'Perhaps we should take tea, and—er—Captain Zhadnov might care to tell us . . .' She turned to catch the eye of the footman, who had recovered his senses and was hovering in the doorway. He made a little bow and went out hurriedly, closing the door behind him.

'Please sit down,' Galina said to everyone in general, but looking at Gennadi as she spoke. She encountered a hostile stare from the iciest pair of eyes she had ever seen, and was glad to move away to her place by the tea-table to escape from them. It was only then that she realised that her mother was also in the room.

'Gennadi Yakovich has been telling me about his adventures,' she said placidly. 'So exciting! I said all along that there was no sign of Death in connection with his card.'

'Were you not shipwrecked after all, then?' Galina enquired, looking in Gennadi's direction, but not quite at him, for his hostility unnerved her.

'I don't know what story has gone about,' he replied

impatiently. 'Perhaps someone would care to enlighten me, and then I'll tell you what really happened.'

Galina looked at Tatya, who had told her about Gennadi's supposed fate, and asked her if she would tell the story, which she did, in much the same words she had used before.

When she had finished, Gennadi gave a snort of impatience, but, as the servants brought in the tea equipage at that moment, he delayed giving his version until everyone had been served. Unfortunately, the footman who handed him his cup and dish seemed to be filled with superstitious dread, which made him extremely clumsy. There was a sudden exclamation from Gennadi, and Galina looked up from pouring tea in time to see the footman sprawling on the floor.

There was a stunned silence for a moment, and then Galina said in a cold, detached tone, 'I will not have my servants struck in my house!' with a slight stress on the possessives.

'*Your* servant is a clumsy oaf, who dropped *your* dish and *your* teaspoon, and fell over *your* footstool!' Gennadi retorted brusquely.

Galina stared at him for a moment, startled by the raw nervousness in his voice, and then she realised that there must be an immense amount of pain and resentment bottled up in this man, who had just returned from a long and dangerous journey to find himself presumed dead and his home in the possession of a stranger.

'I apologise,' she said bravely. 'I was mistaken. Vova, are you hurt?' to the footman, who had scrambled to his feet and was standing scarlet-faced.

'No, indeed, Galina Stepanovna,' he replied in a low, embarrassed mumble. 'I tripped over the footstool. I'm sorry.'

'You may go then. Thank you.' The footmen bowed themselves out, and Galina turned her attention back to

Gennadi. 'You were about to tell us what really happened.'

Gennadi had retrieved the dropped dish and spoon from the floor while Galina was talking to the servant, and had apparently used the few seconds to recover his equanimity, for he spoke in a collected manner, with only a trace of nervousness in his voice.

'As you know, I was under orders to chart the coast of Novaya Zemlya and some of the other Arctic islands nearby. The work proceeded more slowly than the Admiralty had estimated, although I told them in the first place that it would take more than one summer. I decided to winter on one of the islands, but the sea froze earlier than usual, and suddenly—overnight, in fact—we were caught in the ice.'

'You didn't set out to reach the mainland, then?' Lev asked.

'Why should we? We'd supplies enough for at least two years, and the task was unfinished. We stayed with the ship, intending to complete the survey and sail home at the end of the summer just past. Unfortunately, the current carried us northeastwards, towards the area of permanent ice, and the pressures of the moving pack began to crush the ship. We mounted the boats on sledge runners, and when we had to abandon the ship, we set off to sledge across the ice to Novaya Zemlya. There was a storm, and I lost some men, including the two who came back with that idiotic tale. The rest of us overwintered on the island, did as much more of the survey as we could during last summer, and started out to sledge to the mainland about two months ago, and so home.'

'You didn't think to send a message to explain why you didn't return when you were expected?' Andrei asked.

'The Imperial Post doesn't function in the Arctic

Ocean,' Gennadi replied drily. 'In any case, I'd said all along that I expected to be up there for two seasons. If those two idiots hadn't come home with their story, no one would have thought anything amiss! I reported to the Admiralty this morning, having reached Petersburg late last night, and was considerably shocked to find myself officially dead, and disinherited into the bargain!' The underlying bitterness broke through in the last few words.

'Well, I suppose the sailors' story must have sounded convincing, and your uncle had to do something about his property, thinking you were dead, with no other family . . .' Tatya said reasonably. 'Surely the courts will soon declare you not dead?' She ignored the hollow laughs from her brother and Igor, who both knew only too well that Russian courts never did anything 'soon', and could make the simplest case last for years and cost a fortune in fees. 'I suppose the Emperor could do it by decree?'

'That's what the Admiralty suggested,' Gennadi replied. 'And I understand that the matter's already in hand. The real problem is my uncle's will, for I must make it plain that I've no intention of leaving things as they are. The estates need proper management, and they're not a plaything for a girl! Besides, my uncle meant me to have them.' He again turned that coldly hostile glare on Galina, who met his eyes for a moment, then looked away, troubled and unhappy that he should dislike her so much, yet unable to blame him for doing so.

'Of course,' she said equably, stifling her instinctive annoyance at being considered unfit to manage the estates. 'You've every right to object, and I shall . . .'

'Galina!' Andrei, Igor and Lev almost shouted in unison, followed by Sasha's, 'Steady on!'

'Don't say another word about it until you've consulted a lawyer!' Igor said warningly. 'And even then, give the matter some careful thought.'

'May I enquire what business it is of yours?' Gennadi asked brusquely.

'I'm Galina Stepanovna's business adviser and friend,' Igor sounded decidedly prickly himself. 'Not that that is any of your business!'

'Where are you staying?' Galina asked Gennadi. It was the first thing to come into her head in an effort to avert the incipient battle which seemed about to erupt between him and Igor, but she added with genuine concern 'I collect that you lived—live here when you're in Petersburg?'

Gennadi showed a quickly covered trace of surprise and replied uncertainly, 'I've a room in the Hotel London.'

'But you'd be very welcome here,' Galina said. 'After all, this—this is your home, isn't it?' She just managed to stop herself saying 'was', for she was anxious to allay his hostility and show him that he need not regard her as an enemy.

'I hardly think . . .' he began hesitantly, as if he half-wished to accept, yet was too proud to do so.

'I think it would be quite ridiculous for you to stay in an hotel, which would undoubtedly be very dirty and infested with unpleasantness,' Galina's mother said with unexpected decisiveness. 'After all, you must have been coming here to stay nearly all your life, and it's quite hard enough for you to find yourself in this predicament without your being required to be bitten all over by fleas and bugs and given inedible food! We are not exactly short of rooms here, and you have no need to endure any more of our company than you wish. There are two dining-rooms if you prefer to disassociate yourself entirely. We shall quite understand, under the circumstances.'

Galina looked at her mother with surprised admiration at hearing her own thoughts put so clearly and succinctly, and could only add, 'My mother is quite right. I should feel most distressed if you insisted on staying somewhere else.'

Gennadi gave her an odd look, partly puzzled, partly suspicious, and said stiffly, 'I must own that I have been looking forward to the comforts of home after two years in the Arctic. Thank you for your kind invitation. I accept with gratitude.' It was not said very graciously, but to Galina it seemed a triumph, and she was not at all pleased with Igor when he said sardonically, 'And you'll be able to keep an eye on the General's treasures and see that Galina doesn't give them all away.'

Galina expected an explosion, and for a moment Gennadi's lips clamped together as if to contain one, but then he relaxed a little and said fairly mildly, 'Are you here for any particular reason, Igor?'

'I'm cataloguing your uncle's collection,' Igor replied promptly, and with a shade of defiance. Galina recalled that the General had always refused to have such a catalogue made, and presumably Gennadi would share his objections.

'I suppose you should be capable of managing that fairly well,' Gennadi sounded off-hand and only the slightest touch doubtful. Then he rose to his feet and said quite pleasantly to Galina, 'If you'll excuse me, I must be going. I have an engagement to dine with the Navy Minister. If you're sure it will be convenient, I'll call at the hotel on the way and tell my man to bring my kit here.'

'By all means,' Galina replied. 'I'm sorry that you've had such a shocking home-coming. I'm sure everything can be worked out before too long.' She held out her hand and Gennadi crossed the room to take it rather gingerly and brush his lips across her fingers as he bowed. He then took general leave of the others, answering their warm expressions of goodwill with dignified restraint which Galina suspected might cover embarrassment, and was then ushered out by the footman who came in response to Galina's ring.

'Oh dear!' Tatya exclaimed as soon as he had gone. 'How dreadfully awkward it all is. Poor man. I can't imagine what terrible conditions he must have endured in the Arctic! Fancy being marooned on the ice, with no ship and hundreds of *versty* to the nearest land! And then to come home to this situation!'

'And poor Galina, too!' Nadya added. 'What a dilemma!'

'It is indeed,' said Andrei. 'But not one we should discuss, I think. We're all in a difficult position here, for some of us are friends to both parties in the—the matter, and can see justice on both sides. You must consult a lawyer, Galina! I'm sure an equitable situation can be found, but it's a problem for a trained legal mind.'

'Yes, of course,' Galina replied. 'I shall pray about it tonight, and see my man-of-business in the morning. Now, you will still all stay to dinner, won't you? I'd rather not be left alone to worry about the situation all the evening!'

Of course they agreed, having come to dinner in the first place, and everyone made a determined effort to converse about anything at all other than inheritances, Naval officers and law-suits. After a few minutes, Galina excused herself and went to speak to Osya Ivanich, who was casting an eye over the arrangements in the small dining-room.

'Gennadi Yakovich will be staying here until things are sorted out,' she told him. 'Oh—I suppose we haven't put his usual room to another use?' she added with a twinge of doubt.

'No, Galina Stepanovna. He's always occupied the

small suite in the south wing, and that's not been used since—since he was last here.'

He had regained his normal composure by now, and sounded much as usual, apart from the slight hesitation in his last sentence. Galina looked at him speculatively for a moment, and then ventured, 'It must have been a great shock for you when he arrived.'

'Indeed, yes! That's why young Vova was so clumsy, you understand. I'm very sorry for that—he's not usually clumsy. We all thought at first, when they said he was dead, that he might still come back, for there were times before when he was missing for weeks, but it's been so long this time, and we all accepted . . . and then to open the door and find him standing there!'

'You realise that there will have to be . . .? I mean, he will want to contest the General's will. The General left me his property because he thought that Gennadi Yako-vich was dead, and he isn't . . . I expect that, when things are sorted out, he'll be your master.' She watched Osya's face closely, hoping to gain some inkling of his feelings about the prospect, but he maintained the proper lack of expression of a good servant and only bowed slightly and thanked her politely for taking him into her confidence. Then he asked her to excuse him as he must go to see if dinner was ready for her guests.

After he had gone, Galina stood for a few moments, biting her lower lip and wondering what she should do. If she had only herself to consider, there would be no problem, but there were the serfs. It was clear that the General had treated them badly, by her standards, that is, but probably no worse than the great majority of serf-owners in the Russian Empire. Would Gennadi's attitude to them be the same as that of his uncle? She very much feared that it might.

With a little sigh, she made her way back to the Peacock Salon, pausing to look at the Wheel of Fortune as she passed it. The knight was at the apogee again at the moment, and the serf was sprawled in abject submission below him. It seemed all too appropriate.

CHAPTER
TEN

THE MOON

Reflection and imagination/Doubt and misgiving

WHEN she retired for the night, Galina first read a chapter of the history of the Ukraine which Igor had given her, to calm her nerves, and found it inordinately full of bloodshed, distributed impartially between battles, murders and massacres. Then she spent half an hour by the clock thinking, keeping her eyes on the dial to make herself concentrate and remain within the limit she had set, for otherwise she knew that she would go on milling the same ideas about all night.

First, she opened her mind to consider the aspect of the situation to which she had firmly closed it all the evening—her personal reaction to Gennadi's reappearance. He was almost all she had imagined—handsome, direct, courageous, and if he had seemed abrupt, and irritable, it was understandable under the circumstances. He must have arrived in Petersburg very tired and strained after his experiences in the North, and then to receive such a succession of shocks—his uncle dead, himself assumed dead, and his inheritance given to another—even his home lost to him. After all, he had exercised a great deal of self-control, and only flared up a few times, mostly when Igor had provoked him.

She pulled herself up short at that. Why was she

defending him? She must be careful not to confuse her imagined ideal with the real man, whom she did not really know, whereas she did know Igor, and liked and trusted him. There must be a good reason for Igor's dislike of Gennadi, something more than the trivial jealousy of which he had spoken. Somehow, she must make an opportunity to ask Igor to be more explicit. She must know what kind of man Gennadi was.

Why? Not just for her own sake, she hastened to assure herself, but because of the serfs. The well-being of more than two thousand souls would depend on the character of Gennadi Yakovich when he became their owner, and this was a very worrying thought to Galina. Her first reaction on finding that Gennadi was still alive had been to surrender all the property to him, and it still seemed the right thing to do morally, if only she could be sure that he would not treat the serfs as his uncle had done. She had intended to do so much to make their lives better—schools and dispensaries in the villages, better cabins, improved agriculture, and, eventually, freedom. Would Gennadi be prepared to give them anything, or would he keep them in the old wretched poverty and ignorance common to nine out of ten of the people in the Empire?

Obviously, that was the main question out of the many to which she would have to find answers before she could decide what to do about the inheritance, and her time was now up. There was no point in spending any longer on the problems now, so she set them aside and prayed very earnestly for a while.

Before she finally went to bed, she drew back one of the curtains a little and looked out of the long window to see what kind of night it was. Over the houses opposite, across the little river, the moon was sailing in a black velvet sky spangled with stars, their size and brilliance enhanced by a heavy frost which touched with silver the black silhouette of the gateway and railings between the forecourt and the street. The ice on the Fontanka gleamed faintly, and a late home-goer skated past, like a creature of fantasy on the silver surface. A dog howled somewhere, baying at the moon, and another answered. It all seemed vaguely familiar, like a half-remembered dream. Galina shivered, hastened to climb into bed, and slept tolerably well.

In the morning, she went downstairs to the library and took a good look at the portrait of Gennadi, noting with interest how the artist had subtly exaggerated some aspects of his appearance and played down others, and when Igor walked in suddenly, and stopped with a jerk just inside the door as he caught sight of her, she observed dispassionately, 'If ever I have my portrait painted, I'll go to Borovikovsky—he certainly knows how to make the best of one's looks!'

'It's a good likeness, and not much improved on the original—not as much as usual with Borovikovsky, that is—he's a very popular portraitist,' Igor observed wrily. 'How are you this morning?'

'Quite well, thank you, and ready for breakfast,' she replied. 'Are you coming?' she added as she moved towards the door.

Igor hesitated, looking towards his desk, and then said, 'I don't know if there's any point in going on with the work until . . . Yes, I'll come to breakfast.'

'Do you think Gennadi Yakovich won't let you finish the catalogue if he becomes the owner?' Galina asked as they walked along the gallery.

Igor shrugged, 'I've no idea. I can't honestly say that I really know Gennadi's thoughts on the subject. He'll probably see the sense of it, but whether he'll wish me to do the work is another matter. He was always inscrutable, unless he chose to be otherwise.'

Galina made no reply to that, for they were approaching the dining-room and she was wondering whether Gennadi would elect to join them for meals, or keep to his own quarters. She was both relieved and anxious when she saw that he was already in the room, serving himself at the side-table and exchanging a few polite remarks with her mother, who was sitting at the table.

Pausing briefly in the doorway, Galina murmured to Igor, 'Please don't make any trouble!' to which Igor replied with a look of mingled innocence and amusement, but, fortunately, did not appear to be offended. He followed her in with an affable 'Good morning' to Gennadi, echoing Galina's own greeting.

Gennadi seemed very quiet, getting on with his breakfast without contributing to the rather artificial conversation, his eyes moving from one speaker to another as if he were trying to discover some deeper meaning behind their trivial words.

Before long, the light chit-chat languished into silence, and then he ventured to remark, 'I see that you seem to have got rid of a great deal of furniture and so forth.'

'The things have only been put into storage,' Galina replied defensively. 'Nothing has been sold or thrown away yet. I had to have a great deal put out of the way, to make room to move about the house.' She felt herself resenting the implied criticism in his remark, yet regretted the sharpness of her own answer.

'Yes,' Gennadi said mildly. 'The house was rather cluttered. I—er—wondered what had happened to my polar bear, that's all. It used to stand in the Chinese Salon.'

'How uncomfortable,' commented Countess Razumova. 'All those dragons! *Polar* bear?' she added with sudden enlightenment. 'Ah, so that's why it's white! I thought it might have died of old age.'

'Indeed not!' Gennadi was stung to reply. 'It was in the prime of life. I shot it myself, on my first voyage to the Arctic, when I was fifteen. I cured the skin myself as well, and then had it stuffed. I'm very proud of that bear!'

'Oh dear!' Galina said faintly, but was distracted by Igor remarking sepulchrally, 'It has the moth,' with obvious intent to provoke. As he was sitting next to her, she managed to deliver a sharp kick on his ankle with no more visible effect to the others than Igor dropping his knife on his plate with a sudden clatter.

'Shot it?' Countess Razumova queried with interest. 'From my memories of my dear father's hunting exploits, I recall that a bullet usually makes a very noticeable hole. Did you patch it in some way, for I didn't see any sign of damage during the animal's brief sojourn in my room?'

'No. I shot it in the eye,' Gennadi replied *en passant* to his more important question. 'How did it come to be in your room?'

'We were trying to find a more convenient place for it,' Galina explained. 'You see, I wanted the salon cleared, and the bear is rather large. You must have been very close to shoot it in the eye. Surely polar bears are particularly dangerous and ill-tempered?'

'Any kind of bear is entitled to be ill-tempered if someone shoots it in the eye,' Igor could not resist the contribution, but he moved his feet out of Galina's reach as he spoke, and the others quite properly ignored his remark.

'I hadn't much choice,' Gennadi said, sounding almost apologetic. 'I was running away from it when I fell over and caught my foot in a crack in the ice. I'd no wish to be a bear's dinner, and a wounded bear is even worse than a whole one, so I had to be sure of killing it. Er—what did you eventually do with it?'

'Well, it rather alarmed people when they came upon it unexpectedly, so I'm afraid it's in one of the attics,' Galina replied apologetically. 'I'll have it brought down and put in your rooms.'

'Thank you,' Gennadi had lost his air of hostile watchfulness at the prospect of being reunited with his bear, and gave Galina the faintest glimmer of a smile, which softened his features and made her catch her breath and feel quite dizzy.

The meal continued in silence for a few minutes, and then Countess Razumova, to make conversation, remarked, 'I think the display of snuff-boxes in the cabinets along the gallery looks very fine. What a remarkable collection of them the General had!'

'It was an excellent idea of Igor's to set them out like that,' Galina replied.

'Yes. They make an interesting exhibition,' Gennadi said. 'I was looking at them just now.' Then he added, 'Would you have any objection if I stay in my rooms this morning? I'm still rather tired after so much travelling.'

Galina replied with suitable politeness and genuine sympathy, thinking how fatigued he must be by his journey and the shocks he had sustained on his return, and said that he must feel free to do whatever he wished. She went herself to her little office, after giving orders concerning the polar bear, and spent some time ostensibly looking over the household accounts, but in fact sitting staring into space, wondering about Gennadi Yakovich.

Presently, a footman came to enquire if she would receive Cherbatov, the man-of-business for the Zhadnov estates, who had just arrived.

'Oh. Yes, of course!' Galina exclaimed, realising guiltily that she had done nothing about sending for him, or even informing him of the new developments.

He came in looking harassed and more than a little annoyed.

'I find my position most invidious,' he informed her after they had exchanged greetings. '*Most* invidious! I assure you that I am not taking sides in this issue. I can only speak for the Zhadnov property, and it's for the courts to decide to which of you it belongs. I can say or do nothing to pre-empt that decision, you understand?'

'Quite right,' Galina replied soothingly. 'An impartial adviser is exactly what we need.' She rang for a footman, and asked him to request Gennadi to come down if he would be so kind, and kept Cherbatov in general conversation about one or two of the outlying estates until Gennadi appeared.

He paused in the doorway, bade Cherbatov, 'Good morning,' and then looked about him with some surprise, his clear blue eyes taking in the plain, large desk, the neatly-arranged books and papers, and the generally business-like look of the office, the only feminine touch being a vase of hot-house flowers on a side-table.

'I think this used to be a store-room,' he remarked as he sat down.

Galina, over-defensive and expecting a note of criticism, assumed it was there and replied, 'Yes, but I needed somewhere to conduct my business affairs. As you said yourself, the Zhadnov property is not a plaything for a girl.' Gennadi's only response was a slight quirking of the eyebrows, which she found irritating.

'Perhaps you don't expect a female to be concerned in the management of estates,' she went on. 'However, M. Cherbatov has been kind enough to come and give us the benefit of his advice. His responsibility is to the estates, not, at least until the ownership is decided, to either of us, and I'm sure you must agree that the smooth running of the estates and the well-being of the souls dependent on them must be paramount.'

Gennadi's eyebrows quirked again, but he responded quietly, 'Of course.'

'Perhaps you would be kind enough to tell us the exact terms of the General's will,' Galina said to Cherbatov.

'Certainly. I have it with me, as a matter of fact.' He ferreted among the papers in the small valise which he had brought with him, and produced a single dirt-stained quarto sheet. 'Here it is. It's a simple document, but sound enough in law. To explain the circumstances—when I heard of Captain's Zhadnov's—er—demise—presumed demise, that is,—I thought it my duty to go at once to the General. It was not at all easy to find him, you understand, for he was with Marshal Kutuzov's force pursuing the French in their withdrawal from Moscow. Eventually, I found him in a field-hospital near Krasnyi, where he was—well, quite so. It was a terrible place—you can't imagine . . .!' He shuddered and looked nauseated by the memory.

'No need to dwell on it,' Gennadi said quietly. Galina gave him a puzzled look, wondering whether the remark was intended to spare Cherbatov's feelings, or her own, or was merely callous, but the handsome face was inscrutable, and she found no answer in it.

'Indeed no!' Cherbatov pulled himself together. 'I mention it only to explain the condition of the paper. I told him the—er—news, and he said there was no one else of his blood left that he cared to remember, so it (meaning the property) had better go to—er—the Razumova girl. Meaning yourself, Galina Stepanovna. He had a poor memory for names, you understand. I made out a brief will, and he signed it with a doctor and a fellow-patient as witnesses. He died a few weeks later.' He paused for a few moments to show proper respect, and Galina crossed herself. Gennadi belatedly followed suit, and then Cherbatov resumed. 'In effect it states that, the last of his blood-relations having unfortunately perished, the General, being in his right mind, etcetera, gave and bequeathed to his god-daughter, Galina Stepanovna Razumova—he managed to remember your name—everything of which he died possessed, without conditions. That means that you were to have everything, and you could do as you pleased with it,' and he looked over his spectacles at Galina in an anxious fashion, as if to be sure that she had understood.

'So if I choose to give it away, there could be no objection from anyone?' Galina asked thoughtfully.

'None at all. You are free, under the terms of the will, to do whatever you please with it, subject to the law, of course. You may give away all or any part of it, if you choose,' Cherbatov assured her.

'I have not said anything to contest that,' Gennadi said. 'I accept that the will is genuine, and that you are legally entitled to have the property, and to do as you please with it. My contention is that, had my uncle not been told that I was dead, he would not have made that will at all. Am I right, Cherbatov?'

'Well—er—' Cherbatov was disconcerted to find himself about to give a plain, one-word answer, and temporised, 'You must understand that I was officially informed of your demise by the Admiralty, and undertook to convey the news to your uncle—to the General.'

'No blame attaches to you,' Gennadi assured him, 'but as a result of hearing that news, he made the will you have there?'

'Er—yes,' Cherbatov was trapped.

'Had he not received that news, his previous will would have been executed when he died?' Gennadi continued, and again Cherbatov was forced to a simple, 'Yes.'

'And what were the terms of that will?'

Cherbatov again ferreted in his valise, and produced a small, clean bundle of papers tied round with pink tape.

He untied and unfolded them, with much crackling, smoothed them out, and said, 'After the usual preliminaries, including your uncle's full titles and all his decorations, and a list of his land estates and properties . . .' he turned over one sheet after another until the came to the last, '. . . it says that, after his debts have been paid, and despite your past impertinences and strange ideas, as you, Gennadi Yakovich, are his sole surviving blood-relation, he gives and bequeathes to you all the property of which he died possessed, without condition. In essence, the same as the other, but with a different beneficiary.'

Galina sat quite still, staring at the leather top of the desk before her, the words she felt she should utter almost on her lips, held back only by this dreadful uncertainty about the character of Gennadi. *Why* did Igor dislike him? How would he treat the serfs? She hardly heard Cherbatov continue, 'There is, however, a codicil to this will.' It was not until her name was mentioned that she realised that he was saying, 'In it, the General added that he bequeathed his god-daughter, Galina Stepanovna Razumova, one thousand roubles for her dowry.'

There was a brief silence, and then Gennadi said briskly, 'Well, that seems clear enough. At the moment, I'm still legally dead, but as soon as that situation is remedied, I intend to contest the will—the one which was executed, that is—on the grounds that it was only made because my uncle thought me dead, and that the earlier will expressed his real wishes. Perhaps I should add that there is a certain necessity for me to do this. I have no property myself, and no income save my naval pay, which, in common with all such payments, is not intended to be adequate for a man's sole support! My uncle made me a generous allowance while he was alive, which has presumably now ceased.' This last was said in a mildly ironic tone which did not invite sympathy, pose a question, or do anything but state an accepted fact.

'Well, of course . . .' Cherbatov replied nervously, shaken out of his dignity and confidence by having given two plain answers already.

'Then pray resume payments at once. Retrospectively,' Galina found no difficulty in uttering this time.

'I wasn't begging,' Gennadi said sharply, while Cherbatov, at the same time, objected, 'But the Captain is, if you'll forgive the term, officially—er—deceased!'

'I don't see what difference that makes,' Galina told him. 'If it disarranges your accounts to make payments to a deceased person, then put them down to my personal expenditure, but give the money to Captain Zhadnov. And there is no question of anyone begging. I don't suppose you asked your uncle for the allowance, but you accepted it, quite rightly, from an estate in which you had an interest, so we'll continue it on that basis until the whole matter is cleared up, at least, just as I shall accept the thousand roubles dowry when—and if—you win the case.'

Her sudden switch in mid-speech from Cherbatov to Gennadi, still in the same business-like tone, disconcerted the two men for a moment, then Gennadi, recovering first, made her a slight bow and said, 'Yes, ma'am! As you say. Thank you,' with that glimmer of a smile which had set Galina's blood-pressure awry before, but this time it was a little stronger, and the effect was consequently increased.

'Of course, you are perfectly entitled . . .' Cherbatov began, 'Yes, as you say. Quite so. It shall be arranged.'

'At once,' Galina added.

'Of course. This is without prejudice to the outcome of a possible legal contest concerning the rightful ownership of the property.' Cherbatov recovered himself and adopted his most pettifogging and pedantic tone. 'You do understand, Countess, that your action, albeit dictated by motives of altruism and kindness, might be construed as an admission . . .?'

'I understand quite well, thank you,' Galina said kindly, wishing that men would not assume that all females were bird-witted. 'I choose to continue payment of the allowance to Captain Zhadnov because it is a charge on the estates which I have inherited from my godfather and I consider that I should so continue it, as my godfather would have wished. Does that make it tidy for you?'

'Ah! Eminently suitable!' Cherbatov looked quite pleased. 'I shall have a document drawn up to that effect for your signature. Now, I think that there is nothing further to be done until the matter of the Captain's legal status of existence has been settled, and I have an appointment at the Ministry of Justice to see someone about that, so if you will excuse me . . .'

'Oh dear! Lawyers!' Galina murmured when he had gone.

'He means well,' Gennadi pointed out. 'He's honest and conscientious, which might be thought to outweigh his other characteristics.'

'Other?' Galina looked at him with large, questioning eyes, for he sounded as if he might possibly be joking.

'He's also pedantic and boring.' Gennadi looked at her for a moment, and then said seriously, 'You're an interesting person. You seem to have been very busy in the short time since you came to Petersburg.'

'Busy?' Galina was immediately on the defensive again, and yet felt sorry that it should be so.

'I gather that you've already made a number of friends, you've set to work to sort out this oriental bazaar of Uncle Yuri's, you've made the house habitable, brought the children out of banishment, married off half the household, and did I understand rightly that you've been to Kiev?'

'You've not been idle yourself,' Galina commented tartly, disconcerted that he had already discovered two things of which his uncle would certainly have disapproved.

'It's necessary for the captain of a ship to know exactly what's going on, from keel to topmast and stem to stern,' he replied with a shrug. 'And it becomes a habit. Why Kiev? My uncle had no land in that area, only a little property in the city. Was there some trouble over it? Not enough to take you such a distance in winter, surely?'

Galina considered evading the question, but decided that she had done nothing to be ashamed of, so that determined little chin tilted defiantly and she replied, 'I expect you know that your uncle lent some money to a Count Bednyak, who has an estate near Kiev?'

'No. My uncle didn't consider it necessary to tell me very much about anything. Was it a large sum?'

'Three thousand roubles.'

'Well-secured, presumably, knowing my uncle.'

'Very. His whole estate was the security.'

Gennadi's eyebrows quirked, but he made no other comment.

'The Count wrote to tell me that he couldn't pay, because he had suffered bad harvests and diseased crops, and he had to save his serfs from starving. The loan fell due at the end of December. I thought it best to go down to Kiev and look into the matter. Luckily, he had a pair of valuable vases, so Igor Grigorovich bought them for the Emperor, and that was more than enough to repay the principal.'

'And the interest?' Gennadi's face was unreadable.

'I let him off that, as he'd had so much worry and bad luck. The General had planned to get possession of the estate, I gather.'

'Naturally. Yuri Sticky-fingers didn't lend money for charitable purposes. What about Count what's-his-name? Bednyak. Presumably he's still in the doldrums financially?'

Galina had never heard of the doldrums, but she guessed his meaning and replied, 'I've arranged for a supply of good seed to be sent to him. Wheat, because his main trouble was caused by growing rye every year, and not rotating his crops at all. I explained to him about disease cycles, and the better market for wheat in the towns . . .' She tailed off, for Gennadi was staring at her in an odd manner.'

'You amaze me!' he said after a moment. 'I suppose you gave him the seed?'

'Of course not. His pride was hurt more than enough by having to write to me. I sold it to him at a fair price.'

'Fair to whom?'

The confusion of Galina's feelings, the suspicion that this man, who could have been her ideal, was in fact no better than his uncle, and the faint smile which accompanied the question, caused her to flare up suddenly, and she snapped, 'When I say "fair", I mean fair to everyone concerned, whatever you may mean by the word! In any case, what I did is my business, not yours! When the courts hand over the estates to you, I've no doubt you'll do as you please with them, and be as fully entitled to do so as I am and have been while they're in my ownership. Yes, I've let the house-serfs marry—at least you can't undo that!—and I've let them have their children with them, though I expect you'll banish them again. Yes, I'm having the contents of the house catalogued, and I'm returning as many as possible of the stolen things to their rightful owners, and you'll just have to wait until you're the owner to put a stop to that! I had every intention of freeing all my serfs as well, and I'm only sorry that there won't be time to do it now. I've done a great many things which you won't like, and I don't care. Your uncle was a thoroughly greedy, grasping tyrant, and I pray that I never become like him—and you would do well to make the same prayer!' With that, being on the brink of bursting into tears, she fled from the room before Gennadi could even get to his feet, let alone say anything.

The winter-garden was nearby, and, whereas the rest of the house seemed to be full of servants, that was a place where no one ever appeared to go. In fact, Galina wondered how it was kept so well-tended as she had never seen a gardener there. She went into it, sat down on a rustic seat in a grotto amid ferns and tinkling water, and shed a few tears to relieve her feelings, and then wondered miserably what she should do.

She still felt morally bound to hand over everything to Gennadi Yakovich, for the story of the two wills left no doubt in her mind that he was the General's true heir, and it was bad enough for him to return from that dreadful journey to find himself given up and well-nigh forgotten, without having to fight for his rights as well, but what about the serfs?

She thought back over the things he had said during the incredibly long time since his appearance yesterday evening. Had he struck Vova, or had the man really tripped? What had he said about the servants' children? 'Brought them out of banishment'? He had known that they existed, then. If only she could remember whether he sounded approving or disapproving. Perhaps neither —he seemed such an inscrutable man! His face wasn't exactly expressionless, but very hard to read, and his voice was the same—pleasant, sometimes ironic, sometimes irritable, but usually . . . What? One couldn't call a voice unreadable, but something of the sort. His smile was . . . rare. That was not the word towards which her thoughts tended, but the memory of that smile was too disturbing to think about.

After letting her mind wander in this disjointed fashion for a while, she sighed, stood up, and started to leave the garden. Snow was falling on the glass roof, pattering faintly like the march of a company of mice, but in here it was as warm as a summer's day, and the air was scented by flowers.

Rounding a large stone vase full of cascading stems covered with little red flowers, she was surprised to come upon a gnarled, bearded old man in an earth-stained kaftan, on his knees weeding. He stood up as she appeared, bowed, and tugged a shaggy grey forelock.

'Good day, Galina Stepanova,' he said in a rusty voice, speaking Russian. 'I was just tidying up a bit, ready for Gennadi Yakovich. He likes it tidy—no weeds and everything just so. I expect he'll be coming to look round soon—he usually does most days, when he's home. He says there aren't any flowers at sea.'

'You keep the garden very well,' Galina commented.

'Well, we try, the two boys and me, but there's not much joy in it when no one comes to look. Old Master never did—didn't know a flower from a cabbage, that one! It's been grand since you came, cutting flowers for the house every day, and now Gennadi Yakovich is back to look round and ask the names of things.'

'You're pleased that he's returned, then?' asked Galina.

'Oh, indeed—no offence, Galina Stepanovna, but he's a good man. Always interested in what people are doing, and says when he likes something, and don't shout much when they're wrong!'

'I expect you know that he will probably be your master before long?' Galina said.

The old man looked troubled. 'Oh, mistress! We don't know what to think, or which to pray for! You're a good mistress, the best—but we know Gennadi Yakovich is really the heir. If only we could have you both!'

Galina smiled a little sadly at that, shook her head, and then went on her way, but not before the old man had picked her a spray of scented pale pink flowers and presented them with a dignified bow. Galina thanked him, then realised that she did not know his name.

'Old Mischa,' he said. 'That's all—just Old Mischa.'

Igor was at work in the library, engrossed in a long list. He answered politely when spoken to, but clearly had quite three-quarters of his mind on his work, so Galina left him to it and went in search of her mother, only to find that the Countess had gone out shopping and would not be back for luncheon, as she intended to take it with a friend.

Galina wandered up to her bedroom, meeting the polar bear with attendant footmen on the way, feeling a little irritated with Igor for being more interested in porcelain than in herself, with her mother for departing from her usual stay-at-home habits, with Gennadi for not being the perfect hero of her imagination, and mostly with herself for being irritated. She spent the rest of the morning reviewing her wardrobe, and went down to luncheon determined to be polite—distantly so, but certainly polite—to Gennadi.

He was not there. A footman presented a note from him in which he expressed regret that he would not be able to take luncheon or dinner at home as he was bidden to the Admiralty, and expected to be there for several hours, and then to dine at the Palace—he did not say with whom.

Igor appeared, but talked exclusively of Sèvres, Chantilly, Wedgwood and Capodimonte, with mention of other manufactories, which normally would have interested Galina, but today made her feel inclined to throw a selection of their wares at him, piece by piece. Of course, she did nothing of the sort, but responded courteously when he paused for breath, which was not often, so she was able to pursue her own thoughts most of the time, coming, of course, to no conclusions.

After luncheon, she ordered her carriage and went to see Tatya, who welcomed her warmly, sat her down in a comfortable chair in the garden room, served her with tea, and then said, 'How are you, my dear? Do you wish to talk about it?'

'I don't know what to think, or what to do,' Galina said despairingly. 'I can't make him out at all! I know it's less than twenty-four hours since he came back, but I can usually form some sort of an idea of a person's character at a first meeting, and I can't at all with him! What is he really like, Tatya?'

Tatya looked a little taken aback at this outburst, but she considered for a moment, and then replied, 'He's very brave and very intelligent—the two don't always go together! I've never heard anything against his character—he doesn't drink overmuch, or gamble to excess, or any of the other things which cause scandal. He's sometimes rather blunt in his speech—for instance, Anna Volkhova, poor soul, once tried to—to flirt with him, and he told her quite plainly, and in public, that she'd do better to pay more attention to her own husband, and less to the husbands of other women. She laughed, of course, and made some unpleasant innuendo, to which he replied, "Rubbish!", and then she asked, "Oh, are you secretly married, then?" and he said, "To my ship, Princess until I find a female to excel her." which really quite *annoyed* her! Otherwise . . .' She thought again, then shrugged. 'Otherwise, I find I know very little about him. You see, officers in the Navy are so seldom in Petersburg. I know he was in the Corps of Pages with Andrei and Igor, but then he transferred to the Naval Academy when he was thirteen or so, and has been at sea most of the time since, so even they don't really know him all that well. All I can say is that everyone's pleased to see him when he comes on leave—at least, all the people one counts as having an opinion that matters. I've never heard anything to his discredit. I'm sorry I can't be more helpful.'

Galina sighed. 'Thank you. It's his attitude to things that worries me. This morning, he made several comments and asked some questions which made me think that he might share his uncle's ideas about the serfs, and—oh, he wasn't exactly critical, but I had the impression that he objected to everything I've done. On the other hand, he must be very shocked, and worried about his situation, and resentful of my having what should have been his. Once or twice he's given just a glimmer of being—well—more as I imagined he might be. I don't know what to think, or what to do.'

'There's no need for you to do anything for a while yet,' Tatya said gently. 'He has to be declared legally alive again before he can take any action over the will, and that will take some time, with the Emperor so far away with the Army. Don't worry, dear. You'll have time to find out about his character and opinions before any decisions are made. Perhaps you can both agree to some sort of compromise solution.'

'Yes, of course,' Galina said, sounding unconvinced. 'I'm being silly. Oh, if only he could have been more like his portrait!' A statement which no doubt would have pleased Borovikovsky, but it made Tatya bite her lip and look troubled.

CHAPTER
ELEVEN

THE WHEEL OF FORTUNE

The reaping of what has been sown / The close of a cycle

GALINA did her best to be patient and to draw Gennadi into conversation without becoming defensive, but she found it difficult. He was out a great deal, and when they did meet, he seemed reluctant to enter into discussion about any subject other than the most trivial. If she mentioned anything to do with the household or the estates, he seemed to draw back, his eyes becoming wary and the muscles about his mouth tightening as if he was clamping his lips shut.

To make matters worse, she became increasingly aware that Igor had been right. She had fallen in love with Gennadi's portrait, and despite the caution and mistrust which filled her mind, her heart had no reservations about him at all. By New Year's Eve, she had to admit to herself that she loved him, despite the differences between the real man and the ideal, and yet every time she spoke to him, she seemed to build the wall between them higher. Almost everything he said put her on the defensive. Even a comment on the weather had her searching his face covertly for some underlying meaning, and she could feel herself becoming as prickly and disagreeable as a porcupine, however hard she tried to be calm and reasonable.

At breakfast on New Year's Eve, he said, 'I observe that the servants had new clothes at Christmas. Are you planning New Year gifts as well?'

It was said in a tone of mild enquiry, yet immediately her hackles rose, and she heard herself say sharply, 'No, I am not! I gave them at Christmas. Another departure from the Zhadnov tradition, I'm glad to say!' Then she suddenly remembered Osya's words when she had asked him if the General gave Christmas gifts to his servants—'Gennadi Yakovich used to give something at New Year when he was here, but he wasn't a rich man, you see.'

There was a moment's silence as she stared at Gennadi, her eyes very wide and startled, and her hostility suddenly evaporated. She saw the look of withdrawal in his eyes change, first to puzzlement, then to concern.

'Is something wrong?' he asked.

'Yes, I am,' she replied contritely. 'I'm sorry.' There was a great deal more that she would have liked to say, but nothing would come, and, in any case, both Igor and her mother were at the table, the Countess reading a letter from her husband in Tver, and quite oblivious of the small drama going on before her, and Igor apparently absorbed in stirring jam into his glass of tea.

'Perhaps we're both wrong,' Gennadi said quietly. It sounded like a peace-offering, but Galina was too wretched to reply, and left the room as soon afterwards as she reasonably could.

It took her nearly an hour to sort her way through a jumble of imperfectly remembered words and looks, trying desperately to recall exactly what Osya, Igor and Old Mischa had said about Gennadi, and how they had looked when they said it, trying to remember just what Gennadi had said in their various exchanges—his actual words, not the interpretation she had put on them at the time. Eventually, a new picture of him emerged, but she still had doubts and misgivings. After all, she had been wrong before, and she might still be wrong! Above all, there was still the shadow of Igor's dislike for him. She must tackle Igor, and somehow persuade him to tell her the truth.

He was, as usual, in the library, on his knees before a packing-case which appeared to contain teacups. He looked up as Galina entered, and said, 'Not a samovar among them, and no two alike!' then, seeing the serious expression on her face, 'What's the matter?'

'I want to ask you something, Igor,' she said nervously. 'It's not my business, but I really need to know, or I wouldn't ask.'

Igor stood up, perfunctorily brushing the knees of his trousers, moved a quantity of assorted bric-à-brac from the seats of two chairs, set one for Galina, and sat on the other himself.

'Ask, then,' he invited.

'Why do you dislike Gennadi Yakovich? The real reason, not the one you gave me before, about being jealous of him.'

Igor's face lightened, although he did not actually smile. 'Ah, so you *are* in love with him!' he exclaimed. 'Well, well! I'm sorry to disappoint you, my dear, but that *was* the real reason. You see, when I first knew Gennadi, we were both seven years old. He was tall, agile, clever, good at everything, as fair and handsome as an angel, confident of himself and his position in the world, because he was Russian, and the only nephew of a rich misogynist uncle. He rarely failed to do very well at anything he tackled, and he'd already learned to control fear. I, on the other hand, was a weedy, under-sized child for my age, dark and ugly, ungainly, nervous, so anxious to get things right that I usually got them wrong, homesick, short of money, prey to nightmares, and Ukrainian.'

Galina was listening intently, her eyes fixed on his

face, expecting him to go on with an account of teasing or bullying, but instead he continued, 'Gennadi was usually kind to me, in the offhand manner of a Lordly Being to a Lesser Mortal, and he even fought off other fellows who thought it might be amusing to bully me. Looking back, I can see that he was remarkably kind, for I didn't give him much thanks—I was a surly, disagreeable child. I suppose I resented his being everything that I couldn't be. Anyway, eventually, when we were about nine, I discovered that there was something I could do which he couldn't—I could irritate! I don't think I need try to explain—you've seen me do it. I found that I could apply little pin-pricking remarks and comments which goaded him until he lost his temper, and I'm afraid I've gone on doing it ever since. There's no particular malice in it. It doesn't really mean anything, and he knows perfectly well why I do it—he took the trouble to tell me once! He just accepts it now, like a horse accepts flies—he flicks his ears and tail, and even stamps a hoof, but they don't cause him serious concern. I don't dislike him—in fact I admire him very much, but I'm jealous, that's all, just as I told you.'

Galina, having screwed up her courage to hear something to Gennadi's discredit, felt quite deflated. 'Oh. Well, thank you for telling me,' she said, sounding as flat as she felt.

'Of course,' Igor went on encouragingly, 'he's not perfect, by any means! He was quite conceited in his youth, but the Navy knocked that out of him. He's proud and touchy about matters of honour and so forth, and the fact that he had to accept an allowance from his uncle must have been a bitter pill, but no one can live on an officer's pay in either Service. It's a marvel the General didn't stop it, really, for he wasn't inclined to put up with insubordination from anyone, but I suppose Gennadi's being his only relation softened him a little, and to give old Yuri his due, he did respect people who stood up to him.'

'Insubordination?' Galina asked, her attention caught by what she suspected Igor might have meant.

'Downright mutiny at times!' Igor grinned reminiscently. 'They used to have some furious rows on the rare occasions when they were both home on leave at once. Yuri Semyonovich was a boyar of the old sort—he'd have been happy in the time of Ivan the Terrible! He was all in favour of down-trodden serfs, hanging, flogging, rapine, plunder and all the other good old customs. Gennadi, on the other hand, is a Westerner, enlightened, liberal in his views . . . You can imagine how the fur flew!'

Galina could hardly believe her ears, for this was the answer to all her doubts and fears. If only she had asked Igor before!

'Is this really true?' she asked tremulously.

'Of course. Why . . .?' Igor broke off, looked searchingly at her, and then said, 'Oh, so that's the trouble! I couldn't understand why you were treating him like an enemy to humanity. I thought it was some sort of elaborate courtship ritual! You've been thinking that he shared his uncle's views? Oh, my poor girl! Why ever didn't you let the man speak for himself?'

'But everything he says seems to be a criticism of what I've done!' Galina said despairingly.

'Everything he says? But you never let him say anything! If he ventures a remark or asks a question, you leap on him, beak and talons, and bite his head off! For goodness' sake be quiet and *listen* to him!' Igor exclaimed, looking vastly amused.

'Yes, I will,' Galina said shakily. 'That is, if he ever speaks to me again.'

'He will,' Igor said, smiling to himself. 'A man who can lose a ship in the Arctic and still bring most of his crew home isn't going to be defeated by a slip of a girl!'

'Yes,' Galina said thoughtfully. 'I mean, no. Thank you, Igor. I'm very grateful to you.'

'Anything to oblige,' he replied gently. He was still smiling, but in a sympathetic fashion. 'I hope the course of true love goes smoothly for you now.'

There was something in the way he said it, some slight stress on the 'you' which caught Galina's attention, and as she rose and walked to the door, she looked back and asked tentatively, 'Didn't it for you?'

'No,' he replied seriously.

'I'm sorry.' She paused, then, even more tentatively, 'Was—was it Tatya?'

'No. Someone else—you don't know her. It's four years ago now, over and done with. She married Another.'

'There'll be someone else,' Galina tried to encourage him, for he sounded very sad.

'I don't think so.' He had been standing by his chair, but now, the note of finality in his voice echoed by his movement, he returned to the packing-case, and remarked, 'There must be a couple of hundred of odd cups in here. Extraordinary!' and Galina left him.

She went in search of Gennadi, but he had gone out, and soon after she had to leave the house herself to attend a luncheon and skating party. She returned home briefly to change her clothes, then went to dine with the Valyevs, feeling miserably that, at this rate, it might be days before she saw Gennadi again, and she would have liked to put things right with him, if he would allow her to do so, before the year ended.

Her fellow-guests for dinner were the same as those who had attended that first dinner she had gone to in Petersburg, which now seemed so long ago,—the Valyevs, who this time were her hosts, the Orlovs, Tatya, Igor and Sasha. After the meal, they naturally

went together to church, choosing to attend the St
Nikolai Cathedral, that beautiful blue, white and gold
creation in Russian Baroque, known as the Sailors'
Church, with its detached campanile rising like a giant
wedding-cake from the banks of Kryukov's canal.

The friends held a brief debate outside, hurriedly
because the night, although fine, was bitterly cold, and
the number of people hurrying past to the service made
conversation difficult, to decide whether they would go
to the lower church, which all but Sasha dismissed as too
low-ceilinged and claustrophobic, preferring the main
church above it. Sasha admitted cheerfully that his
preference was based entirely on a dislike of dragging his
wooden leg up the stairs, but, with Andrei and Igor
assisting, one on each side, he fairly flew up the half-
dozen flights.

The upper church was a revelation to Galina, who had
not seen it before. The elaborate gilded iconostasis, the
icons which were set against each elaborately-carved
column, the richly-robed priests, the great choir, and the
throng of people from every rank of society, all shim-
mered in a haze of incense and the golden light of
thousands of candles. The building was full of music and
light, and a subdued religious joy which overcame the
cold and hunger of the poor people, and even defeated
for a while the smug self-satisfaction and frivolous gaiety
of the rich.

There was a constant current of movement in the
congregation as people tip-toed from icon to icon with
their candles, pausing to light one and pray, bowing
repeatedly and crossing themselves with solemn, sweeping gestures, then going on to the next, slipping unobtru-
sively between the worshippers who were following the
chanted service, joining full-heartedly in the magnificent
singing. All the time, people were drifting slowly out of
the side doors, and more were entering, so that there

was a constant smooth, quiet flow of movement, like water eddying round the great pillars.

Galina and her friends moved with the stream, borne by it further into the central nave, and then, suddenly, Galina came face to face with Gennadi. 'Where else,' she thought 'but in the Sailors' Church?'

His face was impassive, and she wondered if he ever showed his feelings, but he certainly looked very slightly taken aback when she held out her hand and greeted him with a friendly smile, albeit speaking in the softest whisper because of their surroundings.

She could do no more than smile and murmur, 'Good evening,' as his lips brushed her fingers, his eyes watching her face warily, and then the others were round about him, exchanging handclasps and whispered greetings. Then, somehow, he became part of their group and remained with them until the end of the service, when they all left together, and it was Gennadi who gave Sasha an arm down the stairs in a matter-of-fact, unobtrusive manner which Galina, now as partisan as she had so recently been suspicious, thought admirably tactful.

Outside, the little group drew aside from the stream of homegoing worshippers to bid one another a happy and blessed New Year, having to shout above the joyous clangour of the bells, which were clashing out from the campanile, answering the hundreds of others all over the city and beyond, spreading blessing and celebration across Holy Russia.

'I've some news,' Gennadi informed them, his voice, trained to shout down a gale in the wildest ocean, carrying through the brazen clamour of the bells without much difficulty. 'I'm officially alive, by Imperial Decree!'

'Already?' Igor shouted back incredulously.

'Empress-Mother!' Gennadi bellowed. There was a flurry of congratulations, the men shaking his hands and banging him about the shoulders, the ladies clasping his hands, all smiling and trying to congratulate him and express their pleasure at once, amid the noise of the bells and the shouts of greeting, crying of children and singing going on amongst the crowds around them.

Galina, suddenly self-conscious, hung back for a few seconds, then gathered her courage and went towards him, last of all, in such a rush that, as he seemed to step forward, they virtually collided, and she found to her surprise that she had actually kissed him fleetingly on one cold cheek.

At that moment, the bells suddenly stopped, and his startled 'Galina?' rang out clearly, but everyone took advantage of the comparative silence to congratulate him all over again, and Galina was able to draw back and cover her confusion by pulling the hood of her sable cloak forward to hide her face. It was a moment or two before she realised that the only illumination came from the moonlight reflected on the snow and the flickering streetlamps beyond the churchyard, so it was too dark for anyone to see her expression.

As they walked towards their carriages, Igor asked Gennadi if he was returning home, to which he replied that he was, but he had his own carriage, so he followed Galina's to the house, and then joined Galina, Countess Razumova and Igor in the Peacock Salon for a glass of wine before retiring. He told the Countess his news, and explained that the Navy Minister had taken him to dine with the Empress Dowager a few evenings before, and she had, after questioning him about his adventures, offered to use her powers as Regent in the Emperor's absence to issue the decree, to save him having to wait for a despatch to go all the way across Europe to the Emperor, who was somewhere between Frankfurt-am-Main and Belfort.

He gave Galina two or three searching looks during the general conversation, and she wished very much that she could have a few minutes alone with him, but there was no opportunity, and she had to be content with smiling at him rather self-consciously and, she suspected, artificially, whenever their eyes met. He eventually gave her a brief flicker of a smile in return, and with that she had to be satisfied, hoping that she might be able to speak to him privately in the morning.

She was not, however. She slept late, and found that he had already gone out when she went downstairs. Osya informed her that he had made his usual presentation of money to the house-serfs, and had mentioned that he expected to be out all day, and his valet was even now packing his full-dress uniform to take somewhere for his use in the evening. Galina could have wept with vexation that he would go on thinking her unfriendly and disagreeable for yet another day.

She was herself engaged to go with her friends to the customary great fête at the Winter Palace, when the Emperor allowed thirty thousand of his subjects, from all classes of society, to wander freely through the state-rooms of his Petersburg residence.

The crowds were quite frightening, for everyone who could get a ticket took advantage of the opportunity, and, for all its vast scale, the Palace could only just accommodate such numbers. Time and again, Galina found herself cut off from her friends in a press of peasants, servants, poor labourers, soldiers, fashionable ladies and gentlemen, seamstresses, street-cleaners, coachmen, officers of the two services, and court officials. The smell of unwashed humanity, or, rather, unwashed clothes (for even the very poor usually went to the bath-house before visiting the Palace) was quite overpowering at times, and she was thankful when at last it was time to withdraw to a range of rooms on the second floor which had been arranged for the convenience of those who had been favoured with an invitation to the dinner and ball to be held in the evening.

Irina, Tatya and Nadya joined her in a little circle of chairs in one corner, where they took tea and chatted about the things they had seen during the afternoon while they rested, amid a couple of hundred other ladies doing the same, and then their maids arrived with their evening toilettes, and there was a great flurry of dressing, hair arranging, preening and competition for access to the rather limited numbers of mirrors available.

Dinner was served at round tables in four large salons, which opened into one another, and after that there was dancing in the white ballroom and the two smaller rooms at either end of it. As had become usual, Galina's programme filled quickly, and it was a relief to her that it was customary to divide one dance between two or more partners, particularly when Gennadi suddenly appeared before her, completely the hero of her dreams in his full-dress uniform, which, although much less resplendent than that of most of the Army officers and Court officials, nevertheless made him look particularly handsome and distinguished.

'Have you anything left for an undeserving villain?' he enquired with apparent seriousness.

'N-no,' she managed breathlessly. 'Only for a misjudged and ill-treated hero! Oh, Gennadi Yakovich! I'm truly sorry I was so horrible to you!'

The blue eyes searched her face warily, and then he said, 'I've not given you much reason to do otherwise. Now, I wonder who gave me a good character, or did you receive a flash of illumination from my guardian angel, as I did from yours?'

'Igor Grigorovich . . .' she began uncertainly, wondering what he meant, then broke off, for her partner for the dance just beginning had come to claim her. Hurriedly, she handed Gennadi her programme. He scribbled in it and managed to give it back to her before she was whisked away, but it was not until some time later that she had a chance to look at it, and found that he had given himself the latter part of a waltz towards the end of the ball, which seemed an age away.

The time arrived eventually, however. Galina's partner for the first part of the waltz was Prince Nikolai, who danced extremely well, but conversed somewhat stiltedly, with long intervals between remarks, giving Galina plenty of time to look about for Gennadi as she was swung and whirled about the room.

At first, she failed to locate him, and wondered if perhaps he had left, for she had seen little of him during the evening, and nothing at all since supper, but presently he came in from the corridor running alongside the ballroom with another naval officer, and stood talking to him for a while, and then came purposefully through the maze of dancers to claim her.

She could hardly find her voice to thank Prince Nikolai, let alone make any sort of conversation with Gennadi, who said very little himself. He danced competently, but not as well as Prince Nikolai, and commented that he was a little rusty at the exercise.

'We don't have many balls at sea,' he offered in explanation. 'Mermaids don't dance, of course, and it's difficult to practise with the floor going up and down in two or three different directions at once.'

Galina was so overwhelmed at finding herself actually in his arms that she only replied, 'Yes, I suppose so,' instead of laughing. She had reverted to the dreadful self-consciousness of a young girl at her first dancing-lesson, and was horrified by the blushes which would keep rising to her cheeks, and the remarkably silly things she heard her own voice uttering from time to time. By the end of the waltz, which was only a couple of rounds of the patterned floor, she felt that the whole ball had been a total disaster, and even her apology to Gennadi had been inept and inadequate. On the way home, she snapped at Dasha for no particular reason, and snubbed Igor quite sharply when he remarked that she seemed to be on better terms with the Handsome Hero. She had a good cry when she was alone in her own room, and felt a little better.

In the morning, she had a lengthy and difficult interview with Cherbatov, who protested repeatedly at all her suggestions, and then took luncheon with Tatya, seizing the opportunity to tell her what Igor had said about Gennadi, and unconsciously giving away a great deal about her own feelings in the process. Afterwards, she and Tatya went to a sledging-party.

The event had been organised by one of Tatya's Beaux, an indolent and extremely wealthy young man called Tolya Lenivov, who had never made the slightest attempt to serve the Emperor in any way—a most unusual phenomenon in the Russia of that time. He owned a large summer residence along the Tsarskoe Selo road, where his gardeners had laid out a winding route of packed and polished snow through the grounds, wide enough for two sledges to run side by side in safety, so that races could be held.

Galina had never been on a racing sledge before, and had the sense to say so, for she could see that a passenger in one would need to know at least what to do. The vehicles were lightly-built and small, mounted high above the runners and as easily overturned as a rowing-boat. The runners were shod with polished steel and there was just room in each sledge for the driver and one passenger beside him. A trotting horse was harnessed to each sledge in the usual way, but a second animal, a galloper, was attached to a long rein, and was trained to run out at either side, or in front, as the driver wished, preferably with much showy leaping and prancing.

'A beginner!' Tolya exclaimed, as if he found this

particularly pleasing, when Galina spoke up. 'Now, you must go with a really good driver. Gennadi Yakovich, will you take a novice?'

Most of the men among the guests were gathered round the dozen sledges, inspecting them and choosing which each would drive. They were all well-wrapped-up in heavy coats and ear-flapped caps, for the day, although fine and sunny, was very cold. Galina failed to recognise Gennadi, or even to realise that he was there until Tolya called him, and apparently he also failed to recognise Galina in her hooded sable cloak until he came closer to answer Tolya.

'By all means! Who . . .? Galina Stepanovna? Good afternoon.'

Galina went with him to the sledge which he had chosen, praying that she would not make a fool of herself again and turn the afternoon into as bad a fiasco as that precious half-waltz had been the previous night. Her prayer was answered, for all went well this time. Gennadi settled her into her place, and set off round the course, driving slowly and looking carefully at the bends and corners as he explained how she should adjust her position to incline her weight to left or right on the bends, only he, of course, said port and starboard.

She soon had the idea, and he drove on a while in silence, concentrating on the horses, which were strange to him, and occasionally calling to one or other of them in Russian, using a combination of endearments and mild insults which seemed to convey his meaning to the animals quite satisfactorily.

'So Igor spoke for me, did he?' he said at length, still watching the course and the horses. 'He's always been a good friend, in the intervals of goading me to murder him. If the courts do eventually find in my favour, I assure you that I shall take good care of the serfs and let them marry and have children as much as they like, within moderation, and I'll not cheat any poor landlords out of their estates, or whip footmen for falling over their feet, or building ice-mountains in all the court-yards. I'm sorry about what I said the day we first met—implying that you couldn't manage the estates. I was wrong—you're more capable and competent than most men, and I'm sorry that I have to try to rob you of your fortune. I'll see that you get your dowry, of course, as my uncle intended, and more besides.'

'It doesn't matter,' Galina said quietly. 'I don't mind, now I know you'll do the things I wanted to do.'

'You won't mind not being rich?' Gennadi asked, looking in her direction. Her hood hid her face, and he leaned forward a little to see inside it, but the galloper, sensing that his driver's eye was no longer upon him and being a foolish beast and a poor judge of character, seized the opportunity to perform a spectacular caracole and slewed the sledge round, nearly overturning it. Gennadi took corrective action almost instinctively, and called the galloper something most uncomplimentary in a voice more suited to a violent storm in the Cheskaya Gulf than a frosty afternoon on a quiet country estate. A number of icicles fell from the trees, and the gal-loper suddenly became a very sedate and well-behaved beast.

'Not really,' Galina replied when order had been restored. 'It's pleasant to be rich, of course, but it carries so much responsibility, and I find that difficult to carry entirely by myself. If one was to marry the sort of man who would share in one's interests, of course, it would be different . . .' She stopped, thinking that she was letting her private thoughts run away with her tongue.

'Yes.' Gennadi did not sound as if he had read any-thing into the impersonal way in which Galina had spoken, although he again leaned forward to peer inside her hood. 'I must say that you seem to have a very thorough grasp of administration, and some interesting ideas.'

'For a female,' Galina added.

'By any standard. After all, there's no reason why a female shouldn't be able to manage estates. We've had some most successful Empresses, even if some of them have used unconventional methods. I must admit that my experience of female activity is limited, as I've been at sea so much, but it appears to me that incapable females are so by choice rather than lack of ability.'

Galina decided it would be better to steer the conversation away from such a controversial matter, and enquired if his voyages had taken him to many foreign countries, which provided a safe subject for the rest of the tour of the course, and then the races started, and there was no more time for conversation.

Gennadi won all his races, Galina managed to keep calm and lean in the right direction, once she had mastered the difference between port and starboard, helped at first by a slight push or pull from Gennadi, but he soon saw that it was no longer necessary and concentrated on his steering, cutting corners and stealing the inside course on bends in a thoroughly hair-raising fashion, and out-shouting everyone else, which seemed to please his own horses, while discouraging those of his opponents. It was very exciting.

After the racing, which continued by the light of the moon and flares when the early darkness fell, an informal dinner was served in the house, followed by a concert, then conversation and supper, but Gennadi left to keep another appointment after dinner, and Galina plucked up her courage when he bade her goodbye to ask him if he would spare her a little time for a business discussion after luncheon the next day. He gave her one of his direct, searching looks, but agreed without comment.

Cherbatov called again in the morning in a mild fit of sulks, but he brought the papers for which Galina had asked, and she explained her reasons all over again, and, as he had had time to think about them overnight, he eventually agreed that she was possibly acting responsibily. He had brought a clerk with him, and the two of them witnessed Galina's signature before they left.

Gennadi appeared at luncheon, and amused Countess Razumova with a lively account of an interview he had endured during the morning with an elderly and very deaf admiral, who, it emerged, thought Gennadi was the captain of a ship which had been rammed by a whale off the coast of Norway.

Galina listened with interest, her amusement dampened by nervous anticipation, and afterwards went to the Peacock Salon and sat down facing the door, holding herself very straight and trying to still the fluttering sensation in her stomach.

Gennadi entered a couple of minutes later, apologised for keeping her waiting, then took a chair at her invitation, his face as watchful and inscrutable as ever.

'It's just about—about the property,' Galina began nervously. 'I thought—well, if the courts settle it, they'll take forever, and the costs will probably be very high, and while it all drags on, the serfs won't know who owns them, and they'll be unsettled, and everyone will suffer . . . Anyway, I thought . . . it seems more sensible if I just sign it all over to you, so I've had M. Cherbatov draw up a deed of gift . . .' She produced a sheet of paper from her reticule and handed it to Gennadi, who took it with a brief 'Thank you' and read the contents through two or three times.

'I don't know what to say,' he said eventually, sounding disconcerted.

'It's obvious that the General wanted you to inherit his property,' Galina said. 'I've felt all along, ever since you came home, that it was wrong for me to hold on, that I ought to give it all to you. The only reason why I didn't do it at once was because . . .'

She hesitated, and Gennadi finished for her, 'Because you thought I was like my uncle, and you wanted to protect the serfs from me. Galina, this is an extraordinarily generous gesture you've made, and I'm grateful to you, but mainly because it now makes it possible for me to make a suggestion myself, which I think—hope—may be a better solution to the problem, and a fairer one. May I speak?'

'If you wish,' Galina replied, wondering what was coming.

'Why don't we share the property? I'm away at sea much of the time, and I'd feel happier about the serfs and everything else if I knew that a competent person who shared my beliefs was looking after things in my absence. Cherbatov's a good fellow, I know, but he's a paid servant and, quite rightly, won't take the responsibility for action in an emergency. All those souls need someone to turn to with their problems, someone who cares about them and has the authority and the will to act.'

'Are—are you asking me to be your steward?' Galina asked, puzzled.

For the second time in a few minutes, Gennadi looked disconcerted, which must have been a record. 'Not exactly,' he replied. 'I was thinking more in terms of marriage. I wondered if you would care to be my wife.'

A flood of colour rose to Galina's cheeks, and all she could utter was a small, choked, 'Oh,' but Gennadi did not appear discouraged by her apparent lack of enthusiasm, for he continued, 'Of course, I'm not only thinking of the serfs—I'm thinking of myself as well, I confess. You see . . .' he hesitated and looked at her with a certain diffidence. Being an observant man, he saw that her eyes were shining, not flashing with indignation, so correctly assessing his chances, he continued more boldly, 'I happen to have fallen in love with you.'

Galina was still speechless, so he went on encouragingly, 'I thought, the first time I saw you, that you were beautiful, and so full of character. You're like a ship—a lovely lady, with a will of your own, and with the right man for your captain . . . It's a partnership, you see, a ship and her captain. When they're right for one another, there's nothing they can't do . . .'

Far from being insulted at being likened to a ship, Galina thought she had never heard anything so beautiful and poetic, and her whole face was illumined with delight, although she still failed to find her voice.

'So what do you think?' Gennadi stood up and moved towards her, and Galina rose to her feet as if in a trance. When he was quite close, he looked into her face with an expression which made her feel quite weak-kneed, and said, 'Will you marry me, Galina?'

'Yes,' she managed in a faint croak. He put one finger under that determined little chin and said '*Moya dushka!*' Galina wondered why she had ever thought his eyes were cold. They were warm and soft now, and so clear that she could see in them how fine a man he was. Then he took her in his arms and kissed her in a very competent fashion. If she had any remaining doubts about him, about herself, about what it felt like to be in love, they melted like the Neva in the spring thaw, and she was swept away in the surge of his feelings and her own, as if the great river itself was carrying her.

Some time later, Igor entered from the library, carrying a large, jewel-encrusted cross of the Orthodox variety with three cross-arms. He found the happy couple sitting sedately on a sofa, and appeared not to notice that they hastily shifted apart to a more proper distance at his entry.

'This,' he said, brandishing the cross (with some difficulty, for it was very heavy) 'belongs to the church of the Assumption in Smolensk. Would you like it returned?'

'How do you know?' Gennadi enquired mildly.

'It's engraved on the base,' Igor replied with a certain relish, which made Galina smile.

Gennadi exchanged a glance with her, then replied to Igor's question, 'Yes, I think so.'

'A wedding-present, shall we say?' Igor asked as a parting shot, and closed the library door behind him before either of them could reply.

Galina and Gennadi looked at one another and laughed, and then forgot all about him, and, indeed, everyone else except each other, while outside in the gallery, the Wheel of Fortune, whirred, clicked, and moved on.

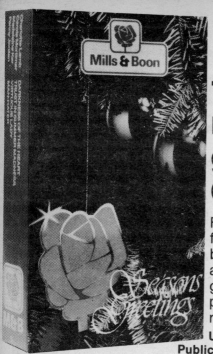

How to join in a whole new world of romance

It's very easy to subscribe to the Mills & Boon Reader Service. As a regular reader, you can enjoy a whole range of special benefits. Bargain offers. Big cash savings. Your own free Reader Service newsletter, packed with knitting patterns, recipes, competitions, and exclusive book offers.

We send you the very latest titles each month, postage and packing free – no hidden extra charges. There's absolutely no commitment – you receive books for only as long as you want.

We'll send you details. Simply send the coupon – or drop us a line for details about the Mills & Boon Reader Service Subscription Scheme. Post to: Mills & Boon Reader Service, P.O. Box 236, Thornton Road, Croydon, Surrey CR9 3RU, England. *Please note: READERS IN SOUTH AFRICA please write to: Mills & Boon Reader Service of Southern Africa, Private Bag X3010, Randburg 2125, S. Africa.

Please send me details of the Mills & Boon Subscription Scheme.

NAME (Mrs/Miss) _____ EP3

ADDRESS _____

COUNTY/COUNTRY_____ POST/ZIP CODE_____
'BLOCK LETTERS, PLEASE

Mills & Boon
the rose of romance